Kill for a Million

Don't miss any of Janet Dailey's bestsellers

The Calder Brand Series
Calder Brand
Calder Grit
A Calder at Heart
Calder Country
Calder Strong

Rivalries
One in a Million
Lie for a Million
Kill for a Million

The Frosted Firs Ranch Series
Evergreen Christmas

The New Americana Series
Paradise Peak
Sunrise Canyon
Refuge Cove
Letters from Peaceful Lane
Hart's Hollow Farm
Hope Creek
Blue Moon Haven
Lone Oaks Crossing
The Champions
Whirlwind
Whiplash
Quicksand

The Tylers of Texas
Texas Forever
Texas Free
Texas Fierce
Texas Tall
Texas Tough
Texas True
Bannon Brothers: Triumph
Bannon Brothers: Honor
Bannon Brothers: Trust
American Destiny
American Dreams
Masquerade
Tangled Vines
Heiress

Kill for a Million

JANET DAILEY

kensingtonbooks.com

KENSINGTON BOOKS are published by

Kensington Publishing Corp.
900 Third Avenue
New York, NY 10022

After the passing of Janet Dailey, the Dailey family worked with a close associate of Janet's to continue her literary legacy, using her notes, ideas, and favorite themes to complete her novels and create new ones, inspired by the American men and women she loved to portray.

All Kensington titles, imprints, and distributed lines are available at special quantity discounts for bulk purchases for sales promotion, premiums, fund-raising, educational, or institutional use.

Special book excerpts or customized printings can also be created to fit specific needs. For details, write or phone the office of the Kensington Special Sales Manager: Attn. Special Sales Department, Kensington Publishing Corp., 900 Third Avenue, New York, NY 10022. Phone: 1-800-221-2647.

Library of Congress Card Catalogue Number: On file

ISBN: 978-1-4967-4482-1
First Kensington Hardcover Edition: May 2026

ISBN: 978-1-4967-4488-3 (ebook)

10 9 8 7 6 5 4 3 2 1

Printed in the United States of America

The authorized representative in the EU for product safety and compliance
is eucomply OU, Parnu mnt 139b-14, Apt 123
Tallinn, Berlin 11317, hello@eucompliancepartner.com

Kill for a Million

CHAPTER ONE

U.S. Interstate 40, mid-August

The midday sun glimmered on the surface of the freeway, creating mirages that evaporated like water with the changing light. Heat shimmered in gossamer waves above the moving traffic. Beyond the ribbon of asphalt, the Arizona desert spread like a sea of brush and cactus, all the way to the distant hills.

Roper McKenna kept his hands on the wheel and his gaze fixed on the road. This was no time for wandering thoughts. The Dodge Ram 3500 truck was towing precious cargo.

Inside the luxury-class trailer, emblazoned with the Culhane Ranch logo, three valuable performance horses were on their way to the biggest show in the country—the Run for a Million reining event in Las Vegas. Millie, a gifted young filly, and One in a Million, a semi-retired champion, were the backup horses. Fire Dance, the competition horse, was a flashy bundle of nervous energy. If that energy could be controlled, the flame-red stallion had the talent to carry Roper to a million-dollar victory—a prize that would be split with Fire Dance's owner, rancher Chet Barr.

Roper had promised himself that, for the week ahead, he would put his worries aside and focus on the competition. But it wasn't easy to forget that he was the prime suspect in the murder of his former employer, wealthy rancher Frank Culhane—or that he'd fallen hard for his new boss, Frank's sexy, spirited widow, Lila.

Lila had planned to make this trip with him. But she was back home in Texas, recovering from snakebite under the care of her daughter. When—and if—Lila felt strong enough, the two women would be flying to Vegas for the big show. Roper worried about her; but for now, even that concern would have to be put aside.

In Lila's place, Roper had brought along his twenty-year-old half sister. Cheyenne was easy company, but they hadn't talked much on the long drive. They were both preoccupied with their own thoughts.

A petite, dark-haired beauty, Cheyenne was already a celebrity rodeo star. But she was weary of the rodeo life and eager to try a new sport—cow cutting. Hayden Barr, the son of Fire Dance's owner, would be competing in this year's cutting event. He'd offered to take her behind the scenes to meet the riders and see the horses—maybe even find one to buy. Roper could sense her anticipation—but was it for the horses, or was it for Hayden?

"Hungry?" he asked her. "We'll be taking the off-ramp to Highway 93 at Kingman. We could stop for burgers."

"No, let's keep going," she said. "After the horses are unloaded, we can get a good dinner in Vegas. We should be there in a couple of hours."

"Your choice." Roper checked his mirrors, signaled, and moved into the outside lane for access to the off-ramp, coming up in a few miles. The freeway here was edged with a sloping embankment that dropped off to the right.

A gravel strip and a cable barricade along the shoulder provided a measure of safety. All the same, Roper gave himself plenty of room. With three precious horses in the trailer, he couldn't be too careful.

A glance in the side mirror warned him of the massive semitruck with a green Peterbilt cab approaching from behind in the lane to his left. Roper held steady in the outside lane. The semi had plenty of room to pass him. The driver wasn't even honking the horn. But the huge truck was coming up fast and close—too close.

Roper's pulse slammed. A warning screamed in his head. The bastard was about to sideswipe him.

The horses! God, the horses . . .

As the huge rig came up even with the trailer and began to cut over, Roper floored the gas pedal and swung onto the shoulder. The barrier cable snapped as a wheel broke over the rim of the embankment. He could feel the crumbling edge as he kept moving forward, pulling the horse trailer along the shoulder.

He felt the sickening shift of weight and the strain on the gooseneck hitch as the edge crumbled under the outside wheels. Metal screamed as the giant rig roared past, gouging a crease on the side of the truck and back along the length of the trailer.

In the next instant, the semi moved on to vanish amid the heavy traffic. The truck and horse trailer were left with their outside wheels jutting over the embankment.

Roper glanced at Cheyenne. She hadn't cried out, but her face was deathly white. She tugged at her seat belt. "The horses—"

"Stay put! We can't open that trailer till we get to a safe place."

"What if we roll?"

Roper shook his head. "There's nothing we can do for

them here. I'm going to try to pull us back onto the road. Don't move or try to get out. Just tighten your seat belt and lean toward me. If we start to go over, pull up your knees and protect your face."

The truck's engine had stalled when the semi cut past them. Cheyenne leaned left over the console to help balance the weight and willed herself to keep perfectly still. The slightest motion could cause the rig to tip. She pictured the forty-five-degree slope of the embankment and the twenty-foot distance to the bottom. Even if she and Roper survived the rollover, the horses wouldn't. They would be tossed around and hurt so badly that they would almost certainly have to be put down. But Roper was right. Any effort to help them here would only worsen the odds of a crash.

She held her breath as Roper applied the hand brake, shifted into neutral, and turned the key in the ignition. What would they do if the truck wouldn't start? Freeze in place? Wait for help and pray that the rig didn't tumble down the slope?

The starter cranked. The engine coughed and started. Cheyenne took a deep breath. At least they had power. But they were still in danger. The wheels that remained on level ground had to find enough purchase to move the truck off the edge of the embankment. And the engine needed enough torque to pull the heavy trailer to safety.

Beads of perspiration stood out on Roper's face as he geared down, released the hand brake, and eased the gas pedal to the floor. The engine roared. The wheels spun, and the truck teetered, straining against the sagging weight of the trailer.

Cheyenne tried to remember the prayers her mother, Rachel, had taught her as a child, but she didn't have her mother's faith. She could only brace against the dash, her lips forming one word, *please . . . please . . .* again and again.

Suddenly, as if by a miracle, the wheels caught the solid surface. The truck crawled forward. The gooseneck hitch groaned as the trailer was dragged, inch by inch, back onto level ground.

Cheyenne began to breathe again. They were all right. But what about the horses?

"Stay put." Roper's voice rasped with emotion as he guessed her intent. "We can't check the horses till we get off the freeway."

"Yes, I know." Cheyenne sat up. As her thundering pulse slowed, she remembered the looming semitruck, the shock of impact, and the screech of crumpling metal. She put up a hand and felt the sore spot on her head. It was tender, but nothing to worry about now.

"That big truck had plenty of room. The driver didn't need to move over." She took a deep breath. "He didn't even honk. That wasn't an accident, was it?"

Roper's only response was a shake of his head. What wasn't he telling her? Why would someone want to harm them—even kill them?

Looking through the windshield, Cheyenne could see a flashing light. A highway patrol cruiser had pulled in front of them, blocking the flow of traffic from the outside lane. The trooper was motioning Roper to follow him.

Roper pulled into the lane behind the cruiser. There were no thumping noises to indicate a flat tire or damaged wheel, which was good. But all Cheyenne could think about was the horses. Even if they weren't badly hurt, they would be terrified. She lowered the side window and listened, trying to hear them kicking and screaming through the high window slots in the trailer. But the traffic noise and the laboring truck engine muffled any sounds she might have heard.

They reached the exit and followed the cruiser down the off-ramp, into the empty corner of a Walmart parking lot. The trooper parked, climbed out of the cruiser, and motioned Roper into a space with plenty of room around it.

The truck came to a stop. Cheyenne unfastened her seat belt and jumped to the ground. She could hear the horses now, snorting, shrilling, and slamming against the sides of their confining boxes. She reached for the bolt that secured the rear door. There was no way the horses could be let out of the trailer here. But at least she could check on them.

"Wait, Cheyenne. Don't open the door without me." Roper was on the ground, talking with the trooper as they inspected the damage to the rig. The long crease was ugly, but it hadn't penetrated the steel skin of the truck or trailer.

"I'll give you a permit to drive with the damage." The trooper was filling out a form on a clipboard. "We'll be on the lookout for that green Peterbilt that sideswiped you. Too bad you didn't get a license number."

"It was all I could do to keep the rig on the shoulder," Roper said. "But that semi had plenty of room to pass—a clear lane next to me. The driver cut over with no warning and tried to push me past the edge. Did you see it happen?"

The patrolman stared at him. "No. I came along after the damage was done. If you're saying it was deliberate, you're talking attempted murder."

"That's the idea. But I don't believe it was personal. The driver was more likely a hired hit man. If you catch the bastard, I'll want to know who paid him. Thanks for your help, Officer. You have my cell phone number. And now, if you'll excuse me, I need to look after these horses."

As the cruiser drove away, Cheyenne turned to face her

brother. "What's going on, Roper?" she demanded. "If somebody was trying to kill us, I need to know about it."

"This has nothing to do with you, Little Sister." Roper turned away and walked back toward the rear of the trailer. "Don't worry, I've got it handled."

Roper unfastened the lock and slid back the bolt at the base of the door. Cheyenne could hear the horses slamming against the sides of their stalls and whinnying in distress. She stood back, watching as the door rolled upward and daylight flooded the inside of the trailer.

The three horses were wild-eyed, snorting and bucking in their stalls. Their fear tore at Cheyenne's heart. These innocent animals had no idea what had just happened to them. They had felt safe inside the trailer. Then they'd been flung violently to one side, their hooves scrambling for a hold on the slanted surface. No wonder they were terrified.

Roper knew better than to approach them. He kept his distance in the trailer, his expert gaze examining each horse for any visible sign of injury.

From where Cheyenne stood, the horses looked sound enough. But they would need close inspection by a vet once they were unloaded at South Point. Damage to the vital bones and tendons in their legs could be hard to spot at first. And there was no telling how long it would take for them to settle down and allow themselves to be examined.

Roper closed the door, walked back to the truck, and climbed into the driver's seat. As she took her place beside him, Cheyenne sensed her brother's dejection. He'd left the Culhane Ranch with high hopes of winning the Run for a Million on Saturday. If none of the horses he'd brought was fit to compete, the show would already be over for him.

But there was more. Even before the so-called accident,

she'd noticed his somber expression and long silences. And she'd overheard what he was telling the highway patrolman—that the truck and trailer had been sideswiped deliberately.

Despite their age difference, she and Roper had always been close. But now he sat behind a wall of silence. What was wrong? And why wasn't he telling her about it?

She got out her phone and began texting. Roper glanced at her, frowning.

"I hope you're not telling our mother about this. She'll only be worried."

"I'm texting Hayden," Cheyenne said. "He planned to meet us at the trailer entrance to South Point. I'm just letting him know we'll be late. As for Mother, I don't tell her anything. She fusses over me like an old biddy hen." She imitated her mother's voice. "*Guard your honor, Cheyenne. Remember what the good book says—Who can find a virtuous woman, for her price is far above rubies.* Good Lord, you'd think this was the 1800s!"

"Mother means well," Roper said. "You're her only daughter. She wants to protect you."

"I'm a rodeo girl, Big Brother. I know how to protect myself, especially from cowboys."

"And Hayden?" Roper's voice had taken on a teasing tone.

Cheyenne hesitated. She hadn't spent much time with Hayden Barr, but she liked him. He was handsome, from a good family, and seemed genuinely nice. He'd even promised to introduce her to cutting competition and offered to help her get the training she needed.

But past experience had taught her not to accept anyone at face value. Until she knew Hayden better, she would proceed with caution. Only if she felt completely safe would she give him her trust.

Roper was waiting for her reply.

"I'm giving it time," she said. "For now, that's all I can tell you."

It was a sensible answer, from a good place inside her. Still, when she thought of Hayden, she felt a prickle of unease. From the depths of her memory, a voice whispered a warning—one she had learned to heed.

Danger . . . don't assume that anything is what it seems.

Chapter Two

FBI Agent Sam Rafferty surveyed the main arena of the South Point Equestrian Center. This afternoon, a Tuesday, the seats were empty. But in the days and nights ahead, fans would be swarming in to watch trainers and non-pro riders show their horses in bucking, cutting, herding, and reining competitions.

The last and biggest reining event of the week, the Run for a Million, was scheduled for Saturday night. By then, it would be up to Sam to have someone—most likely Roper McKenna—under arrest for the cold-blooded murder of Frank Culhane.

Nick Bellingham, Sam's boss at the Bureau in Abilene, had given Sam one final week to solve the case. Succeed, and he would be solidly in line for Nick's job. Fail, and the blot on his record would haunt the rest of his career.

The hell of it was, Sam liked Roper and had trusted him enough to let him come here and compete. After all, the man was innocent until proven guilty. But Sam had a job to do. And Roper, despite his sworn claim of innocence, had opportunity, means, and motive in spades.

The opportunity would have come easily. At any time,

even in the middle of the night, Roper could have invented an excuse to lure Frank into the stable where the murder had taken place. Roper's only alibi had been furnished by his mother, who claimed he'd been at home all night. But mothers could lie, and they often did.

Roper worked with horses and would've had no trouble getting his hands on the 18-gauge hypodermic that had injected a fatal dose of fentanyl into the back of his wealthy boss's neck. The hypodermic, already identified as the murder weapon, had been found by two young boys in the creek that ran past the McKenna Ranch.

As for motive, Roper had two reasons to commit murder. Frank's death had freed him to win his late boss's place in the Run for a Million. And now Roper was evidently sleeping with Frank's glamorous widow, Lila.

The case looked like an easy win. But there was a problem. Every shred of evidence against Roper was circumstantial. If the case came to trial, a smart lawyer would have a good chance of getting an acquittal. If Sam failed to find proof that would hold up in court, he would be forced to walk away, leaving the high-profile case unsolved.

Of course, there was always the chance that someone else was guilty. Lila herself was not above suspicion. Neither was Frank's ex-wife, Madeleine, the mother of his two children, Darrin and Jasmine. Darrin and his wife, Simone, were determined to inherit Frank's house and ranch. And Madeleine, rumored to have mob connections, would do anything to help them. Sam would be remiss to rule out any of them.

An eyewitness would be a godsend. But only one pair of eyes had seen the violent crime that ended Frank Culhane's life—the eyes of Frank's prize stallion, One in a Million. Horses were sensitive, intelligent animals. The murder would be buried in the big bay roan's memory for as long as he lived. But the stallion would keep the secret.

After checking the time, Sam took an exit from the arena to the open lot where Roper was expected to arrive with the horses. Sam would be keeping an eye on him. He would also be questioning anyone who might have light to shed on the murder case. He didn't relish collecting dirt on a man he'd come to respect. But he'd sworn an oath to perform his job.

Not that he'd kept to the tenets of that oath, Sam reminded himself. Falling in love with Frank's daughter, Jasmine, had been a serious breach of conduct—especially since Jasmine was still on his list of suspects. That was why they'd put their relationship on hold until this case was closed. Sam was getting impatient to hold her in his arms again. But he couldn't let that guide his decisions now.

Between the trailer lot and the arena, the complex of sheds, docks, and cattle pens swarmed with activity. Trucks were rolling through the Pyle Avenue gate, lining up their trailers to be unloaded. Horses snorted and whinnied. Cows bawled. Country music blared from a hidden speaker. The torrid Las Vegas air smelled of dust, diesel fumes, and manure.

Sam had transferred to cowboy country from a job in Chicago. Today he was dressed in faded denims and a plaid shirt, complete with boots and a Stetson. But he was still a city man, and this milieu felt as alien as a planet scene from *Star Wars*.

He found a strip of shade against the immense barn and settled back to watch and wait. Someone else appeared to be waiting, too. It took a moment for Sam to place the dark-haired cowboy checking his phone nearby. Then he remembered seeing him at the Culhane Ranch, when he'd delivered the spectacular red stallion Roper would be showing. He was the son of the horse's owner.

Sam had done his homework at the time. Hayden Barr was heir to a horse-breeding dynasty on a big ranch outside Wichita Falls. Since he had no possible connection to Frank Culhane's murder, Sam had dismissed him from memory.

Now Hayden had turned toward the gate where the Culhane rig was driving in. Viewed from the front, everything looked fine. Only as the truck turned, swinging the trailer into view, did Sam see the ragged scrape, like the mark of a giant claw, that ran from the truck's front wheel and along the trailer to the end. The damage had the look of a deliberate sideswipe—maybe with the intent to cause a fatal crash.

Something similar had happened to Lila Culhane weeks earlier when someone had tampered with her Porsche, causing a rollover that could have killed her. The so-called accident had been clumsily arranged by Lila's stepson, Darrin, who'd been saved from arrest by his mother. Darrin was still out there and still scheming to get his father's widow out of the way. Maybe this was another attempt.

But today, Sam could see that Lila wasn't in the passenger seat. Instead, it was Roper's younger sister, Cheyenne, opening the door and jumping to the ground.

Hayden strode toward the rig. Cheynne met him partway. They exchanged a few words as Roper backed the trailer into position and climbed out of the cab. Then they joined him at the rear of the trailer.

Sam watched from a distance, where he could see inside as Roper raised the rear door. Sam could imagine what he was thinking. The collision that damaged the trailer would have thrown the horses into a panic. Even if they weren't physically injured, the high-strung animals might be too traumatized to perform.

The horses bucked and squealed, showing the whites of their eyes as Roper lowered the ramp. Motioning Cheyenne and Hayden back, he stepped into the trailer. He spoke to them in a soothing voice, but they continued to lunge at the sides of their boxes, as if they were fighting to break out of the trailer and bolt for freedom.

One in a Million was the steadiest of the three. Once Roper had clipped the lead rope onto his halter, the big bay roan allowed himself to be led, snorting, quivering, and eye-rolling, down the ramp and into vast barn where an air-conditioned stall would be waiting. Roper would give him a few minutes to settle down before coming back for the other horses.

Hayden and Cheyenne waited outside the trailer, talking and watching the horses. Sam weighed the idea of joining them and asking a few questions, but decided against it. Cheyenne had been on the rodeo circuit at the time of the murder. Neither she nor Hayden would've had anything to do with Frank's death.

Cheyenne had noticed the FBI man watching them. She knew who he was. He'd questioned her family members about Frank's murder. At the time, he'd asked her about Roper's relationship with his boss. She'd answered truthfully that Roper had never complained about Frank. That had ended the conversation.

But what was the federal agent doing here now? Could Roper be more deeply involved than he'd let on?

Frank Culhane might have deserved to die. But her brother wouldn't have killed him. Roper had respected the man. They'd worked well together. And even if that weren't true, Roper was no killer.

But what about the incident with the semi? Was someone trying to kill him? Something wasn't making sense.

When she had a chance to talk with her brother alone, she would face him down and force him to tell her everything he was holding back. She wasn't a child. If Roper was in trouble, she would support him any way she could.

Roper had returned, carrying an extra lead rope, which he handed to Hayden. The next horse to unload would be Millie, leaving the wildly struggling Fire Dance for last. As the two men approached, Millie tossed her head and backed against the rear of her box. She whimpered as they got the ropes on her. Dread tightened Cheyenne's throat. She knew horses. Millie was in pain.

She stifled a moan as Roper and Hayden led Millie out of the stall. The beautiful white-faced filly was limping painfully. Her right hind leg, visibly broken, jutted at an angle.

Roper's throat moved as he swallowed his emotion. "Let's get her to a stall and send for the vet."

"Do you think a vet can save that leg?" Hayden asked. "I've seen injuries like that. It might be kinder to put her down."

"We'll see." Roper's expression masked his thoughts, but Cheyenne knew that he had to be devastated. "She's Lila's horse," he said. "After I get the vet's opinion, Lila can make the final call." He turned to Cheyenne. "Keep an eye on Fire Dance until we get back. Don't get too close. He could kill you, given the state he's in. If you're worried about him, lower the door."

"Leave Hayden here with Fire Dance," Cheyenne said. "I can help you get Millie to a stall and stay with her for the vet."

"Fine." Roper passed Hayden's lead to Cheyenne. "Damn it, there's a place reserved in hell for the driver of that truck!"

"We need to talk about that—and a few other things," Cheyenne said.

"Not now. Let's go." He led the limping Millie off the ramp with careful steps.

Cheyenne walked close, supporting the filly's injured side. Her eyes misted as she stroked the satiny neck. "Oh, Millie, darling," she whispered, "I'm so, so sorry."

Roper sat on a bench outside the arena, watching the setting sun bleed crimson streaks across the desert sky. The barn, with its 1,200 climate-controlled stalls, was swarming with activity, but here, the evening was quiet. With the rig safely parked in the trailer strip, Cheyenne had gone to dinner with Hayden. They'd invited him along, but Roper had no appetite. After the hellish afternoon, it was time to phone Lila. He dreaded giving her bad news. But she'd be waiting for his call, and he needed to hear her voice.

In a world that seemed to be spinning out of control, Lila had become his anchor. She was as strong as she was beautiful—a widow who could have her pick of wealthy, respectable men. Why she would choose a simple cowboy with bad luck dogging him like a hungry coyote was more than Roper could fathom. He would take the love she gave him, but he had his pride. He wouldn't claim her under the law and heaven until he could offer her the life she deserved. That meant clearing the murder charge and making a name for himself as a trainer and money-winning rider. He hoped Lila would wait. But he wouldn't blame her if she came to her senses and walked away.

She would have been here with him now. But before the trip, she'd stumbled against a wheelbarrow of loose hay, reached out to steady herself, and been struck on the arm by a small rattlesnake. After antivenin treatment in the hospital, she was recovering at home, under the care of her daughter, a nursing student at Texas Christian University. But Roper was still worried about her. He wouldn't breathe easy until he made sure she was all right.

He needed to talk with her for another reason. That sideswipe on the freeway had been no accident. The driver had meant to cause a deadly crash. Only luck and the fast-moving traffic had kept him from finishing the job.

There was no question that the man had been paid. Roper could imagine why and by whom. Maybe Lila could confirm that his hunch was right.

He scrolled to her number and made the call. Her husky "Hello" stirred a tightness in his chest.

"It's me, Boss." The last word emerged as a caress. "How are you? Resting in bed, I hope."

"Actually, I'm on the patio, by the pool, with a glass of iced tea. Gemma's been hovering over me all day. I told her I needed some time alone. I was hoping you'd call now. How was the drive to Vegas?"

"I'll tell you in a minute. But first I want to know about you. How's the pain?"

"Not too bad. I'm mostly just feeling tired. But I'm beginning to think fate has it in for me. I've been rolled in a car, knocked down by a horse, bitten by a rattler . . . Heavens, what's next? I feel like a magnet for disaster." She gave a wry chuckle. "That's enough whining from me. How was your trip?"

Roper steeled his emotions. Lila had been hurt repeatedly. He was about to hurt her again. "Before I tell you about the trip, I need answers to a couple of questions."

"Go ahead." A note of caution had crept into her voice.

"How many people knew about your plan to drive to Las Vegas with me?"

She hesitated. "Not many. Mariah knew, of course. And Gemma—I always let my daughter know where I'll be."

"You didn't tell Darrin and Simone?"

"No. Why should I? We're barely on speaking terms. But Mariah could have mentioned it to them—or even passed it on to Madeleine if they're in touch."

Lila's answer matched Roper's suspicions. Mariah, the Culhanes' longtime cook and housekeeper, was loyal to Frank's first wife. She also kept in touch with Frank's son and daughter-in-law. If they'd known about Lila's plans, they would have expected her to be in the truck with him.

"So, who knew that you'd decided to stay home?"

"Probably just Gemma. I'd already given Mariah the week off to visit her sister in California. The stable hands might have seen me, but they wouldn't have paid much attention. They had orders from you." She fell silent for a moment. "Why are you asking me these questions, Roper?"

He told her about the incident on the freeway. "It couldn't have been an accident. I can't help thinking that whoever hired that semi driver expected you to be in the truck with me."

"So a fatal rollover would have killed us both." Her voice quivered slightly.

"It makes sense. We know who wants you out of the picture. They already tried it once. And taking me with you would be a bonus. They'd have you out of the house and me out of the stable—a double win."

"But how could anyone be so cold—and with the horses in the trailer? Are you sure Darrin and Simone were behind it?"

"Them or their mother. We know that Madeleine's got the connections to put out a hit—if she's even in the country. But unless the police find the truck driver, and he talks, we've got no proof of anything."

"So there's nothing we can do?"

"For now, just be wary of them. Don't put yourself in a situation where you could be hurt."

A beat of silence passed between them before she spoke again.

"I'm sorry, Roper. If your hunch is correct, I'm partly to blame for what happened. Is your sister all right?"

"She's fine. She went out to dinner with Hayden Barr tonight. The rig took a beating, but the damage is insured."

"What about the horses? Were they hurt?"

Roper took a deep breath. It was time for the bad news.

"The horses were shaken up when the trailer tipped. One in a Million was spooked, but he doesn't appear to be hurt. Fire Dance was so crazy wild that Hayden and I, and Sam Rafferty, who was close by, could barely get him out of the trailer and into a stall. The last time I checked, he wasn't letting anybody near him. He doesn't seem to be injured, but I don't know if he'll be calm enough to show on Saturday night."

"So Sam is there. I was wondering where he'd gone."

"He's keeping an eye on me. I can tell he's under a lot of pressure to close the case, but I can't let that worry me this week. I told him about the so-called accident, so at least he's aware that something's going on."

"What about Millie? You haven't mentioned her."

Roper lowered his voice. "I'm sorry, Boss. Millie was hurt. She has a shattered left leg, most likely the shaft of the tibia. It's bad. The vet can do surgery and attach a metal plate, but he says she'll always be lame. She won't be able to run or carry a rider."

"Oh, Roper." Lila gave a moan of dismay. "Is she in much pain?"

"The leg's been splinted to keep it stable, and she's had shots of phenylbutazone for the pain. But the surgery will need to be done soon—unless you choose to put her out of her misery. She's your horse. It's your call."

Lila took a ragged breath. "I was in the stall when Millie was born. I hand-raised her after her mother died. She had so much potential, so much spirit. With time and experience, she could have become a champion like her father." The words ended in a sob. "If I love her, I won't force her to suffer, Roper. And I won't force her to live out her life as a cripple, knowing she can't run free."

"So you're asking to have her put down?" Roper's voice was gentle, but there was no way to soften the impact of the question.

"Yes." Lila was weeping now, forcing each word. "It's the only kind thing I can do for her. Have her body shipped home in a refrigerated truck. I don't care how much it costs. I'll have the grave dug and bury her here on the ranch, next to Million Dollar Baby."

"I'll take care of everything," Roper said. "I'm sorry that I can't be there with you. If I hadn't decided to take her—"

"Don't even think it. This wasn't your fault. I'll be with you later in the week when I come to see you ride."

"Maybe you shouldn't try to come," Roper said. "You may not be strong enough to make the trip. And the way things are going here, you might not have much to see."

"I'll be the judge of that. I love you, Roper. No matter what happens—"

"I love you, too, Boss." He cut her off. "As for what happens, let's not talk about that. All we can do is make the best of now."

"I'll be there. You can plan on it—oh, here's Gemma. Got to go."

The call ended abruptly, leaving Roper gazing at the phone in his hand. Steeling himself, he slipped it into his pocket and went back inside the barn. He needed to check on the two stallions. After that, it would be time to make arrangements for the end of Millie's beautiful, young life.

But he wasn't letting this tragedy go—especially given that the likely target had been Lila. He wouldn't rest until the driver of the green Peterbilt had been punished and the person who'd hired him had faced justice—the law's or Roper's own.

* * *

Darrin Culhane hurled his cell phone against the far wall of his home office. It splintered the glass of his framed law-school diploma, where it hung next to a photo of him shaking hands with George W. Bush.

Leaving the glass shards on the floor, he stormed into the living room, where his wife, Simone, dressed in leggings and a baggy tee, was watching one of the endless TV reality shows she favored. A bowl of chocolate ice cream rested on the growing bulge of her belly. She'd been pretty before, and full of life. But her pregnancy had turned her into a slob. Darrin could scarcely stand the sight of her. At first, he'd been happy with her pregnancy. He'd wanted an heir. But why couldn't women churn out babies without getting fat and cranky?

She looked up as he walked in front of her, blocking her view of the screen. "So what was that noise and clatter about?" she asked.

Darrin picked up the remote and switched off the TV. "That was the goon we hired to drive that truck. He forced the rig off the road, but it didn't go all the way over, and he didn't get another chance. The Highway Patrol was right there."

"Is he keeping the money we paid him?"

"You have to ask?" Darrin kicked an empty pizza box across the floor. "But he sounded nervous, like he might be in trouble. Oh, and he caught a glimpse of the woman in the truck. She was a brunette, definitely not Lila. So it's just as well that the rig didn't crash. But now it's back to square one for us."

Simone set the bowl on the coffee table. "Now what? Have you got any more brilliant ideas?"

"We can still fight Lila in court. We've got a good case.

She's not a real Culhane, and she never gave Dad any children."

"But that could take months. And we could still lose. When we were married, you promised me we'd inherit that house when your father died. We were going to raise our children there, entertain guests, become *the Culhanes.*"

"That was before I knew about the terms of the will."

She stood to meet his gaze, her blue eyes blazing with determination. "We can't just give up. Can't your mother arrange something else?"

"You know Mother's gone off the radar. Not even a phone call or a blasted text. That was why we had to arrange for the truck driver on our own, with one of Mother's shady friends."

"Why doesn't your mother just die? At least we'd have her money. That remission was almost too convenient. I'm beginning to suspect the bitch never had brain cancer in the first place."

Darrin's hand struck the side of her face in a slap that sent her reeling backward. "Say what you want about me," he snapped. "But there'll be no disrespecting my mother in this house. If you ever call her that again—"

"I could leave you, Darrin." Simone had regained her footing. She glared up at him, her voice shaking as she spoke. "I could pack up and go home to my parents. Or I could go to the police and tell them everything I know about you and your mother and her friends. You'd never see me or this baby again."

Startled by her vehemence, Darrin froze. This was something new, meek little Simone standing up to him. Maybe the pregnancy had roused a protective streak in her. "You wouldn't dare," he said.

"Wouldn't I? Hit me again and find out."

Darrin took a step backward. "I'm going out," he said. "I'll be back after you've come to your senses."

"Fine." Simone picked up the remote, turned on the TV again, and settled back onto the sofa. "Pick up a couple packets of Oreos on the way home."

Darrin snatched up his keys and stalked out the front door. Even with the sun gone, the night air hit him with a blast of heat. His twelve-year-old Mercedes was parked in the shade of a willow tree. The damned house didn't even have a garage.

He climbed inside, cranked up the AC, and turned on the windshield wipers to wash off the saucer-sized bird splatter that was blocking his vision. With the motor purring, he switched on the headlights and drove out through the gate. He needed a drink, and the Jackalope Saloon, which had begun to feel like his home away from home, was open.

For two cents, he would send Simone home to her rich parents in Dallas. But that would be a reckless idea. For one thing, she was carrying his baby—his heir, hopefully a son. If she could prove that he'd hit her a few times, she might be able to get full custody. Also, Simone knew enough about his under-the-table activities—including tax evasion, an investment scam, and two failed hits on Lila—to get him disbarred and probably jailed as well.

Simone would play all sweet and innocent. But she wasn't blameless. Her demands for a better lifestyle and her constant whining about the Culhane house had driven him to do things he wouldn't have dreamed of doing before they were married. His self-respect had long since flown out the window. That was mostly—if not all—Simone's fault.

No thanks to her, he was sinking ever deeper into this dirty morass. And he could see no way out.

He was pulling into the parking lot outside Jackalope's when his cell phone rang. The caller was unknown. Darrin was about to dismiss the call. But maybe it was from a potential client. He could always use new business.

He took the call. "Hello?"

"Am I speaking to Darrin Culhane?" The muffled voice sounded disguised.

"Yes. Who's calling, please?"

"You don't know me. But I know you. We need to talk."

Darrin's nerves had begun to crawl. "Talk about what?"

"You'll find out. Are you going to Las Vegas for the big horse show?"

"We're still talking about it."

"If you go, we can meet there. No need to look for me. I'll find you." There was a silent pause.

"Wait, damn it!" Darrin exploded. "Who the hell are you?"

The mysterious voice chuckled. "I'm your brother, Darrin."

Chapter Three

Cheyenne had shared a pizza with Hayden in a noisy restaurant a few blocks from the arena complex. Hayden had offered to take her to an upscale place downtown, but after the incident on the freeway, she was too emotionally drained to enjoy good food. She was also worried about the horses. They were Roper's responsibility, but she loved all horses, and she cared deeply about these three animals.

Roper had phoned her about the decision to euthanize Millie. Cheyenne had seen the injury. She had been around horses all her life, and she understood why it had to be done. Still, she was heartsick. The beauty, the talent, the training, the hope, and the innocence of a young animal, all lost for nothing. She burned with silent anger.

She and Hayden had walked to the restaurant by way of a side street. Now they took a different route back to the equestrian complex, a narrow shortcut connecting a shabby motel, a shuttered pawnshop, and a couple of dimly lit bars. Beyond the jagged line of rooftops, the lights of Las Vegas gleamed like distant stars. Cheyenne might have been nervous walking this way alone, but with Hayden at her side, she felt safe enough.

They chatted comfortably on the way. Hayden was easy to be with. Cheyenne found herself liking him more and more. But she hadn't come to Las Vegas for romance. Hayden Barr was her ticket to a new career.

"I'm looking forward to meeting your family." He guided her along the uneven sidewalk with a touch at the small of her back. His eyes kept a sharp lookout for any moving shadows. "Will they be coming to watch your brother compete in the Run for a Million?"

"Some of them plan to be here. Just so you'll know, Roper's my half brother. His father died in a rodeo when he was young. Our mother remarried another rodeo rider and had the rest of us—me and my three brothers."

"So you're the only girl?"

"That's right. And rodeo's in our blood. My father was crippled by a bucking bull. He's been in a wheelchair for as long as I can remember, dribbling Jack Daniel's into his coffee to dull the pain. He's part of the reason I want to break out of the pattern. Even though I don't ride buckers, my luck might not last forever. I worry about my brothers every time they ride out of the gate."

"What about your mother?" Hayden asked. "Is she anything like you?"

"Hardly!" Cheyenne forced a humorless laugh. "My mother is a saint! She can quote whole chapters of Scripture from memory. And she lives every verse. Not that I'm complaining. She raised us to be decent and respectable. She cooks great meals from scratch, on a shoestring. The house is so clean you could eat off the floor; and she's taken care of Dad without help for years. I respect my mother. But, believe me, I wouldn't be like her for all the golden thrones in heaven!"

Hayden chuckled. "So will I get to meet this amazing lady?"

"Probably. She dotes on Roper, and I know she wants to watch him ride. I think my brother, Stetson, is planning to drive her to Vegas. If she comes, she'll be sharing my hotel room."

Cheyenne could have bitten her tongue. Why had she mentioned the room? Was she sending a subconscious message—that if Hayden wanted to sleep with her, he'd have to move fast? Heaven help her, that was the last thing she'd intended. She lengthened her stride, moving ahead of his guiding touch.

"And what about the rest of your family?" he asked. "Will they be coming?"

"Rowdy and Chance will be out on the circuit. I don't know about my dad. He'd be hard to bring, but if he stays home, he'll need somebody to stay with him. What about your family?" she asked, changing the subject. "I know your father will want to see you compete and see Roper show Fire Dance. Will there be others?"

"Nope. Just me and my dad. My mom died of cancer when I was"—he took a breath—"when I was fourteen. That would be eight years ago. Dad's had a few women in his life, but he never remarried, so there's just the two of us. He'll be coming in a day or two. He flies his own plane, so I can't be sure when he'll get here."

"That's interesting about your dad. Do you fly, too?"

"I do," Hayden said. "But the horses don't. I drove here with my cutting horse, Steely Dan. And I'll be driving him back to Texas with Fire Dance after the big show's over. I just hope Fire Dance will be fit to compete."

They were passing the motel, a two-story stucco building with a walkway along the second floor and a moldering pool out front. A row of lights along the roofline cast shadows over dimly lit parking lot.

The orange neon NO VACANCY sign in the office window

sputtered on and off, but the vehicles that crowded the parking lot—mostly older cars and pickups, a couple of farm wagons, and a bobtailed semitruck—made it clear that the rooms were full. A scantily clad woman, tucking cash into the pocket of her cut-off shorts, slipped out of an upstairs room and descended the stairs. As the light caught her face, Cheyenne could see that she wasn't a young girl. Maybe she had children at home. Or maybe she just needed drug money.

As the woman vanished among the vehicles in the parking lot, Cheyenne's gaze fell on the bulky outline of the semi, parked without a trailer, at the far end of the lot. Her pulse lurched as she recognized the squared lines of a Peterbilt—a common enough truck. But what were the chances that it could be green?

What she was imagining was next to impossible. There had to be hundreds of Peterbilts, even green ones, on the road. But Cheyenne knew she couldn't pass by without a closer look.

Hayden caught her arm as she stepped off the sidewalk. "Whoa! Where are you going?"

"That truck!" She strained against his clasp. "It could be the one. I need to check it for damage."

"You mean the one that sideswiped your rig?" He pulled her back onto the sidewalk. "What are the chances, Cheyenne? That semi could be anywhere by now. Damn it, even if you're right, that parking lot could be dangerous, especially for a pretty young woman like you. You don't know what—or who—could be out there."

"Are you coming with me or staying here?" She twisted free and started back into the parking lot.

With a muttered curse, Hayden caught up with her. "All right. Let's get this over with."

They wove their way among the parked vehicles, Hayden guiding the way with the flashlight on his phone. There was little human activity at this hour, but the crumbling asphalt was littered with cigarette butts, spots of chew, and occasional drug needles. A rat scuttled across their path.

Under light, the Peterbilt truck was green, just as Cheyenne remembered. If it had sideswiped the trailer rig, any damage sustained would be on the passenger side of the cab. Heart pounding, she directed the beam of Hayden's phone light.

There it was. The outside edge of the heavy bumper, which had caught the side of the blue Dodge pickup, was streaked with blue paint, as was a shallow scrape along the passenger side door.

Cheyenne's pulse broke into a gallop. "This is the one!" she whispered. "This is the truck!"

Hayden began taking pictures with his phone—closeups of the damage and the license plate and shots of the entire vehicle. He was doing his best to help. But as she watched him, the memory of the crash surged afresh—the roar of the semi and the scream of metal, the fear of hanging over the edge of the road, and the terror for the horses. Because of this truck, and its driver, a precious filly would pay with her life.

Cheyenne's roiling anger heated into rage. If she'd had a crowbar or a pickaxe, she would have shattered the glass and mutilated the metal. If she'd had a knife, she would have slashed the tires. All useless. Nothing could undo the harm that had been done.

Hayden had almost finished taking photos when the glaring beam of a flashlight, blindingly bright, froze them where they stood. As their eyes adjusted, the stocky figure of a man in jeans and a black tee came into focus. One hand held a powerful flashlight. The other hand aimed a revolver.

"What the hell do you think you're doing?" The gritty voice was a match for his pudgy, brutal-looking features. Cheyenne could sense his flinty eyes taking their measure. Neither she nor Hayden had a weapon. The man could shoot them both, right here.

He fixed his gaze on Hayden. "Put your phone on the ground and kick it toward me."

When Hayden hesitated, the man's voice dropped to a growl. "Do it, mister. And no tricks, or I'll shoot your girlfriend. She won't look so pretty after that."

Hayden did as he was told. Keeping the gun aimed, the man crushed the phone with a stomp of his thick-soled motorcycle boot. Would he really fire that gun? Not likely, Cheyenne reasoned. He might be a hit man—and probably was. But this wasn't a contract situation. He had nothing to gain and everything to risk by shooting a couple of nosy strangers.

Still, she couldn't be sure enough to make a move. And there was Hayden's safety to think of as well as her own.

His gaze shifted to Cheyenne, eyes narrowing. "Hey, I know you, girl. You were in that horse rig that blocked me on the freeway out of Kingman. I could barely get around you. Tell your driver he should've been more careful. He could have caused a bad accident."

Cheyenne's temper flared and erupted.

"An accident!" Heedless of the danger, she spat out the words. "We were in the outside lane. You had plenty of room to pass. But you moved over and crowded us off the shoulder. You almost killed us! And a beautiful horse will have to be put down because of you."

Hayden was nudging her to stop, but the words kept coming. "That was no accident! You did it on purpose!"

The man lowered the gun. A slow smile creased his ugly face. "Prove it, lady. Try to prove it was anything but a fender bender. I'm sorry about the horse, but you've got nothing." He kicked the broken phone across the asphalt. "You can have that back. Now get out of here before I decide to make trouble."

Pocketing his phone, Hayden took Cheyenne's arm and guided her back through the maze of parked vehicles. Only as they reached the sidewalk did he speak. "Damn it, Cheyenne, you scared me to death. I was afraid we were both going to get shot. What were you thinking?"

"I wasn't thinking," she said. "I was furious—the way he was talking, as if he'd done nothing wrong. Do you think you can recover those photos you took?"

"I don't know. I'll try. At least I remember the license plate number. We can give that to the police. But the man was right about one thing. Unless we can prove he was carrying out a hit, we've got nothing. You're talking property damage. He dented a rig and injured a horse. That's a misdemeanor. And now he's claiming it wasn't even his fault."

"At least we've seen his face," Cheyenne said. "We can always look at mug shots or work with a sketch artist to find out whether he's a hit man."

"Maybe. But again, you'll have to convince the police he's worth their time."

"I hear you. Let's go check on the horses." Cheyenne strode ahead as the barn came into sight. Hayden's long legs kept pace with her. Clearly, he seemed to think she should forget the incident on the freeway or leave it to Roper. But she couldn't forget what had happened. And she wouldn't be at peace until justice had been done.

* * *

The inside of Barn A, where the horses were housed, was a sea of numbered stalls, arranged in long double rows. Concrete pillars rose like trees in a forest, supporting the vast roof, which also sheltered a vet clinic, a feed store, offices for the judges and barn manager, and a double row of wash racks that also served the adjoining Barn B. A passage on the south side of the barn led to the casino and the hotel lobby.

Cheyenne and Hayden savored the cool air as they entered on the north, from Silverado Ranch Boulevard. The lights had been dimmed, but they could see well enough to follow the stall numbers and find their horses.

Hayden's cutting horse, a brown-and-white paint gelding, was dozing. He raised his head, instantly alert, as Hayden opened the stall gate and ushered Cheyenne inside.

"This is Steely Dan," he said. "Best horse I've ever ridden. I can't wait to have you see him in action."

Cheyenne stroked the silky coat. The horse was in superb condition. "He's beautiful," she said.

"Beauty is always a plus," Hayden said. "But what really counts in a cutting horse is what they call cow sense—the instinct to follow a cow and keep it under control. That instinct can't be taught. It's bred into them. Remember that when you choose your own horse."

"I've heard people compare cutting horses to border collies," Cheyenne said. "Would you agree with that?"

"In a way, I suppose. A smart horse is every bit as intelligent as a dog." He slipped an arm around her shoulders. "Come on. Let's go check on the other horses."

His touch was warm and supportive as they moved along the row of stalls. But Cheyenne felt a chill of dread as she braced for what she would find. Maybe Roper would still be in the barn. That would make things easier. And they could also tell him about finding the truck and driver at the motel. But the hour was late, and Cheyenne knew how tired he must be. When they came to the three stalls assigned to the Culhane horses, there was no sign of him.

Both stallions were traumatized. One in a Million was standing in his stall with his head at the gate. He appeared calm; but he showed the whites of his eyes and flinched when Cheyenne reached up to stroke him. The oats in his feeder hadn't been touched.

Fire Dance was wild-eyed and quivering. When Hayden, who knew the horse well, spoke to him softly over the gate, the red horse laid back his ears, bared his teeth, and lunged for him.

Hayden stepped back, shaking his head.

"Do you think he'll be all right to show?" Cheyenne asked.

Hayden sighed. "He's going to need time. All we can do is hope he recovers before the Run for a Million."

The stall between the two stallions had been assigned to Millie. It was empty. The spirited filly, so full of grace and promise, was gone. Was she still in the vet clinic, scared, confused, and in pain, unaware of the IV needle that would soon end her suffering? Or was she already lying cold under a canvas, her body waiting to be loaded and hauled away?

Shaking with grief and anger, Cheyenne burst into sobs. She pressed her hands to her tear-blinded eyes, but the flow, like a river in spring thaw, went on.

"It's all right, Cheyenne." Hayden's arms circled her, drawing her in to huddle against his chest. "Go ahead and cry, girl. I'm here."

He rocked her, his hand massaging her back, his lips nibbling a trail along her hairline. "There . . . there," he murmured. "That's it. Let it go."

His free hand cupped her chin, tilting her face upward.

For a moment, Cheyenne feared he was going to kiss her. “No—not now!” She turned her face away. She liked Hayden, but this wasn’t the time or place.

“Are you all right, Cheyenne?” A familiar voice spoke from somewhere behind her. As Hayden released her, she turned to find Roper standing next to the stall. He looked haggard and drawn, his eyes bloodshot, his jaw shadowed with stubble.

“I’ll be fine.” Cheyenne took the clean handkerchief he offered and dabbed at her eyes. “What about Millie?”

“It’s over.” Roper’s voice was drained of emotion. “The body’s on the way back to Texas in a refrigerated van. Lila wants to bury her on the ranch.”

“We found the green semi that hit you. And we found the driver.” Hayden related the incident at the motel, ending with the driver’s dismissive words.

“The hell of it is, he’s right,” Roper said. “We can talk to the police. But if we can’t prove there was a hit involved, this won’t even be worth their time. It’s a damned traffic ticket—a dented rig and a horse that had to be put down.”

“You look exhausted, Roper,” Cheyenne said. “You need to go to your room and get some sleep.”

“You don’t look too chipper yourself, Little Sister,” Roper said. “I need to spend more time with the horses. Go on up to bed. I’ll see you in the morning.” He raised an eyebrow. “That’s an order.”

“You’re not here to give me orders,” Cheyenne said.

“You can say that when you’re twenty-one. Until then, I’m the boss. So get going.” He was teasing her now, coaxing away her tears, something he’d often done when she was growing up. Roper had been her hero, her protector from the wild antics of her three roughneck full brothers. He still took his role seriously.

"Watch yourself on the elevator," Roper said. "At this hour, you don't know who you'll be riding with or what condition they might be in. Get in with a crowd if you can."

"For heaven's sake, Roper, I'm a rodeo girl!" Cheyenne protested. "If I can fend off drunken cowboys, I can certainly make it to my hotel room on my own."

"I'll go along and see her safely upstairs," Hayden offered. "All right, Cheyenne?"

Cheyenne sighed and nodded. More arguing would be childish and a waste of time. She turned away and started for the casino and hotel entrance on the south side of the barn.

Catching up with her, Hayden placed a guiding hand on the small of her back. A jolt of awareness shot through her body. The message was subtle but clear. She willed herself to ignore it. She was too emotional and too tired for any kind of sensible decision.

The casino was a bedlam of noise—the piercing dingding of slots, the clatter of roulette wheels, the slap of cards, and the rattle of dice. The shouts of dealers rose above the blare of country music from the audio system. Lights flashed. Customers hunched over machines and around tables, crowding shoulder to shoulder. Armed security guards with two-way radios flanked the doors and slunk like coyotes along the fringes of the crowd.

Cheyenne and Hayden made it to the elevator bank. In response to the button, a nearby set of doors slid open. The elevator was empty.

Cheyenne stepped inside, with Hayden behind her. She laughed as the doors closed. "See? You and Roper didn't have a thing to worry about. I would've been perfectly safe, riding up to the fourteenth floor in an empty elevator."

Hayden pushed the floor button, then turned toward

her. "Who said anything about an empty elevator?" he teased. "I'm here."

He caught her hands, swung her around, and caught her close. His mouth captured hers in a deep, demanding kiss. Cheyenne went rigid, for an instant. Then, with a little moan of resignation, she surrendered, softening against him, opening her mouth to the sensual invasion of his tongue. She closed her eyes. She hadn't meant to let this happen, but he was kind and gallant, and he knew how to kiss. After a hellish day, maybe this was what she'd needed.

As his tongue invaded her mouth, her body began to stir—the faint pulsing between her thighs, the pleasant ache as her nipples tightened beneath her bra. The fingers of his free hand found the hem of her T-shirt and meandered slowly up her back. His touch sent shimmers over her skin. Her breath quickened. Was this what she wanted? She was too tired to think.

The elevator stopped with a slight bump. The doors slid open to reveal a prim-looking matron in a flowered dress with a white lace collar. Hayden and Cheyenne broke apart as the woman stepped into the elevator. "Sixteenth floor," she huffed, giving them a sour look. "I'd press the button myself, but you're standing in the way."

After Hayden had obliged her, the woman turned to face the doors. Spine rigid and head held high, her attitude made it clear what she thought of their behavior. Hayden shifted his gaze to Cheyenne and winked. Cheyenne suppressed a giggle. This was like a scene from a silly romantic comedy. She leaned against him, possessed by a strange light-headedness.

The elevator stopped for them at the fourteenth floor. As the doors closed behind them, they clung together in helpless laughter. It felt good. More than good, Cheyenne thought. Tired as she was, she was beginning to feel alive again.

"What's your room number?" Hayden asked.

Cheyenne recovered her breath. "Fourteen forty-four, down that hallway on the left. Go on. I can make it from here."

"Oh, no, you don't. I intend to do my gentlemanly duty." Offering his arm, he walked her down the empty hall to the room at the end. "Where's your brother staying?"

"Right across the hall in fourteen forty-five. He thinks he needs to look out for me. He's as bad as my mother."

"But you do rodeo. How do you stay safe?"

"I go with my brothers. Not that they care what I do when we're on the circuit. I've learned to look out for myself. That's one reason I want to do cutting. I'm tired of being babysat. In a few months, I'll be twenty-one. By then, I want to be on my own."

"You're on your own right now. We just saw Roper in the barn."

"True, but he could be back anytime."

They had reached the door. As Cheyenne stepped in front of him and lifted her key card out of her shirt pocket, Hayden's arms slid around her from behind. When he pulled her against his lean body, she felt the first quiver of fear. But she willed herself not to resist. She was no fool. She knew what he had in mind. But maybe it was time. Maybe letting Hayden make love to her would blot out the memory that had terrorized her dreams for the past two years. She needed to break free of it. Why not now, with a man she liked and was beginning to trust?

His hands slipped under her shirt and moved upward to cradle her breasts through her bra. Cheyenne's breath caught. Her pulse skittered.

The key card flew out of her hand.

Landing on its edge, it flipped over and came to rest near the toes of two dusty, well-worn boots. A callused hand reached down and picked it up.

Hayden released her and took a hasty step to one side. Hot-faced, Cheyenne stared down at her feet.

"Here's your card, miss." The man spoke with a gruff undertone. Taking the card he thrust at her, Cheyenne forced herself to look up. A sun-weathered face scowled down at her. He was tall, his dark brown hair untrimmed and windblown, his silvery eyes framed in lines of weariness.

His gaze took in her flushed face and rumpled shirt. "Are you all right?" he asked her.

Cheyenne found her voice. "Yes, thank you. I'm fine."

"Not every cowboy you meet here can be trusted," he said with a stern glance at Hayden. "My room is right next door, and the walls are thin. If you need any help, make some noise. I'm a light sleeper. I'll hear you."

Was he thinking that Hayden had picked her up on some street corner? She had to admit she looked the part of a buckle bunny, with her tight-fitting jeans and fitted black T-shirt. And after what he'd seen as he came down the hall, what else was he to think?

Should she set him straight? But he was a stranger. She didn't owe him an explanation.

"This isn't what you think," Hayden said. "I was only showing Miss McKenna to her room."

One dark eyebrow tilted upward in evident disbelief. Then he shrugged. "Whatever you call it. And now, if you'll excuse me, I've had a long drive from Ten Sleep, Wyoming. It's past this cowboy's bedtime." He unlocked his room, stepped inside, and closed the door behind him.

Still burning with humiliation, Cheyenne turned to Hayden. "I think you should go," she said. "We've had enough excitement for one night."

"Yeah." Hayden nodded. "That cowboy has a way of spoiling a good time."

"A way? Does that mean you know the man?"

"Everybody knows him," Hayden said. "That's Buck Tolson, the national cutting champion. I competed against him last spring at Cave Creek. I was in first place until he came out last and beat me by five points. But that's not going to happen again. This time I've sworn to beat him—and he's just given me another reason to leave him in the dust."

CHAPTER FOUR

Sam finished an early breakfast at the hotel coffee shop and walked outside to collect his thoughts. The eastern sky was washed with hues of rose and peach. The desert breeze smelled of sage, tobacco smoke, and exhaust fumes. Traffic rumbled past on nearby Interstate 15.

Time was flying, and Sam was no closer to finding Frank Culhane's killer than he'd been when he left Texas. He had the rest of the week to either solve the case, write it off as unsolved, or arrest Roper, based on unproven evidence, and take a chance on a trial.

For Sam, the acquittal of a man he respected would come as a relief. But it would leave Frank's murder unsolved, justice unserved, and a permanent blot on his own record. He had days to find solid answers.

The Shootout, a free-for-all match to fill eleven of sixteen reining slots for next year's Run for a Million, would be held on Friday. Contestants could make up to three runs on three different horses. That was what Roper had registered to do. But one horse was gone. If the others were too traumatized to show, he would be out of the competition.

Maybe that was just as well. If Roper was found guilty of murder, by this time next year he'd be behind bars.

But what if Roper was innocent? Sam asked himself. What if, while he waited for Roper to slip up and show his hand, the real killer was still out there, hiding in plain sight?

Thoughts churning, Sam walked around the hotel and entered the arena complex, where the Shootout was scheduled to take place.

What if he'd taken the wrong approach—letting the evidence overrule his own intuition? Maybe it was time to back off and look at the larger picture—the suspects on his list and any others he might have overlooked.

Whether he liked it or not, that included Jasmine and her mother.

Lost in thought, he found himself wandering on a random path through the vast building. Now he was walking down a corridor that led past offices, dressing and workout rooms, and an emergency medical clinic. At this early hour, most of the doors were closed.

Arranged along the wall, in the spaces between the doors, were framed photos of men and women who had made contributions to equine sports—champions, horse breeders and trainers, business investors, and others.

Sam stopped short at the sight of a familiar face. There on the wall was a framed photo of a smiling Frank Culhane.

Sam had viewed Frank's remains. He'd also seen stock photos in the tabloids and the murky private-eye shots of Frank in a motel doorway with his young mistress. But only now, looking at the portrait of a man in his prime, dressed in a blue western shirt with a Native American bolo tie, his tanned, rugged features framed by a mane of silver hair, did Sam get a sense of the person Frank had been in life. The face in the picture exuded power, confidence, and magnetism.

What would motivate someone to kill such a man? Envy? Revenge? Ambition? Greed? Fear? Even love?

This week Sam would make it his mission to find out. He would track down and interview anyone who had known Frank Culhane, including the family. If he could find the truth about why Frank had been murdered, he would have a new lead to his killer.

From his place in the barn, Roper could hear the sounds of the rookie and non-pro events starting up. Fans were pouring into the nearest of two arenas. Horses were being saddled and warmed up. Soon the judges would take their places, and the first event would begin.

Today was Wednesday. The Shootout would take place on Friday. Riders who'd competed in past Shootouts claimed that it was even more stressful than the final Run for a Million. Any qualified rider—man or woman, pro, non-pro, or rookie—could enter, so the field was large. At the end of the long day, eleven spots in next year's Run for a Million would be awarded, as well as a handsome cash prize. For the winners, the uncertainty would be gone. They would have prize money and a full year to train. Roper had hoped to be among them. But if neither of his horses was fit to enter, he could already be out of the running.

The remaining five places would be awarded at the Cactus Classic in March. That was where Frank had won his spot. Roper could only hope to do the same. Right now, all he could do was work with the two stallions, in the hope that at least one of them would be ready for Saturday's million-dollar run.

For now, he'd resolved to plan his days. He would go

ahead with his life as if there were no clouds on the horizon. But the specter of a wrongful conviction and a lifetime behind bars haunted him day and night. No more freedom. No more horses. And no more Lila, his beautiful boss, whose warm passion had awakened him to a new life.

He knew that Sam Rafferty was watching his every move, waiting for a slipup that would justify an arrest. Sam was the kind of man Roper would value as a friend. But Sam had sworn an oath to uphold the law. There was no question that, when the time came, he would put duty before friendship.

He glanced at the time on his phone, resisting the urge to call Lila. This wouldn't be a good time for her. The van with Millie's remains would be arriving sometime this morning. The cowboy who ran the ranch's miniature backhoe would have the grave dug. He'd be waiting to help move the body to its resting place and blanket it under Texas earth. Lila showed a tough face to the world, but Roper knew that her heart was as tender as a child's. Today that heart would be breaking. After the cowboy left, she would lay flowers on the fresh grave and cry her eyes out. He only wished he could be there to hold her.

He would give her some time. Then he would call and tell her not to come to Las Vegas. The trip would tax her strength. Worse, it could be dangerous. If the hit on the freeway had been meant to take her out, another attempt on Lila's life could be made at any time. She would be far safer at home.

Even if she were to come, she could be making the trip for nothing. There was a chance that neither of the stallions would be fit to perform on Saturday.

But that couldn't be allowed to happen. He owed it—to Lila, to Chet Barr, and to himself—to see that Fire Dance was ready to compete, and that One in a Million would be there for backup.

Starting now, he had the rest of the week to work with them and get them ready. If he failed, it wouldn't be for lack of trying.

After silencing his phone, to avoid any startling sounds, he focused his full attention on the horses. Both stallions had nibbled at their oats. But they were chuffing, snorting, and stamping their hooves. When Roper reached out to Fire Dance over the gate, the wild-eyed sorrel laid back his ears and thrust his head forward, baring his teeth in a clear threat to bite.

One in a Million was more approachable, still rolling his eyes, snorting, and tossing his head, but no longer trying to kick. Roper took a calming breath. Then, whistling a familiar tune, he took a brush and a clean towel, stepped into the stall, and closed the gate behind him. It was a risky move. The powerful stallion could easily kill him. But One in a Million had never known anything from his trainers but trust and gentleness. He snorted and quivered but didn't strike out.

Roper extended the brush and towel, letting the horse sniff them. The big roan usually enjoyed being groomed. But this time his head jerked upward. He backed away, his rump crashing into the back of the stall.

Roper stood his ground, speaking softly. "It's all right, big boy. Nobody's going to hurt you. I know you had a big scare, but you'll be fine now."

As he eased closer, Roper began to sing, his voice low and calming. The song was one that Frank used to sing as he brushed the stallion's glossy roan coat.

"As I walked out in the streets of Laredo . . . As I walked out in Laredo one day . . ."

One in a Million's ears pricked forward with sudden interest. Continuing to sing, Roper moved the brush lightly over the stallion's withers and down his shoulder. He heard the release of breath as the powerful body began to relax.

Roper kept the brush moving. It was a start. But with Fire Dance still wild with terror in the next stall, he had a long way to go. With luck, One in a Million might be ready to show. But unless he could ride Fire Dance into the arena, Chet Barr would be one angry owner.

Sam was crossing the hotel lobby, headed for the barn to speak with Roper, when he recognized the young woman coming out of the elevator. Petite, with stunning eyes and a cloud of dark hair, it could only be Cheyenne McKenna.

This morning she looked shower fresh, her hair flowing in damp waves. She was dressed in a blue denim shirt and fresh jeans. Back in Texas, he'd interviewed her just once. Mostly, he'd asked about Roper's relationship with his former boss. She'd had little to say, as she was spending most of her time on the rodeo circuit. But someone in her family—maybe it was one of her brothers—had mentioned that Frank had offered to train her in reining, and she'd turned him down. Maybe there was more to the story than what he'd heard.

"Excuse me, Miss McKenna." Sam was close enough to be heard. "Do you have a few minutes? I have some questions for you."

She turned, the half smile on her face vanishing. "I've already told you what I know, Agent," she said. "Besides, I'm on my way to meet someone."

"This won't take long," Sam said. "Come on, I'll buy you some coffee. By the time you drink it, we'll be finished."

She shrugged. "I really can't refuse the FBI, can I? Fine, don't bother with the coffee. Just get it over with."

He led her to a nearby waiting area furnished with several upholstered settees. Sitting, she faced him, a guarded expression on her stunning face. According to the tabloids, she'd turned down modeling and movie offers. Sam could believe it.

"I'm trying to learn more about Frank Culhane," Sam said. "I understand you knew him."

Her only reaction was a subtle widening of her eyes. "I did know him," she said. "But I had nothing to do with his death, if that's what you're asking."

"No. I already know you were away when he was killed. But I understand you spent some time with him. He offered to teach you reining."

"Yes, he did. I said no. Why are you asking?"

"I'm just trying to gain some insights into Frank's personality," Sam said. "Can you tell me why you turned him down?"

"Yes." Her voice was steady, but her hands clenched and unclenched in her lap. "I was only eighteen, but I could tell that I was dealing with a control freak. He wanted to take me under his wing and take over my life."

"What did he do when you refused his offer?"

"What could he do? I left. I never spoke to him again."

"What about your family? Were they involved in your decision?"

"No. Roper wasn't working for Frank then. He was still in Colorado selling our old ranch. And my parents had never liked the Culhanes. They treated our family like trash, always looking down their noses at us. I didn't need anybody's advice. The decision was all mine."

"How did you feel when you heard that Frank had been murdered?"

A shocked expression flashed across her face and vanished. She was under control once more. "I was surprised, of course," she said. "But Frank was no friend of mine. To tell you the truth, I can't say I felt anything at all."

Abruptly, she rose to her feet. "I believe I've answered enough questions, Agent. Unless you have something of vital importance to ask me, I'll excuse myself and be on my way."

Sam stood. "Thank you for your time, Miss McKenna. If I have any more questions, I'll be in touch."

"I hope you find Frank's killer soon," she said. "We all need to put this trouble behind us and move on with our lives."

Sam watched her walk away, her stride lithe and energetic. Young as she was, she was surprisingly self-possessed. But then, she was a celebrity in the rodeo world. She'd faced fans, reporters, and probably her share of unruly cowboys.

But something told him there was more to her relationship with Frank than she'd let on. He'd seen it in her expressive eyes when he'd asked her about Frank's death. She'd been just eighteen when he'd offered to train her—and eighteen was a highly vulnerable age. Had she loved the man or hated him? Whatever feelings she'd had toward Frank Culhane, Sam would bet that indifference wasn't one of them.

But did those feelings have any connection to his murder?

Cheyenne hurried through the lobby and passed into the barn. Hayden would be waiting for her at his horse's stall. He had promised to show her around the facility, introduce her to some cowboys, and watch them exercise their horses in the practice arena. She wouldn't be allowed to ride one—that would be asking too much. But at least it would guide her thinking about the kind of animal she wanted to own.

She'd started the day in a state of happy anticipation. But the encounter with Sam Rafferty had dampened her spirits. Why had the FBI agent grilled her about her relationship with Frank? She certainly hadn't killed the man—although she might have wanted to. Any number of people could confirm that she and her three brothers had been on the rodeo circuit when the killer struck.

So why had the FBI man been so persistent? Did he suspect someone else close to her? Someone like Roper?

A chill passed through Cheyenne's body. Roper couldn't be a killer—he was too kind, too decent. But he'd been close to the ranch. He had access to the stable at all hours. He had won Frank's place in the Run for a Million—and he seemed to be spending a lot of time with Frank's glamorous widow.

A leaden lump congealed in her chest. Sam Rafferty would have every reason to suspect that Roper had murdered his boss. So why hadn't Roper been arrested? Did the agent need more proof? The thought of Roper behind bars triggered a dizzying surge of fear. He could already be in danger. But there was no way Cheyenne would ever believe that her brother was a murderer.

She hadn't seen Roper since last night. He hadn't answered her knock on the door to his room this morning, and her call to his cell phone had gone to voicemail. True, sometimes he turned his phone off when he worked with horses. But she needed to talk to him now. Whatever was happening, she needed to hear the truth.

Intent on finding her brother, she made her way up and down the long rows of stalls. The barn was a busy place this morning, with horses being fed, groomed, and led out for exercise or competition. Stalls were being cleaned, the reeking manure hauled away in wheelbarrows. Water was running in the shower racks.

Cheyenne remembered how to find Roper's stall numbers, but Hayden would be expecting her by now. He might even be out looking for her. She didn't want to meet him until she'd spoken with Roper. And she certainly didn't want Hayden to know that Roper could be a murder suspect. Avoiding him, she took a circuitous route, checking each aisle as she passed.

Turning a corner, she slammed hard into the solid figure of a man. Dazed by the impact, she stumbled backward against the corner of a stall. A hand reached out, capturing her fingers in its big, roughened palm. She allowed herself to be pulled upright.

"Are you all right?"

The deep voice, with its gritty undertone, was familiar. So were the words. Cheyenne had heard them last night, in the hall outside her hotel room.

Her cheeks blazed as she looked up into the glacial gray eyes of Buck Tolson.

"I—I'm sorry," she stammered, still unsettled. "I should have been more careful."

"No damage done." He released her hand. "Are you looking for your boyfriend?"

"He's not my boyfriend." Annoyance deepened the flush in her face. "Not that it's any of your business. You don't know me, and you don't know him."

"Then take some advice from a man who's seen too many other young women get hurt. These cowboys aren't here for romance. Picking up girls like you—that's just their way of blowing off steam. That one you were with last night—by the time his wheels hit the freeway, he'll have already moved on."

"Girls like me?" Cheyenne bristled. It was obvious that the man didn't recognize her. "What do you think I am?" she demanded. "A buckle bunny? Maybe even a pro? Whatever you're assuming about me, you couldn't be more wrong."

"What I think of you doesn't matter." His voice was

calm—maddeningly so. "I'm just trying to do you a favor. If you're smart, you'll pack your gear and get out of Vegas before this town ruins your life."

"Who do you think you are, telling me what to do?" Cheyenne was seething now. "You sound just like my mother!"

Without waiting for his response, she turned and stalked away, down the row of stalls. She was already worried and upset about Roper. The last thing she needed was a stranger telling her how to live her life—a life he knew nothing about.

Buck watched her until she disappeared from sight. He should probably have kept his damned mouth shut. But his sister's suicide last year had set off something inside him—a compulsion to speak up when he saw a young woman on the edge of trouble. Maybe if someone had said those words to Katy, she'd still be alive.

Blond, pretty, and full of fun at eighteen, Katy had come with him to a cutting event here in Las Vegas. The cowboy she'd met had taken her virginity and left her broken. The morning after his championship run, Buck had found her in her hotel room, her system full of alcohol, barbiturates, and anything else she could lay her hands on. There were signs of rough, consensual sex, but the coroner had ruled out foul play in her death. Katy had done this to herself. Luckily for the cowboy, he was nowhere to be found. If he ever saw the heartless bastard again, Buck would make him pay.

With their parents gone, Buck had been responsible for his sister. He would never forgive himself for her death. He'd been speaking to Katy in his mind when he'd warned that dazzling brunette about her boyfriend. His intentions had been the best. But he'd only succeeded in making her angry.

It was time he faced the truth. Rescuing a hundred girls wouldn't save Katy or bring her back. He needed to stop before it became an obsession. This week, he was here in Las Vegas to defend his cutting championship, and right now, his horse needed a workout.

Chief, his rangy buckskin gelding, was waiting down the row. The nine-year-old American quarter horse nickered and butted his head against the gate as his owner approached. At fifteen and a half hands, he was tall for a cow horse, but he was as light-footed as a cat, able to turn on a dime, with instincts that could anticipate a cow's every move. Buck had been offered a quarter of a million dollars for Chief. He'd turned the wealthy buyer down. Some things were worth more than money.

As he reached for the saddle pad, Buck noticed the horse in the next stall—a sharp-looking brown-and-white paint. A memory stirred. That horse and its rider were hard to forget. Buck had bested them in last year's cutting championship. They'd been leading until his high-scoring run left them in second place.

Hayden Barr, that was the rider's name. As for the face that went with it . . . Something was familiar. A new connection.

Buck muttered a curse as the mental picture came clear. It was Hayden Barr he'd seen last night in the corridor of the hotel, fondling the spunky brunette who'd just now gone storming off down the row of stalls.

Small world. And none of his concern.

With a mental shrug, Buck turned his full attention to the horse. It was time to forget the lady and go back to minding his own damned business.

Cheyenne found Roper with the stallions. He was standing outside Fire Dance's stall, coaxing the horse to take a carrot through the bars of the gate. So far, Fire Dance was having none of it. He'd backed into the far corner of the stall, where he was snorting, tossing his head, and baring his big, yellow teeth.

Cheyenne stopped a few paces behind her brother. "We need to talk, Roper," she said.

"I'm busy. Does it have to be now?" His attention was fixed on the stallion.

"I'm afraid so. There are things I need to ask you. Urgent things."

With a sigh of impatience, he dropped the carrot into the stall and turned toward her. "Did you see Hayden? He was here looking for you a few minutes ago. Now he's gone upstairs to check your room. If you showed up, he said to keep you here."

"Fine. That will give us a few minutes to talk."

"That's all the time I have. What's this all about, Cheyenne? Is it Hayden? Has he been pushing things too far?"

"If that were the problem, I could handle it myself," she said. "No, it's something more serious."

He waited for her to go on. He knew, of course, what she was going to ask him. He'd probably known all along.

"Sam Rafferty stopped me in the lobby," she said. "He asked me about Frank, about my relationship with him, and about yours. He seemed to be looking for a reason you might have to kill him." Her eyes met his, their gaze unflinching. "I know our mother swore that you were at home when Frank was murdered. I thought that was the end of the trouble. But is it? I can tell you're worried about something, and not just the horses. Roper, does the FBI still suspect you of murder?"

He took a breath. She sensed pain in the jagged rush of air. "You know I didn't kill him, don't you?"

"Of course. I'd fight to the death to defend you."

"Thank you, Little Sis." He squeezed her shoulder. "But

even that might not be enough. I seem to be the perfect suspect. Motive, means, and opportunity. Sam Rafferty even tells me they've found a piece of evidence—the murder weapon, I'm guessing. But it's all circumstantial. There's no witness and no prints or DNA to tie me to the crime."

"But you could still be arrested, couldn't you?"

"Yes. But Sam agreed to let me come here and compete as long as I behave myself. It's a safe bet on his part. Any attempt to escape would make me look guilty as hell."

"Oh, Roper!" Heartsick for him, Cheyenne shook her head. "What about your boss, Mrs. Culhane? She could have killed Frank. It would've served him right. I heard that he cheated on her."

"Lila's not part of this. She was better off when Frank was alive. At least she wasn't fighting Frank's kids for the ranch."

She studied him a moment. "You're in love with her, aren't you?"

"That's between Lila and me. I trust you to keep it to yourself."

"Of course. Mother would have a fit. How much does she know about the FBI investigation?"

"I haven't told her anything. But Sam's talked with her a couple of times. She confirmed that I was home all night, and that sometime after midnight I heard barking and got up to chase a skunk off the porch. I caught the dog and shut him in the barn so he wouldn't get sprayed. When I came back inside, wearing nothing but skivvies and the boots I'd pulled on, Mother was in the kitchen, in her robe, so she could truthfully say she saw me—and add that I wouldn't have gone anywhere without clothes."

"And that's not enough of an alibi?"

"Sam claims that parents will say anything to protect their children, so he can't accept the story as proof."

Roper glanced down the row of stalls. "Here comes Hayden. I hope I've satisfied your curiosity."

The last words stung. "It wasn't curiosity," she said. "I'm worried about you. I want to help if I can."

"If you want to help, Little Sister, keep quiet and don't interfere. Understand?"

"Yes, but . . ." Cheyenne's words trailed off as Hayden came within hearing. He was smiling, ready to show her around as he'd promised.

Coming down in the elevator this morning, Cheyenne had been excited about the day ahead. Now it was as if a bank of storm clouds had rumbled across the sky, blotting out the sunlight.

Fixing a smile on her face, she strode forward to meet Hayden.

Chapter Five

Sheltered by the patio umbrella, Lila sat in her favorite chair beside the pool. One hand cradled her phone as she waited for the ring and the one voice that would give her comfort.

Burying Millie that morning had left her drained. As the dirt clods fell from the backhoe onto that lifeless body, she'd felt as if they were crushing her heart. But she'd stayed until the backhoe had finished the grave and been driven off to the shed. Then she'd arranged a few wildflowers in a heart shape on the fresh earth, whispered a word of farewell, and allowed her daughter to escort her back to the house.

Gemma had never been fond of horses—or any other kind of animal. She had tolerated her mother's grief but not really understood it. However, she was competent and caring with people, qualities that would make her an excellent nurse when she graduated from the program at TCU.

Gemma had seated Lila on the patio, checked the dressing on her arm, and brought out her customary glass of iced tea. Then she'd disappeared inside the house to do her schoolwork. Lila sipped the tea. It was too sweet, not the way she liked it, but at least it was cold.

The mid-August day was already getting hot. The late-morning sun cast glints of gold on the surface of the pool. Hummingbirds buzzed among the honeysuckle blossoms where the vine grew over the wrought-iron fence. After a sleepless night and emotional morning, Lila was tired, but she wanted to take Roper's call outside, where it was peaceful and private.

Mariah, who had returned unexpectedly last night, had begun rattling pans in the kitchen. Lila had given her time off to visit her sister, but evidently the two of them had quarreled, and now Mariah was back home. The longtime Culhane cook was none too pleased that Gemma had moved things around in her kitchen. The banging and clanging of pans was her way of showing displeasure.

Once Lila would have been glad for Mariah's return. But now that she'd learned the woman was acting as a spy for Darrin and Simone, all trust was gone. No place in the house was safe from Mariah's sharp eyes and ears.

Lila was getting drowsy when the phone jangled. Checking the caller ID, she felt her pulse quicken.

"How are you doing, Boss?" The undercurrent of tension in Roper's voice told Lila that things weren't going well for him.

"The burial's done," she said. "I know that death is part of having animals, but I loved that sweet girl. I'm sad, but I'll be all right."

"I know you loved her. So did I. Lila—"

"How are things with you?" She cut him off. When he called her by her name, it tended to be when he had something serious to say. She wasn't sure she was ready to hear it. "How are the stallions?" she asked. "Are they settling down?"

"One in a Million's coming around, though I haven't tried to saddle him yet. I'm most worried about Fire Dance. No one can get near him, not even Hayden. He could have an injury that's giving him pain, but the vet's not seeing anything from outside the stall. It sucks that I'll probably miss the Shootout. I might have to miss the big event as well. But that can't be helped. It's the horses that matter."

"I'm sorry." Lila ached for him. "Hopefully, this is the worst of it. I'll see you tomorrow when our flight gets in. Things are bound to be looking up by then."

"That's what I'm trying to tell you, Lila," he said. "You mustn't come. It's not a good idea anymore."

"What?" Lila gripped the phone, which she'd nearly dropped. "Of course, I'm coming. We've got the plane tickets and the hotel reservations. We talked about this."

"I know we did. But you're barely out of the hospital. You need to rest."

"I can rest in the hotel. I'll have two full days and most of Saturday to take it easy before the Run for a Million. And Gemma will be with me."

"Yes, but there's more. That so-called accident on the freeway was probably meant for you. If someone wants to kill you, you'll be setting yourself up as a target here. And think about this. What if I don't have a horse I can show? You'll have made the trip for nothing."

"What if you do have a horse? What if you win, and I'm not there to see you? I'm willing to take that chance, Roper. You can expect me Thursday evening. I'll call you when we're checked in."

Before Roper could argue, Lila ended the call. With a sigh, she laid the phone on the side table. Roper was too stubborn to call her back. And even if he did, she wouldn't answer. She could be stubborn, too, and her mind was made up.

But Lila knew the man she loved. And she understood the real reason Roper was telling her to stay away. Sam Rafferty had followed him to Las Vegas. If Sam decided that the evidence was sufficient to make an arrest, Roper could be led away from the arena in handcuffs.

That sight was one that Roper wouldn't want her to see. But for Lila, it was one more compelling reason for her to be there. If the worst happened, she would start the legal fight for his innocence that very day—that very hour, if she could.

For that fight, she would need her strength.

"Are you ready to go in, Mom?" Gemma had come outside. She was tall, thin, and pale, like Lila's grandmother, her light brown hair trimmed to a manageable pixie cut. Dressed in khaki slacks and a pale green blouse, she was as plainspoken and sensible as she looked.

Lila rose without help and walked across the patio, ignoring her daughter's proffered hand. She'd been babied long enough.

"Mariah said to tell you that lunch will be served at twelve thirty," Gemma said. "I offered to help, but she shooed me out of the kitchen as if I had the plague. I don't remember her being so grouchy before. When I lived here, growing up, she seemed quite nice."

Lila gave her a wry smile. "As your great-grandma would say, there's been a lot of water under the bridge since then. There's a war going on over this house and the ranch. And as far as Mariah's concerned, we're the enemy."

Simone had tried on every outfit in her closet, from flowery summer sundresses to the elegant party frocks in fabrics like silk, chiffon, and lamé that she'd worn back home in Dallas. She'd looked like a tiny-waisted princess back then, floating into her parents' country-club dances and dinners. Now the gowns would no longer fit over the growing lump of her belly. Either the zippers wouldn't close or the full skirts made her look like a pregnant elephant hiding under a tent.

Aunt Cora, her mother's sister, had rhapsodized about how expectant mothers had a special glow about them. But Simone wasn't glowing. She was getting bigger and more repulsive every day. Her husband didn't want to look at her. He didn't even want to touch her, except to punish her.

She was supposed to love the baby growing inside her. But when was that supposed to happen? So far, she felt nothing, except for the awareness that she was carrying the only legitimate Culhane heir.

That was her power. She would learn to use it.

Simone's gowns, stripped from their hangers, lay scattered on the bed. Even if they still fit her, she would have no place to wear them in a flea-bitten, one-horse town like Willow Bend. She was smothering here, with nothing to do but read magazines, watch TV, and get fat on chocolate-fudge ice cream.

Frustrated, she scooped up the dresses and bundled them in her arms. The fragrance of perfumes she no longer wore rose from the delicate fabric as she carried them across the bedroom and stuffed them into the back of closet. Then she pulled on her blue sweats and left the bedroom.

She could hear Darrin's Mercedes pulling into the driveway. He'd been in court that morning. His mood would depend on how his case had gone.

Through the living room window, she watched him climb out of the car. His shoulders were slumped, his tie loosened—a sign that he must have lost. Darrin wasn't a great lawyer or even a good one. She couldn't depend on him to win their lawsuit against Lila Culhane. The attempt at a hit on the freeway had failed, and he didn't seem inclined to try again.

If she wanted to raise her family on the Culhane ranch, in the Culhane mansion, Simone knew that she couldn't wait around for her weak husband to do his job. Their future would have to depend on her.

Earlier that morning, Simone had received a call from Mariah at the ranch house. It appeared that Lila and her daughter would be flying to Las Vegas for the big event. The rattlesnake bite Lila had suffered, purely by accident, had left her weakened. And she would be away from home—a rare chance for Simone to put things right for her future family.

Feet dragging, thoughts churning, Darrin mounted the steps. The property-damage suit he'd lost in court should've been a slam dunk. But he'd found himself so preoccupied with last night's phone call that he'd blown it wide open. His client, now owing the plaintiff $25,000 for the death of a prize bull that had wandered in front of his truck, was probably mad enough to kill him.

Last night's call from an alleged unknown brother had ended without giving him a chance to ask questions. Was it a prank? Maybe some kind of blackmail? Was it fake—or could it be real? Frank Culhane had been a notorious womanizer. But so far, aside from Miss Crystal Carter's unborn baby, no illegitimate bastards had turned up. So why now?

Another question: What should he do about the phone call? Ignore it? Hire an investigator? Meet the caller in Las Vegas?

And what was he supposed to tell Simone?

Once the words were out, they couldn't be taken back. He would wait on sharing the secret with his wife, Darrin resolved as he crossed the porch to the door. That would buy him time to make his own decision about the phone call.

Simone met him at the door with a cold Michelob from the refrigerator. "Listen to me, Darrin," she said, handing him the beer. "I've made a new plan. Today I'm going into Abilene to buy some new clothes."

He gave her a puzzled look. "That's okay, I guess, as long as you don't spend too much. What—?"

"I said listen to me, Darrin. One way or another, we're going to get that house. Cancel your appointments for the rest of the week. We're going to Las Vegas."

He brightened. This was just the coincidence he'd been hoping for. "You know, I've been thinking the same thing," he said. "We could use a break. You go shopping, and I'll get our tickets."

Sam waited until the end of the day to phone Nick, his boss at the Bureau in Abilene. He hadn't looked forward to the call. He'd hoped to have good news for the man who needed it so desperately. But the day had only brought him more dead ends.

"I've been trying to learn more about Frank while I'm here," he said. "Nobody seemed to like him much. Cheyenne McKenna called him a control freak. I spoke with one of the judges who mentioned that Frank had a thing for young women."

"No surprise there," Nick said. "We already knew that."

"A jealous boyfriend could've killed him," Sam said. "But on the ranch in the middle of the night? That doesn't make sense. I'm guessing the killer was someone he already knew and knew well."

"Which brings us back to Roper." Nick sounded weary. "Or if not Roper, maybe you should take a closer look at Frank's daughter, Jasmine. She was right there, and we've only skimmed the surface of her relationship with her father. The fact that she found the body doesn't clear her of the crime."

"True." Sam felt a stab of dread. Not Jasmine. She was so gentle. And she'd adored her father. Sam had never heard her say a word against him.

"What about that syringe the boys found in the creek?" Sam said, changing the subject. "Is the lab still working on it?"

"They were. But it's been put aside for now. There's nothing new to report. As you know, we're pretty sure it's the murder weapon. But there are no prints or DNA that could tie it to any of your suspects. If any evidence was there, it was probably washed away in the water. Oh—and we checked Frank's phone records. The last call he took on his cell phone was from a burner. That call could've lured him to the stable. But, of course, we can't trace it."

"Well, keep me posted." Sam had already known what the answer to his question would be. Otherwise, he would have heard.

"How about you, Nick?" he asked. Sam's old friend was battling cancer. He had chosen to hold off treatment until Sam could get back to the Bureau and replace him. Sam knew that every delay worsened the odds against his survival.

"My first chemo session is set for Monday," Nick said. "I won't be much good after that, so I'll need somebody in charge here."

"I'll be there, Nick. You can count on me. But it's a shame you never took down Louis Divino. After all those years of trying to nail him, you deserved that victory."

"Oh—I didn't tell you," Nick said. "Divino's gone. Some boater on Lake Travis hauled his body up with the anchor. He was shot through the head with a .38, at close range, back to front. Probably a gang killing. I'm glad somebody got the sonofabitch, even if it wasn't me."

"Do you know who's taken over in his place?"

"I haven't a clue. I guess that'll be your problem. Good luck with it."

"Take care of yourself, Nick. I'll be there for you, I promise." As he spoke, Sam felt a lump rise in his throat. If ever he needed to keep his word, it was now—to the man who'd been his friend and mentor since the early days of his career with the FBI.

After ending the call, Sam crossed the floor to the north-facing window of his hotel room. Opening the curtains, he stood watching the sky darken into night. The lights of Las Vegas spread below him like a vast, illuminated Persian carpet. So many lights. So many people. So many heartaches.

As his frustration overflowed, Sam mouthed a curse. Why couldn't he just wrap up this case, go back to Abilene, and take up where he'd left off with Jasmine? All he needed to do was place Roper under arrest for murder. Then he would be free to get on with his life.

So why didn't he—when every shred of evidence pointed to Roper's guilt?

Sam's thoughts were scattered by the jangle of his phone, which he'd left on the coffee table. Striding back across the room, he picked it up and took the call.

"Sam?" The husky, feminine voice stopped his heart.

The last time they'd spoken—a furtive call on a burner phone—she'd been in Austin, taking care of her terminally ill mother. She'd sounded nervous, he recalled, but she'd assured him that everything was all right. It was only later that he'd begun to worry about Louis Divino and his connection to Madeleine. When he'd called again later to warn Jasmine, she hadn't answered. He'd left a voicemail on the burner phone and waited for a reply that never came. He'd worried about her, but he'd known better than to try again.

Now, Divino was dead, and here she was. Stunned, he found his voice. "Are you all right, Jasmine?"

"I'm fine." He heard a muted sob. "Oh, Sam, I've missed you so much!"

"Where are you?"

"I'm here, in Las Vegas. I just got in from the airport. I'm staying at the Excalibur. I can't wait to see you."

Could this be real—or had his fantasies gone to his head? "How did you know where to find me?" he asked.

"Mariah called me as a favor to Mother. You know how much Mother likes you and wants us to get together. She keeps talking about her future blue-eyed grandchildren."

"Your mother?" Sam felt the vague sensation of having fallen down a rabbit hole. "But isn't she sick? Isn't she . . ."

"Dying?" Jasmine laughed. "Oh, Sam, you know Mother. She didn't really have a brain tumor. It was all an act—a way to get some things she wanted. She's fine. In fact, she ordered me to leave her. I've been staying in LA with a friend from my old Hollywood days, so it was just a quick flight to Vegas. I can't wait to be with you. Can you come to me tonight?"

Yearnings too long denied surged through Sam's body. He stifled a groan. "Jasmine, I'm still on this case."

She was silent for a moment—not a good sign. "We've behaved ourselves for weeks, Sam. Don't we deserve a break?"

When Sam didn't reply, she plunged ahead. "We can be careful. I'm being careful now. I'm calling you on the room phone, not my cell. And I'm not even staying in your hotel. But the Excalibur is close—just a short cab ride or a nice walk."

"Jasmine, I can't—"

"Why not? Nobody knows us here. Who's going to find out?"

"Jasmine, listen—"

"Blast it, Sam, I'm not going to beg you," she snapped. "If you care more about your silly rules than you do about me, that's your loss. In case you change your mind, I'm in room 1620. But I won't call you again. I have my pride."

The call ended with a click. Sam checked the impulse to hurl his phone against the wall. He loved Jasmine to the depths of his wretched soul. He loved her with a hunger so intense that it kept him awake at night. He wanted to spend his life making love to her, building a home, and filling it with their children.

But why, in the name of heaven, did she have to show up here now?

Sam laid the phone on the coffee table and sank onto the sofa with his head in his hands. He reminded himself of the vow he'd taken as an FBI agent. And he thought about Nick, putting his cancer treatment on hold to buy him more time for this case.

"Maybe you should take a closer look at Frank's daughter, Jasmine. She was right there, and we've only skimmed

the surface of her relationship with her father. The fact that she found the body doesn't clear her of the crime."

Nick's chilling words rose in his memory. Much as he might want to ignore them, Sam knew he had to give them the weight they deserved. He'd dismissed Jasmine as a suspect because she'd insisted she loved her father—and he'd taken her at her word because she was sweet and sincere and passionate. Then, when he'd fallen in love with her, he'd stopped asking questions.

Now duty compelled him to raise those questions again, if only to himself. Meanwhile, if it became known, a romantic relationship between the investigating agent and one of the suspects could blow a court case wide open.

Still fighting the urge to get up and go to her, Sam picked up the remote, switched on the TV, and clicked through the channels. Settling on a mindless zombie-invasion movie, he forced himself to watch it to the end. Then, still battling temptation, he showered and went to bed.

Wide awake, he lay in the darkness, listening to the whir and bump of the elevator down the hall and the faint sound of voices passing his door. Jasmine's image tortured his thoughts—her laughing face, with its petal-like, kissable lips, her small but perfect breasts, made to fit the hollows of his hands, her golden legs parting to draw him into her silken warmth.

Logic argued that there was no chance she'd murdered her father. She was too warm and loving, too tenderhearted to take a life. Yet he remembered the time she'd snatched his service pistol out of its holster and fired it to kill a fatally injured antelope from the game farm that had run in front of her jeep. After it was done, she'd shed tears. Jasmine was surprisingly strong, but she wasn't a killer. Sam believed that with all his heart. But his work ethic demanded that he treat her as a suspect until proven otherwise.

If he didn't go to her now, they would be finished. After traveling so far to be with him, Jasmine would never forgive him for putting his job ahead of their love.

But she was right about one thing. Las Vegas was a city of strangers. He might be known here in the South Point complex. But no one on the street or in the Excalibur would recognize him or Jasmine. Surely, they'd be safe, especially if he only saw her in her hotel room.

But there was still the ethical question. If he saw her, he'd be breaking the rules, putting the case and his career in jeopardy. He could always claim that he was investigating her as a suspect, but that would be the height of hypocrisy.

Right now, the only sure thing was that he loved her. And if he didn't go to her, he would lose her.

Torn, he swung out of bed and walked to the window. Somewhere out in that sea of lights Jasmine waited alone. Was he strong enough to honor his vow and break her heart? Or was he already too late?

Jasmine turned over in bed and checked the glowing numbers on the digital clock. Twelve twenty-seven. She should have known that Sam wouldn't be coming.

Sitting up, she untangled the sheets that had twisted around her legs. She'd tossed and turned as she struggled with the terms of her new reality. Sam might love her in his way, but he valued his work more, and she couldn't expect him to change.

She had come to a painful decision. Tomorrow morning she would reschedule her return flight, pack her suitcase, and leave Las Vegas. And she wouldn't cry. A man who would put his job ahead of his woman wasn't worth a single tear.

With a muttered curse, she rose and made a short trek to the bathroom. Before climbing back into bed, she stripped off the sexy black nightgown she'd worn and pulled on an oversized gray cotton T-shirt. She was exhausted. Maybe now that she had a plan in place, she'd be able to get some sleep.

Closing her eyes, she took deep breaths and willed herself to think positive thoughts. She was going to be fine, she told herself. She already had a job offer from an animal-rescue group out of Lubbock. She'd worked with them to find homes for the poor creatures salvaged from Charlie Grishman's game farm. The pay would be minimal, but she didn't need the money. She needed the satisfaction of doing some good in the world. At least she would have that.

Sam could take his job and shove it!

As her body relaxed, she began to drift, then to dream. But this dream wasn't about Sam, shaped by longing and frustrated love. It was the nightmare, etched so deeply into her brain that she would never be free of it.

She was back in her mother's Lake Travis condo, staring into the anthracite eyes of her mother's lover, Louis Divino. Her burner phone, which she'd used to communicate with Sam, lay crushed on the floor between them. Divino had just heard Sam's warning message with instructions for calling his boss at the FBI. Now Divino was going to kill her.

The muzzle of Divino's pistol was inches from her heart. Seconds from now, she would be dead. She willed her last thought to be of Sam, his sweet blue eyes gazing into hers, his strong arms holding her, easing her fall to the floor.

Divino's swarthy face showed no emotion as his finger tightened on the trigger.

Without warning, the deafening blast of a gunshot shattered the silence. Shot from behind, Divino's forehead disintegrated in a mass of blood and tissue.

Jasmine's scream died in her throat as he toppled forward, revealing her mother in the doorway. Her filmy negligee was spattered with crimson. Her manicured hands gripped a Smith & Wesson .38 Special.

Jasmine woke with a convulsive jerk. She was shivering, her body damp with perspiration. What had awakened her? There must've been a sound—but was it the gunshot in her dream, or something real? Her mother had warned her to keep a low profile. A woman taking over the leadership of a powerful mob was bound to have enemies—enemies who wouldn't hesitate to take revenge on her family members.

Jasmine's loaded pistol lay on the nightstand next to the bed, where she'd placed it within easy reach. As she slipped out of bed, a rap on the door made her pulse jump. She'd been right. Someone was out there.

Even if she didn't answer, a locked door might not be enough to keep out an intruder with tools or a master key. With frantic hands, she bunched the pillows in the bed and covered them with a blanket to mimic her sleeping form. Then she stood in the shadowed corner where the opened door would hide her, cocked the gun, and waited.

Seconds crawled past. The knock came again, more urgent this time—and a voice.

"Jasmine? Are you in there? Are you all right?"

Sam!

Her knees went limp. She sagged against the wall. Earlier tonight, she'd been furious with him. But that was behind her now. Sam, her love, had put his misgivings aside and come to her.

Her free hand fumbled with the door chain and opened the dead bolts. Sam opened the door partway and stepped through. As it closed behind him, he caught her close.

For a long, wordless moment, he held her tight. Tears blurred Jasmine's eyes. She let them flow as her body softened against his.

"I didn't think you'd come," she whispered. "I was afraid I'd lost you."

"You should have known I couldn't stay away." His kiss was long and fervent, awakening a flood of sensations that were deeper than lust, deeper than desire. Jasmine had never imagined that it was possible to love someone so much.

Only as he released her did he notice the pistol in her hand. "What on earth—" He eased it from her clenched fingers. "Were you planning to shoot me, Jasmine?"

Before she could collect her thoughts to speak, he looked past her. "What—?" He stared at what she'd done with the bed. "Jasmine, is someone after you?"

Jasmine scrambled for a response. Telling Sam what had happened in the condo and afterward would compromise him and their relationship. It would also endanger her mother. The truth, if it were to become known, could trigger an avalanche of tragedies.

"I'm sorry. It's nothing, really." She gave him an apologetic shake of her head. "I just get nervous when I'm alone in a strange place. I imagine that every footstep going past the door is some evildoer who's going to break in and murder me. When I heard your first knock, it threw me into a panic. You can imagine how foolish I feel now."

He surveyed the hastily arranged bed. "Are you sure

you're all right? I get the feeling there's more to this than what you're telling me."

"I'm fine, especially now that you're here," Jasmine insisted, turning toward him. "Please, let's forget it. I just want to be in your arms."

"And I just want to be in . . . you." He pulled her close. His hands invaded her T-shirt, caressing the naked skin beneath, the curve of her hips, her eager buttocks, her breasts, until her whole body tingled with need.

"Oh, you wicked, wicked man . . ." she murmured as his hand slid down her belly, then lower, setting off a cascade of miniature explosions. "I want you, Sam. I want you so much I can hardly stand it."

"I think you're about to have me." Freeing a hand, he shoved aside the piled covers and lowered her to the bed. It took him mere seconds to shed his boots and jeans. She finished by working the elastic waistband of his briefs down over his jutting erection. She loved the size of him, the baby smoothness and the steely hardness beneath. She loved his manly warmth, the scent of him and the breathy sound he made as he entered. Now he was there, her love, her Sam, thrusting deep inside her where he belonged.

"Welcome home," she whispered.

Afterward, she lay spooned against him, legs tangled with legs. This was her heaven. The world could stop right here and she wouldn't mind, as long as they could stay like this. But a new problem had arisen that could change everything.

She had always been truthful with Sam, even about her past as a party girl. But how could she tell him that her mother, the glamorous Madeleine Carlisle Culhane, had killed her mobster lover and taken his place in the Divino crime family?

Sooner or later, the truth was bound to come out. If Sam

knew she'd kept it from him, he would never forgive her. But how could she betray her own mother, whom she loved in spite of her lawless ways—her mother, who had killed a man to save her life?

Sam had fallen into a doze. Beside him, Jasmine lay awake, listening to him breathe, treasuring each moment, knowing that the time of truth would come—the time when her dreams would crash like birds shot out of the sky, falling dead around her.

Chapter Six

They made love again on the cusp of morning drowsiness, with slow, delicious passion. Afterward, Sam rolled out of bed, pulled on his clothes, and headed for a few minutes in the bathroom. The time had come for him to leave.

Curled between the sheets, Jasmine waited for the lingering pleasure to fade. It was too soon. She wasn't ready to let him go. She wanted to see his face and hear his voice a little longer.

He came back into the room, his face freshly washed and his damp hair finger-combed. Stubble made a sexy shadow along his jawline.

She sat up. "You need to eat," she said. "We could order breakfast from room service."

"That would take at least an hour," he said. "I don't have that kind of time. But we could grab a quick bite in the coffee shop downstairs."

"That would be fine, if you're not worried about being seen."

"Two people having coffee in public shouldn't raise any flags. Let's get going. I can check my phone while you're getting dressed."

"I'll hurry." She flew out of bed. Ten minutes later, they left the room and headed for the elevator. Jasmine was wearing jeans, a loose-fitting Grateful Dead tee, a baseball cap, and the barest touch of makeup. They looked like a couple of tourists who'd gotten in late after a long drive, Jasmine thought. Nobody would give them a second glance.

In the crowded coffee shop, all of the booths were taken. Jasmine and Sam had to settle for a small table in the middle of the floor. Sam ordered plain black coffee. Jasmine took hers with cream and wheat toast. The place was too noisy for private conversation, but at least Jasmine could satisfy herself with watching her man across the table and hoping for another night in his arms.

Sam was sitting with his back toward the coffee shop's wide entrance. Looking past him, Jasmine's eye was caught by a well-dressed couple passing from the direction of the lobby. The tall, thin man was wearing a fedora and a tan, summer-weight sport jacket. The petite blonde on his arm was dressed in white slacks and a matching jacket with a broad-brimmed, black sun hat. They paused and turned, as if checking for a place to eat. For an instant, the woman's eyes made contact with Jasmine's. There was an unmistakable flicker of recognition before they moved on and vanished.

Jasmine's hand shook, splattering coffee on the tablecloth.

"What is it? Is something wrong?" Sam asked.

"No, I'm fine. I just thought I saw . . . But never mind, I was wrong," Jasmine lied, grateful that Sam hadn't spotted the pair. What would Darrin and Simone be doing here in Las Vegas? Did their presence have something to do with her, or with their mother? Clearly, Simone had recognized her. She could only hope that Darrin's scheming wife hadn't recognized Sam as well.

One thing was almost certain. The conniving pair hadn't come to Las Vegas on a holiday. Until she could discover what they were up to, it would be safest to keep Sam in the dark. When she knew more, she could decide when and how much to tell him.

She was already keeping one secret from Sam. Now she had chosen to keep one more.

Standing behind the fence at the practice arena, Cheyenne made her Thursday morning call to her mother. Rachel answered on the first ring as if she'd been waiting with the phone in her hand.

"Hello, dear. Are you all right?" Her natural voice had a sharp tone, which made her sound almost angry, but Cheyenne was accustomed to that.

"I'm fine, Mom. Just watching the cowboys exercise their horses. I'm learning a lot about what makes a good cow horse."

"And what about that young man who offered to help you? Is he behaving like a gentleman?"

"Of course, he is." Cheyenne sighed. Last night after dinner with some of his cowboy friends and their girls, Hayden had escorted her back to her floor. His behavior in the elevator had been anything but gentlemanly, giving her a preview of what she could expect if she welcomed him into her room.

Why not? she'd asked herself. She was almost twenty-one, and it wasn't like she was a virgin. Why not now, with someone who was handsome, well-spoken, and obviously knew what he was doing. She might even let herself fall in love.

She had invited him into the room. He'd lowered her to the bed and gotten as far as unfastening her jeans. But when his hand had invaded her panties, she'd felt the first trickle of panic. Instinctively, she'd begun to push away from him, then to struggle. Hayden had chuckled and continued, evidently taking her resistance as play.

The sound of Roper arriving at his room across the hall had put an end to the drama. Hayden had stood, tucked in his shirt, and zipped his jeans. "To be continued," he'd said, grinning. Then, after making sure the coast was clear, he'd left.

"Cheyenne, are you still there?" Her mother's voice on the phone jerked her back to the present.

"Sorry, Mom, I got distracted. Do you plan to be here tomorrow?"

"I wouldn't miss the chance to see Roper ride. Stetson will be driving. He knows the way."

"What about Dad?"

"I've hired a young man from church to stay with him and take care of the animals. He should be fine."

Cheyenne and Roper had agreed not to tell their mother about the incident on the freeway or the trouble with the horses. Rachel would only worry and probably wear herself out praying.

"Since you're getting here a day early, we'll have time for some sightseeing," Cheyenne said, changing the subject. "There's a lot to see in Las Vegas—the big hotels on the strip, the shops, the shows, and the casinos. You can even drop some change in the slots, maybe win some money. It'll be fun."

Rachel gasped. "Not on your life! I've heard what goes on in those palaces of sin. I wouldn't be caught dead in one. Las Vegas is the domain of the devil. I plan to stay in our room and watch TV or read until time for the big reining event. And I hope you'll stay with me. I get nervous, alone in a big city. Is your brother all right?"

"I suppose so. He's been so busy with the horses that I've barely seen him."

"Well, I made him promise to keep an eye on you. I may need to give him a call about that."

"Oh, please don't bother, Mom. He's got so much weighing on his mind. And I'm too old to need a babysitter. Call me when you get into town tomorrow."

Cheyenne ended the call before her mother could argue and turned her attention back to the practice arena, where several riders were giving their mounts a gentle workout to keep them loosened up for tonight's $250,000 cutting-horse challenge. True to his word, Hayden had given her behind-the-scenes access to the riders and their superb horses. It hadn't escaped her notice that all of the riders were men. Competing on their level would be a challenge. She might have to start with women's events. But she'd never lacked for drive or discipline. She wouldn't be satisfied with anything but her best.

There were several women finalists in the Run for a Million and even more women in an event called Reined Cow Horse, in which riders and their horses competed in reining and then in controlling a single cow. Cheyenne was intrigued. But to compete would require an exquisitely trained horse, and she'd have to master both reining and cutting skills. For now, cutting would be enough.

Clearing her thoughts, she focused on the riders—how they sat their mounts and how they used subtle pressure from their legs to communicate with their horses.

Hayden's paint gelding, Steely Dan, was a beautiful animal, smart and responsive. And Hayden was an impressive rider. Watching the pair, Cheyenne could understand why Hayden had such high hopes.

The memory of last night flashed through her mind. But this was no time to think about what had gone wrong and why. Today, everything was about winning tonight's $250,000 prize and the prestige that went with it.

Now Cheyenne's eyes shifted to Buck Tolson. He sat his rangy buckskin horse with the confidence of a man who has nothing to prove, his posture easy, his narrowed gaze detached, as if no one else in the arena was of any consequence.

Hayden had introduced her to several of the cowboys in the competition. Most of them had already known who she was, and they'd been friendly. Buck Tolson had not been among them.

This morning Tolson had scarcely given her a glance. But Cheyenne could sense the awareness burning between them. He was not a pretty man, but his rugged features were attractive. He looked older than most of the riders. He would be about Roper's age, she calculated. But why should that matter? Only one thing seemed evident. He didn't approve of her being here.

Some of the riders had finished working their horses and were leaving the arena. Cheyenne was waiting for Hayden to dismount when she saw a white-haired man, possibly a judge, come out of the back, catch his attention, and beckon him to the gate.

Cheyenne kept her distance, watching as Hayden dismounted and led his horse to where the older man stood. The two exchanged a few words. Hayden's expression froze, then shattered like a skim of winter ice. The older man laid a hand on his arm.

Cheyenne hurried toward them. Hayden turned toward her, his face pale. "It's my father. His plane went down over New Mexico. He's been taken to a hospital in Gallup, but he's not expected to survive." He shook his head. "I've got to go right now."

"Oh, Hayden!" Cheyenne ached for him. He'd be missing tonight's Cutting Horse Challenge, but at a time like this, that couldn't be allowed to matter.

"Wait, there's something else you need to know." The older man was still speaking to Hayden. "There was a passenger in the plane, a young woman. The medics said she was about five months pregnant."

Hayden stared at him. "Is she—?"

"Evidently, she died on impact. And the baby with her, of course. Was she someone you knew?"

Hayden shook his head. With visible effort, he pulled himself together. "I'll send someone to pick up the horses on Sunday," he said. "If somebody could look after Steely Dan until then—"

"I'll take care of him," Cheyenne said. "I know what to do."

Buck Tolson was behind her, leading his big buckskin to the gate. "I'm sorry about your dad, Barr," he said. "Don't worry about anything here. My horse's stall is next to yours, so I'll be there in case your girl needs help.""

"And you won't have to worry about my beating you tonight, will you, Tolson?" Hayden's tone was shocking in its bitterness. Buck's jaw tightened, but otherwise he didn't respond.

"Just go, Hayden!" Cheyenne said.

For the space of a breath, Hayden glared at his rival. Then he passed his horse's reins to Cheyenne and strode off in the direction of the hotel.

Tolson's gaze narrowed as he took stock of Cheyenne's petite size. "Are you all right with that horse?" he asked.

"I am, Mr. Tolson. My name is Cheyenne McKenna, by the way. I'm not Hayden's girl, just his friend. And I know how to handle a horse."

"Then I take it you know the way to the stalls. Let's go. I'll follow you. My name's Buck, but you can call me whatever you want."

His nonchalance grated on Cheyenne. But she couldn't

fault him for his treatment of Hayden. At least he'd been sensitive enough to know that the man was in distress.

Cheyenne could imagine how frantic Hayden must be. He'd mentioned that he and his father were all that was left of their family. Now, without a miracle, Hayden would be alone. The ranch and the horses would be his. But at such a terrible cost.

She remembered the mention of the young pregnant woman, killed with her baby in the crash. Hayden hadn't known her. Maybe she'd been a neighbor who needed a ride—maybe someone with a family member competing in an event.

They had left the arena and were headed along the rows of stalls in Barn A. Cheyenne kept a tight grip on Steely Dan's reins. The paint gelding was calm, but horses could be unpredictable. With his owner suddenly gone and a stranger leading him, Steely Dan could be feeling some stress.

This morning the barn was a bedlam of noise and activity. With the Shootout starting early tomorrow, dozens of hopeful riders were bringing in their horses. Cheyenne had slept poorly. She was getting a headache. Maybe later, before the 7:00 cutting event, she could go up to her room and lie down. But not yet. She had more urgent things to do.

Once Steely Dan was settled in, she would have to find Roper. He had to be told about Chet Barr's crash and Hayden's departure. Cheyenne had never met Chet Barr, but Roper had spoken highly of him. He would be devastated by the bad news.

Since their arrival at South Point, the two of them had been so busy that they'd barely kept in touch. She needed to spend more time with her brother, especially now, with so much worry weighing on him.

Hayden's horse snorted and tossed his head, almost jerking the reins out of her hand.

"Cheyenne—stop! Get over to the right!" Buck's sharp command reached her ears from behind. Only now did Cheyenne see what was happening at the far end of the row.

A cowboy was struggling to maneuver a nervous palomino stallion into its stall. The horse was resisting the unfamiliar space, snorting, rolling its eyes, and jerking at its lead rope as it tried to back away. The cowboy was doing his best to urge the stallion forward, but the big palomino was more horse than he could handle.

The stallion was becoming agitated. With a sudden scream, it reared and broke free. Trailing its lead rope, it came barreling down the open space between the rows, headed straight for Cheyenne and Steely Dan.

By yanking the bridle and slapping his flanks, Cheyenne managed to swing the paint horse partway to the right. But, too late, she realized that she was still in danger. The move had put her squarely in the stallion's path.

"Get over!" Buck flung himself against her, pinning her against the closed gate of a stall. His body protected her as the three horses collided in a shifting, squealing mass. He kept her shielded through the worst of it, while people came running to break up the melee and lead the stallion away. By the time he released her, she was shaking.

"Stay back," he cautioned her as he caught Steely Dan's reins and then the reins of his own horse. The two geldings were wild-eyed, chuffing and quivering, but with soft words and the calming power of his presence, Buck soon had them under control.

Hot-faced and trembling, Cheyenne took Steely Dan's reins from him. The way he'd protected her, as if she were a child, had left her seething. He hadn't asked permission to invade her space. But his hard body pressing hers against the stall gate, coupled with the danger, had made her pulse race—and stirred something else. She didn't even like the man. But she couldn't deny the shimmering current that puckered her nipples and trickled downward into the depths of her body. She struggled to ignore the feeling. It didn't make sense—her response to a man she barely knew.

He scowled down at her. His deep-set eyes were gray, almost silver, framed in sun-burnished creases. A fresh bruise on his left cheek showed where he'd been grazed by a sharp hoof while protecting her. "Are you all right?" he asked.

She squared her shoulders and took a step back. "Don't worry about me. I'm fine. What about the horses?"

"They look fine to me. But injuries don't always show. Once they're settled in their stalls, I'll phone the vet to check them over. If Chief isn't a hundred percent fit to compete tonight, I won't push him."

"But you're the champion. How can you just walk away from another chance to win?"

"There'll be other competitions, with other cash prizes and other fancy buckles. But there'll never be another horse like Chief." He stepped away from her. "Now, let's get these horses to their stalls and give them some time to settle down."

She walked ahead of him, leading Hayden Barr's paint horse. Buck kept his eyes on her, admiring her easy stride and the way her dark hair hung like a silken veil down her back. By now, he was aware she was a rodeo star. He'd overheard some riders in the practice arena talking about her. But it wouldn't be seemly to tell her everything they'd said.

He could probably have spared her the lecture about the dangers of cowboy romance. She was a little thing, but she seemed savvy and confident enough to handle herself around men. Still, the memory of her in the hotel, with Barr's hands groping under her shirt, made him want to curse and blot it from his mind. She'd insisted that she wasn't his girl. But it sure as hell had looked that way.

Not that it was any of his business, Buck reminded himself. And after the way he'd lectured her earlier, he could imagine what she must think of him. Telling him that he reminded her of her mother wasn't exactly a compliment.

Still, when he'd pinned her against the stall to protect her from the stampeding horse, he'd found himself lingering a few seconds longer than necessary, savoring her warmth and inhaling the fragrance of her hair before he let her go. He wouldn't mind getting to know her better. But not if she was sleeping with Hayden Barr. He didn't need that kind of trouble.

She had disappeared into the next stall with the horse. He could hear her moving—a little grunt of effort as she lifted off the heavy saddle, the soft, feminine sound of her breathing as she removed the pad and bridle and began rubbing the horse with a towel.

He listened as he finished unsaddling Chief and rubbing him down. He was tempted to offer her his help, but if Miss Cheyenne McKenna was the horsewoman he'd been told she was, she wouldn't need his assistance—let alone thank him for it.

Now she was talking to the horse, soothing the nervous animal as she worked. He couldn't catch the words, but he liked the whispery sound of her voice.

Now that he knew more about her, he liked other things, too. She was smart, ambitious, and independent—very much her own woman.

He wouldn't mind spending more time with Miss Cheyenne McKenna. After the vet had checked the two horses, maybe he would invite her to lunch. She might not think much of him, but if he offered to answer her questions about cutting, there was a good chance she'd accept.

Then he could turn on the Tolson charm—and yes, that was a joke. He had about as much charm as a thirty-year-old mule.

Buck finished rubbing down his horse. He was waiting for the vet when he realized that he could no longer hear her voice. Seconds passed, the silence broken only by the sound of the horse munching its feed.

When Buck opened the stall gate to check for Cheyenne, she was gone.

Seated in her hotel room's single armchair, Jasmine faced the door and waited for the knock. She'd given the front desk permission to direct her visitors to her room. She wouldn't be happy to see them, but how could she turn away her own brother and his wife?

The bed had been hastily made to cover any evidence of last night's lovemaking. But something told her they wouldn't be fooled. The only question remaining was what price Darrin and Simone would demand for their silence.

As the elevator dinged on arrival at the floor, her pulse quickened. She waited for the knock before she rose and took her time getting to the door and opening it. She'd never gotten along with her whining brother, and she could barely stand her sister-in-law, who hid her scheming nature behind a mask of vapid stupidity.

"Fancy seeing you here, Jasmine." Simone sashayed into the room, followed by her husband. "And who, pray tell, was that man sitting across from you at breakfast? I daresay he looked familiar. His hair had a cowlick in back, as if he might've spent the night and left the room in a bit of a rush."

Jasmine motioned them to a seat on the foot of the bed, while she took the chair, swiveling it to face them. "Why don't you just get down to business and tell me why you're here?"

Darrin cleared his throat. "As you know, we're still working to reclaim the family home. Now that Dad's gone, Lila has no right to be there."

"And, as you know, I couldn't care less about the place," Jasmine said. "Lila's no friend, but she's your problem, not mine. All I want is to be free of the whole mess. Anyway, I thought you were going to settle your claim in court."

"That could take months," Simone said. "And there's always the chance we might not win. Your brother promised me . . ." She trailed off as Darrin nudged her with an elbow.

"One way or another, we've got to get Lila out of that house," Darrin said. "We didn't plan to involve you. In fact, we thought you were still with Mother. But now that you're here, we could use your help. We're family, Jasmine. You owe that much to Dad's memory."

"Do I?" Jasmine arched an eyebrow. She didn't like where this was going, but so far, she wasn't surprised. "What if I say no?"

"We were hoping not to have to bring this up," Simone said. "But we know what we saw downstairs in the coffee shop. Your FBI lover could lose his job if it became known that he was sleeping with a person of interest in his case."

Jasmine's stomach clenched. She should have known this was coming. But to hear those words from Simone's mouth still came as a shock. "You don't know that," she said. "And even if it were true, you couldn't prove it."

"Oh, couldn't we?" Simone whipped her phone out of her purse and scrolled down the menu. "Take a look at these."

The photos couldn't have been more clear. They showed Jasmine and Sam gazing at each other across the table. The pictures removed any need for an explanation.

Jasmine gasped. "How did you—?"

"Simple." Simone's carefully made-up face wore a triumphant grin. "We paid a waitress to take pictures with this phone. You two were so busy making google eyes at each other that you didn't even notice her."

Darrin leaned toward her, his voice dropping to a conspiratorial low. "So let's talk family business, shall we, Sister?"

Cheyenne found Roper with the two stallions. He was standing inside One in a Million's stall, plying a brush to the big roan's hindquarters. As Cheyenne spoke his name, he dropped the brush, straightened, and turned toward her. His eyes were bloodshot, his jaw unshaven.

"You look like hell, Brother," she said. "When did you last sleep?"

"I got a couple of hours in the night. I'll sleep when this week is over—even if it's on a jail bunk."

"Don't!" She seized his arm. "That kind of talk will only make things worse. You're innocent—you know it, and I know it. So stop tormenting yourself. The Run for a Million is your dream. You've got to be fit to ride on Saturday."

He took a deep breath and changed the subject. "Sam came by to check up on me earlier. A highway patrolman found that green Peterbilt in a gully off I-15, burned to ashes with the driver inside."

Cheyenne shuddered, remembering the man she and

Hayden had met outside that cheap motel. He'd had a gun and could easily have shot them both.

"But why would he be killed?" she asked. "Was it because he didn't run us off the road?"

Roper shrugged. "That, or he knew too much. Maybe he'd threatened to talk if he didn't get paid. Sam thinks that Frank's ex-wife could be behind it. She's got mob connections, and there's nothing she'd like better than to get rid of Lila so her kids can get the house and stables back."

"So that was supposed to be Lila, not me, in your truck?"

"That's the idea."

"Could the first Mrs. Culhane have killed Frank? As his ex, she certainly might've had reason."

"Sam looked into that. He says she actually tried, but Frank died before her hit man could get to him." Roper massaged his back with one hand. "I saw her work the crowd at Frank's memorial service. The woman was a force of nature. I wouldn't put anything past her."

"So, will Lila be coming to watch you ride? I've seen her from a distance, but I've never met her. What's she like?"

"Strong. Brave. Smart. And stubborn. Oh, hell, is she ever stubborn. A bit like you, Little Sis."

"You love her, don't you?"

"No comment." Roper picked up the brush and began stroking along the stallion's back and down his withers. One in a Million exhaled with a long, chuffing breath.

"I was hoping to meet Lila this week. Will she be here to watch you ride?"

"I told her not to come. But, as I said, she's stubborn."

"Mother doesn't like her, or any of the Culhanes—not that she knows them," Cheyenne said.

"Mother will be your problem. Maybe you can do us all a favor and talk her out of coming."

"She'll be fine. She plans to stay in my hotel room until the big event."

"How are things with Hayden?" he asked. "You seem to be spending a lot of time with him."

Cheyenne hadn't forgotten the news she'd come to give Roper. Hesitant to upset him, she had let their conversation become sidetracked. But now that he'd given her an opening, it couldn't wait any longer.

"Speaking of Hayden, something's happened, Roper," she said. "Something awful."

"What?" He stared at her, his arm lowering the brush as if it were a heavy weight.

"Hayden isn't here. He got word this morning that his father's plane had crashed over New Mexico. He's on his way to Gallup."

"And Chet?" Roper's face had paled.

"He's in the hospital. But he's not expected to live. That's all I know about his condition."

"Damn." Roper cursed, shaking his head. "I talked to Chet on the phone last night. He was upset about his stallion, of course, but he didn't blame me. He offered to work with the horse in the hope that we could have him ready to show. I didn't tell him how bad off Fire Dance was."

"There's something else," Cheyenne said. "He had a passenger in the plane, a young woman. She didn't survive the crash."

"Oh, Lord, no," Roper groaned. "Chet mentioned that his girlfriend wanted to come to Las Vegas with him. They'd planned to get married, and she'd always wanted an Elvis wedding. But he said he'd talked her into waiting for a less busy time. She must've changed his mind."

"Did he mention that she was pregnant?"

"No. But that makes sense. Damn rotten luck." Roper sucked in his breath. "Chet was hoping to see Hayden win the Cutting Horse Challenge. I guess that doesn't matter anymore. What about Hayden's horse?"

"I'm taking care of Steely Dan. He's a sweet boy. Hayden said he'd send a driver to load the two horses and take them home to Texas." She paused, glancing down the row of stalls. "How is Fire Dance?"

"Not good," Roper said. "See for yourself. Don't open the gate. Just look over the top."

Fire Dance's stall was two numbers down the row. Dreading what she was about to see, Cheyenne stretched on tiptoe to look over the gate.

The sight of the beautiful sorrel stallion broke her heart. He was wild-eyed, pacing, and tossing his head. When he saw Cheyenne at the gate, he lunged for her, baring his teeth. Reflexively, she jumped back.

"Nobody can get near him, not even to clean his stall," Roper said. "We're sliding food and water under the gate, but he's not taking much."

"Oh, Roper." She blinked back tears. "What's going to happen to him?"

Roper shook his head. "If he can make it home, where he feels safe, he might be all right in time. But he can't stay here. If he's too dangerous to load or be sedated, there'll be nothing we can do but put him down."

Chapter Seven

Darrin hadn't told Simone about the disturbing phone call. But the memory of that voice haunted him like an unwelcome song replaying in his ears. Every place he and Simone walked together—the casino, the shops and restaurants in the Excalibur, the teeming sidewalks, the parking lots, and the horse complex at South Point—he had the prickly sense of being watched. But there was no word, no look or sign, nothing to confirm for him that a long-lost brother was in touch.

Maybe the call had been a prank after all. Maybe the so-called long-lost brother just wanted to rob him, black-mail him, or take advantage in some other way. If the kin-ship was real and the caller was seeking family, he would surely have shown himself by now.

Forget it, Darrin told himself. He had more important things to think about. At the top of the list was getting Lila out of that house, any way he could—and on this, he and Simone were in complete agreement.

Mariah had texted him that Lila and her daughter would be flying to Las Vegas today and staying in a re-served room at South Point—she'd even known the room number. But there were complications. Lila was still recovering from snakebite, so she'd be resting in her room most of the time. And even when she went out, her daughter would be with her. Getting Lila alone would be a challenge.

Running into Jasmine had been a stroke of luck. She hadn't been happy to get involved in their plan, but as Simone had predicted, she would do almost anything to save her FBI lover's reputation and his job.

They'd known better than to tell her too much. As far as Jasmine was concerned, their plan would be to tell Lila that they'd found ironclad evidence to prove that Roper had murdered Frank. Signing the quit-claim deed that Darrin carried in an inner vest pocket would get her possession of that evidence and save Roper from prison.

What they hadn't told Jasmine was that if Lila didn't sign the deed—or even if she did—anything could happen.

Jasmine stood at the window, lost in thought as she gazed out over the cluttered landscape that was daytime Las Vegas. Darrin and Simone's threat to expose Sam had backed her into a corner. She'd had little choice except to agree to their plan.

Her part in it sounded simple enough. The only thing Darrin and Simone had asked of her was that she find a way to separate Lila from her daughter, who watched over the woman like a hawk and who would certainly stop her from signing away her inheritance.

But why not? Jasmine asked herself. She'd never liked Lila, who'd broken up her parents' marriage and ruled the house like a queen for eleven years. Now that Frank was gone, Lila didn't deserve to keep his property. By rights, shouldn't it go to his family?

As for Roper, he didn't strike her as a killer. Especially

since she suspected that Darrin and Simone's claim of evidence was fake. But she wouldn't be hurting him. And she wouldn't be breaking the law. All she needed to do was lure Miss Gemma away from her mother long enough for Darrin and Simone to get Lila alone.

In exchange for this, Jasmine would get the telltale photos deleted from Simone's phone.

The plan sounded simple, even harmless. So why were Jasmine's gut instincts sensing evil—the same evil that emanated from her own family bloodline?

How could she trust her own judgment when her father had been a notorious philanderer, her mother was a mobster, and her brother was a man without conscience, capable of anything that would get him what he wanted? Coming from such a family, how could she not have darkness inside her—a darkness that had let her deny what she'd known from the minute Darrin and Simone laid out their plan.

Her brother had been lying to her. They weren't going to blackmail Lila Culhane into signing away her home—something she would never willingly do. They were going to murder her.

Roper was taking a needed lunch break, eating a cheeseburger and watching the junior reining competition from the sparsely filled stands, when his phone rang. His pulse skipped. The caller was Lila.

"We're here, in the hotel." She was trying to sound breezy, but Roper could hear the exhaustion in her voice.

"I was hoping you hadn't come," he said.

"Why on earth would you say that?" she demanded. "I told you I was coming, and here I am. Gemma just went down the hall for ice, so I have a few minutes alone. What's wrong?"

"I was hoping to tell you later," he said. "You don't need bad news while you're healing."

"Stop babying me, Roper. Your bad news is my bad news. Just tell me."

He sighed. "Since you asked for it, I'll start with the worst. Chet Barr's plane crashed on the way here. He's in the hospital, not expected to survive. Hayden's gone to Gallup to be with him."

There was a pause. Roper could hear her breathing before she spoke. "Oh, Roper, words aren't enough. I met him a few times when Frank was competing. Such a nice man."

"It's a given that Hayden won't be in the Cutting Horse Challenge tonight. He'll send somebody to pick up his horse and Fire Dance at the end of the week."

"How is Fire Dance? Will you be able to show him?"

"There's no way. Something snapped in that horse when the trailer almost rolled, and it hasn't gotten any better. If anything, it's gotten worse. Nobody can get near him. I don't know how they're going to get him back into a trailer and home without sedation. For that length of time on the road, any drug would be dangerous. But that decision will be up to Hayden."

"So you're going with One in a Million?"

"I'll have to. I was planning to use him in the Shootout and save Fire Dance for the final event. But now, I'll be skipping the Shootout altogether. I can't risk him twice. At his age, he's got to be in prime condition for a chance at that million-dollar prize—or even a respectable showing."

"You keep focusing on his age," Lila said. "Maybe it's time you stopped. I was reading the roster of horses that will be competing. One horse is almost fourteen. Another horse is eleven. He won't be the only older horse in that arena."

Passion strengthened her voice. "One in a Million can

do this, Roper, but you've got to believe in him. I know that stallion. Give him your trust, and he'll give you his heart."

"I love you, Boss," Roper said.

"And I love you. If I didn't have a chaperone, I'd invite you up and show you how much. But that'll have to wait. Got to go. I hear Gemma at the door."

The call ended abruptly. Roper finished his lunch, tossed the wrappers in the trash, and walked back into the barn. Lila was right. One in a Million had never failed him. He owed the great stallion his complete confidence.

The news about Chet Barr's crash was still sinking in. What rotten luck, going down in his plane on a clear, calm day, with his son in the cutting finals and his pregnant bride-to-be at his side. The tragedy was senseless. But whatever the cause, Chet was a good man, generous and well-respected. He would be missed.

Assuming Chet didn't survive, his ranch—the house and land, the pedigreed horses, the registered Angus cattle, the airplanes, vehicles, and probably a hefty stock portfolio—would go to Hayden as the only heir. The handsome young rancher would make a fine catch for some lucky woman. Right now, Cheyenne appeared to have the inside track. But he was getting ahead of himself. His sister's happiness meant the world to Roper. But Cheyenne was only twenty, with a mind of her own. Anything could happen.

A tall stranger in jeans, well-worn boots, and a sweat-streaked denim shirt was standing outside Fire Dance's stall. "I hope I'm not intruding," he said "A cowboy at the practice arena told me you had Chet Barr's stallion. I was there when Hayden heard about his father. Awful news. I just came by to see if there was anything I could do. We haven't met. I'm Buck Tolson."

Roper accepted the proffered handshake and introduced himself. The man's name was familiar, but moments passed before it dawned on Roper that he was talking with a national champion.

"A friend of Hayden's is taking care of his cutting horse," Tolson said. "I offered my help, but she seemed to have the situation well in hand."

"I imagine she does," Roper said. "That would be my baby sister, Cheyenne."

"Oh." Tolson's gray eyes brightened with interest. "I should've guessed she was your sister. She got away before I could learn much about her. But that's not why I'm here. One of the riders mentioned that this horse had been traumatized. I've worked with troubled horses as a trainer, so I was curious." He shook his head. "I've been watching this one. He's as bad off as any I've seen. What does the vet have to say?"

"The vet can't get near him. Nobody can."

"He reminds me of a stallion I worked with a few years ago," Tolson said. "Like this one, he'd been traumatized in an accident. I recommended putting him down, something I rarely do. But he was valuable, and the owner insisted we keep working with him. Then one day . . ." Tolson exhaled, as if feeling the pain of a memory. "One day that horse killed one of the stable hands—a woman with young children, as if it could've been any worse."

"So you had to euthanize him?"

"Not me. He wasn't my horse. But yes, it had to be done. A hundred-thousand-dollar stallion. But not worth the life of a young mother. I'll never forgive myself for not having insisted on it sooner."

"And this horse? Fire Dance?" Roper waited for an answer, but Tolson's silence told him enough. The decision wouldn't be his to make.

Tolson had moved to One in a Million's stall. "I remember this big boy," he said. "He was Frank Culhane's horse. One of the great ones. So you'll be riding him in the Run for a Million?"

"That's the plan. He was supposed to be my backup horse, but now it'll all be up to him."

"It's still hard to believe Frank's gone," Tolson said. "And the way he died—even thinking about it gives me chills. Was the bastard who killed him ever caught?"

"Not yet. The FBI is still working on that." Roper struggled to ignore the gnawing sensation in his stomach.

"Any idea who might have done it?"

"No." Roper knew better than to venture a guess. He was innocent, but the killer was almost certainly someone he knew, maybe even someone he cared about. And Sam Rafferty was relentless in his quest to close the case.

"I'll take my leave and let you get back to work," Tolson said. "If Hayden wants to take a chance on the stallion, he can talk to me. But you've already heard what I think."

"I'll pass that on. Still, it's a shame. He's a beautiful animal. And what happened to him was in no way his fault."

"It's almost never the horse's fault," Tolson said. "It's usually the humans who deserve the blame."

He had turned to go, but paused at the sight of Cheyenne coming down the row, looking preoccupied.

"Any word from Hayden?" Roper asked as she came closer.

"Nothing. I'd hoped he might let us know about his father, but I can understand why we might not hear. I'll keep checking my phone."

Buck held back for a moment before he spoke. "I understand this might be a bad time, Cheyenne, but I was hoping to invite you to lunch. You could ask me anything you want to know about cutting. After that, I won't be available. The vet has cleared Chief to perform, so I'll be busy getting ready for tonight's competition."

"That's very kind of you," she replied without hesitation. "I'd be a fool not to say yes."

A faint smile played at the corners of his mouth. "Your choice. Do you have a favorite place?"

"No. Just something close and simple. Let's go."

Roper watched them walk away, chatting but not touching. He'd sensed a subtle vibration between them. But Tolson was older, close to Roper's own age, with a face weathered by some hard living. Roper knew the signs. Hayden would be a better match for her. But Cheyenne was very much her own woman. He could only hope she'd make the right choices.

He moved to the gate of Fire Dance's stall. The stallion laid his ears back, snorted, and lunged. His eyes reflected a nameless terror that no one could ease.

Buck Tolson's chilling account of the stable hand's death was a warning. But if anything could help Fire Dance, Roper vowed, he would move heaven and earth to see it done.

Jasmine's shaking hand hovered over the phone. She was no saint, but she had a conscience. She couldn't look the other way while her brother set a deadly trap for Lila Culhane. And she couldn't be part of his plan.

But if she defied Darrin, and if he used those photos to betray her secret love, Sam's life would be ruined.

She could wait—simply do nothing—or even leave town. But that wouldn't stop Darrin and Simone. She could try to call her mother. But Madeleine had insisted on going no contact for Jasmine's protection. And even if Jasmine could call her, Madeleine hated Lila and would probably side with her son.

There was only one person Jasmine could call for help.

Braced for the worst, she entered Sam's number on the hotel phone. He answered on the first ring and listened without comment as she poured out her story. By the end of it, she was fighting tears.

"I don't know what to do, Sam. My brother is a terrible person, and his wife is even worse. I would do anything to stop them. But none of this is your fault. I can't let them destroy your future because of me."

Sam spoke at last. "Let me be the judge of that, Jasmine. Nobody forced me to fall in love with you. That's something I wouldn't change for the world. As for the rest, you need to step back and let me do my job. Darrin's threat to use those photos is just that—a threat. I'll deal with it."

"But what about Lila? She's got to be protected."

"That's my job, too. I'll handle it. But right now, for the record, I need to ask you some questions—the same questions a prosecutor might ask you. I'll be recording them for your protection and mine. Answer them as if you were under oath."

"Sam, what on earth are you up to?"

"Just do it. Here's the first one. Jasmine, did you kill your father, Frank Culhane, or in any way contribute to his murder?"

"No. Absolutely not." Jasmine became aware that she was trembling.

"Second question. Do you believe your brother, Darrin Culhane, could have killed your father?"

Jasmine hesitated, then answered, "No. Not the way my father was killed. As I told you before, Darrin doesn't have the guts to do that."

"And his wife, Simone?"

"No. She's petite. She doesn't have the height or the physical strength. And she wouldn't have risked her pregnancy in a struggle."

He asked her similar questions about Lila, Roper, and her mother. To these, she gave the same reply: "I don't know."

"Sam, I don't understand this," she said as he finished. "I haven't told you anything you don't already know."

"This isn't for me," he said. "It's for the case file, a record that you've been interviewed—as I've already interviewed others. It's also a cover in case we're seen together, or in case your brother decides to show those photos."

"Fine. But Lila's still in danger."

"I'll talk to her, have her moved to another room, and make sure she doesn't go out alone. And you're to stay out of this. Better yet, leave. Go back to California or wherever you feel at home until this mess is cleared up. One way or another, it won't be much longer. I'll call you from Abilene, and we can decide what to do next."

"So I've come all this way for a one-night stand?"

"We can't be together here, Jasmine. It's too risky. And I've got a job to do."

Jasmine felt her frustration rising. "So I'm to pack my bags, toddle home like a good little girl, and wait for my lord and master to summon me? Listen and listen good! You don't own me, Sam Rafferty, and you never will! I'll come and go as I please. If you want me back, I'll think about it. But never assume you can give me orders!"

Fighting tears, she slammed the receiver down with a bang. Fine. She would stay out of Sam's way—and Darrin's too. They wouldn't even have to know she was here. It would be smart to change rooms. But she wasn't about to leave Las Vegas—not now, when there was so much going on.

When Darrin returned to the room, he found Simone on the bed, propped up by pillows, with a bowl of room-service chocolate ice cream in her lap. An episode of *Real Housewives* blared from the wall-mounted TV.

Darrin picked up the remote from the nightstand and clicked the TV off. Simone looked up at him. "Well?" she asked.

"Nothing." He sank onto the edge of the bed. "Jasmine hasn't called, and she's not answering her phone. When I checked her room, it was vacant. She was gone."

"You're sure?"

"Hell, yes, I'm sure. I looked all over the hotel. The front desk wouldn't tell me anything."

"Well, there you go," Simone said. "You should've known the sneaky bitch couldn't be trusted."

"At least we've got those photos," Darrin said.

"And what good are they now?" Simone's tongue swirled the ice cream from the spoon. "Now that she's gone, who's going to give a damn about two people having breakfast together? Too bad we didn't get a shot of them in bed."

"Our mistake was involving Jasmine in the first place," Darrin said. "I haven't told you everything. That room number Mariah gave us. The room's empty. Lila and her daughter were gone."

"What?"

"You heard me. I'm guessing they were warned by our FBI friend, who got word of our plan from Jasmine."

"Well, whose fault was that?" Simone demanded. "If you hadn't come up with the idea of using your sister—"

"Shut up! The photos were your idea. And look at you—lying there stuffing your face and watching crap on TV while I do all the legwork. You're supposed to be helping me."

"Can I help it if my feet are too swollen for my shoes?" Simone put the empty ice-cream bowl on the nightstand. "If you'd had the brains and ambition to act, the house would be ours by now. You may've killed your father, but you didn't follow through on the house and ranch. Couldn't you, just once, do your job as a man?"

"Wait!" Darrin reeled as if he'd been punched. "Are you saying I killed my father?"

"You were gone long enough, and at the right time. I lied to protect you, Darrin. I lied to the FBI."

"But I didn't kill him!" Darrin's heart battered his ribs like a caged animal. "I left the house after we had that big fight. I drove around looking for someplace to buy a beer, but everything was closed, even Jackalope's. So I came home and went to sleep on the couch. I didn't hear about Dad until the police called the next morning. I can't believe you think I'd murder my own father!"

"Did you?"

"No. I swear to God, I didn't. Do you believe me now?"

"I guess." She shrugged. "I might've respected you more if you had. I've long since discovered that I married a weakling. At least that might have changed my mind."

"Damn you to hell, woman!" Darrin's self-control snapped. In the next instant, he was on her, his weight holding her down, his hands tightening around her throat as he spoke through clenched teeth. "After all I've done for you . . ."

"Darrin . . ." She was fighting to breathe. "The baby . . . *the baby*!"

He let her go and rolled off her. They lay side by side on the bed, breathing hard. Darrin had been angry enough to kill her. But he hadn't and wouldn't—not just because of the baby, but because for now, at least, he needed Simone—perhaps even more than she needed him. They were like two wild animals, hissing and clawing, but depending on each other for survival.

Whatever was to be done, they would do it together.

* * *

For safety, Gemma and her mother had been moved from their comfortable suite on the fifteenth floor to the only vacant quarters available—a bargain-rate room with two single beds and a closet-sized bath. Sliding doors opened onto a tiny balcony with a view of the parking lot far below. The AC was noisy, and the couple in the next room through the wall had what sounded like a toddler in tantrum mode.

Gemma wasn't usually one to complain, but the move struck her as an excess of caution. "If your FBI friend wanted to protect you, why didn't he just post a guard outside our door?" she asked. "We could've stayed in that nice room. Instead, here we are in this little cracker box."

"Sam is just being careful—and if it's any consolation, he says his room is no bigger than this one." Lila was sitting on the bed with her feet up, a book lying facedown next to her. Even dressed in leggings and a tee, with no makeup and her hair caught back in a scrunchie, she possessed a beauty that her daughter would never have. Not that Gemma was envious. So far in this life, Lila's beauty had mostly brought her trouble.

"You heard what he said," Lila continued. "There've been one, possibly two attempts on my life. He has a good idea who's responsible, and so do I. But so far there's been no proof. He'll be using the hotel security cameras to watch that other room. If they show up there, he'll have them. That's the real reason we're here—so he can set the trap."

"I thought he was looking for the person who killed Frank."

"He is. This is related."

"And what about Roper? Does he know you're here?" Gemma had met Lila's horse trainer briefly at Frank's memorial service. She knew about their relationship, but she was far from ready to trust a virile, ambitious man around her vulnerable mother.

"Roper knows we've moved. But we won't be seeing each other until Saturday night, after the Run for a Million. He'll be focused on the stallion—and he'll have family here. His mother and one brother will be coming in tomorrow. And his sister's already with him."

"Have you met his family?"

"No. I mean, the McKennas are neighbors, but we don't socialize with them. I wouldn't have minded. Heaven knows, I don't put myself above anybody. But Frank was adamant about that. And Mariah is even more insistent. She's threatened to quit if a McKenna sets foot in the house. She calls them trash. She'd like nothing better than to see me out of the house and Roper in jail for Frank's murder."

"You seem so sure he's innocent. What if he's guilty?"

"I know him, Gemma. Roper isn't a killer. He respected Frank. He liked his job."

When Gemma didn't answer, Lila picked up her book as if dismissing the subject. "I can tell that you need some time out. Nobody knows we're here. Sam even checked us out of the old room and re-registered us here under fake names. So why don't you get out for a while? Stretch your legs. Explore the shops. Get us some snacks. I feel fine, and I'm not going anywhere."

"You're sure?" Gemma had begun to feel like a caged animal in the small room. Sam had told her to stay put, but the idea of a break was too tempting to resist.

"I won't be long," she said. "Maybe half an hour."

"Take more time if you like. Just call me if you're going to be longer than that. And check around before you come back to make sure nobody's watching you."

"Don't worry, I know who to look for." Gemma fluffed her short hair, checked her scant makeup, and tucked her shirttail in her slacks.

"Call me if you need anything, Mom," she said.

"I'll be fine. Have fun."

Lila's words faded as Gemma breezed out the door. In her time as a busy student nurse, fun had lost its meaning. All she meant to do now was stretch her legs, explore a little, and pick up some snacks for her and her mother to enjoy while they watched tonight's Cutting Horse Challenge on closed-circuit TV.

Stepping out of the elevator on the main floor, she came face-to-face with a life-sized poster advertising a nearby stage show. A spectacular showgirl in a scanty costume and elaborate plumed headdress smiled and posed against a glittering backdrop. That showgirl could have been Lila a dozen years ago—a single mother supporting her child any way she could. Desperate to save that child, she'd broken up Frank Culhane's contentious marriage. Frank's money had paid for ten-year-old Gemma's lifesaving heart surgery. Lila had repaid him with eleven years of wifely devotion. But his first family, to this very day, had never forgiven the woman who'd displaced them.

"I see her, Darrin!" Simone, dressed as a blackjack dealer in a magenta satin shirt, black pants, sunglasses, and a black visor, spoke into her phone. "She just stepped out of the elevator. It looks like she's going toward the casino."

"Are you sure it's Gemma?" Darrin, in cowboy clothes and a red MAGA cap, spoke from the stairwell below the floor where Mariah had told them Lila would be staying.

"It's her, all right," Simone answered. "I'd know your drab little stepsister anywhere."

"Keep an eye on her. Let me know if she heads back to the elevator. Whatever happens, don't let her recognize you."

"I'm not stupid, Darrin."

The two of them had been keeping watch for several hours, hoping to get Lila alone. The next step of the plan would be up to Darrin. He had never killed anyone before. His hands perspired inside his latex gloves at the thought of what he might have to do.

The trick would be to make Lila's death look like an accident. He'd watched enough crime drama on TV to know that wouldn't be easy. That was why he had the gloves and a mask in his pocket, and a piece of pipe under his leather vest. He could push her off the balcony, although he might have to knock her out first. He could even slice her wrists to make her death look like suicide. Or shove her head against the bathroom sink to make it appear that she'd struck it when she passed out. But the balcony was by far the best option.

Darrin was no Superman. Weak as Lila would be from that snakebite, he should be able to overpower her. But, as a backup, he carried a chloroform-soaked rag zipped into a plastic bag. The chloroform, which might be detectable in her lungs, was a last resort, but he couldn't be too careful.

As he came out of the stairwell onto the floor, a horrific thought struck him. If Jasmine had talked to her lover, this could be a trap. Lila might not even be there. He could open the numbered door to find the FBI waiting for him.

A woman with a cleaning cart was coming down the hall toward him. She appeared to be about forty, tired-looking, maybe with a family at home. She could probably use a little something extra.

Slipping a fifty-dollar bill out of his wallet, he held it up where she could see it. "I'll give you this," he said, "if you'll knock on the door of room 1545 and wait until it opens."

The woman hesitated. She looked up and down the hall,

then approached Darrin and snatched the bill with an outstretched hand. After tucking it into her pocket, she moved down the hall to the door and tapped politely.

"Louder! Damn it," Darrin snapped, his nerves crackling like frayed wires.

The woman pounded on the door. Seconds passed. There was no response.

"You've got a passkey," Darrin said. "Open it."

She shook her head. "If I do that for you, I could lose my job."

Darrin held out more bills. "Just open it."

After a nervous glance around, she grabbed the cash from his hand and used her key. Keeping clear of the security camera, Darrin watched the door swing open.

The room was vacant—the beds neatly made, every surface swept and wiped clean, with no sign of luggage or other possessions. As the woman fled down the hall, Darrin studied the number he'd written down. It was the number Mariah had given him.

Stepping back into the stairwell, he called Simone on his cell phone. "This was a trap, but I knew better than to spring it," he said. "Can you still see Gemma?"

"She's in plain sight, watching people play the slots."

"Follow her wherever she goes," Darrin said. "Don't take your eyes off her for a second. If you stay sharp, she'll lead us to her mother."

CHAPTER EIGHT

There wasn't a great selection in the gift shop, but Gemma picked up some chips and dip, a packet of Oreos, and some red licorice strings. She added a couple cans of Diet Pepsi, paid for her purchases, and stuffed a few free napkins into the plastic bag the clerk handed her.

As she crossed the lobby, moving toward the elevators, her instincts began to tingle. She paused, glancing around. Was her imagination running away with itself, or was someone watching her?

The idea seemed foolish, but with her mother in danger, she couldn't afford to ignore her intuition.

Screening herself behind a posterboard display, she scanned the crowded lobby. People were going about their business, some lining up to register at the desk, some headed for the casino, others wandering aimlessly, much as she had done. No one appeared to be paying her any attention.

A flash of bright color caught her eye. A petite, blond woman in a purplish-red, poly-satin blouse stood half-turned away from her. Gemma recognized her outfit. The blouse, worn with black pants and a black visor, was the uniform of a card dealer.

The visor was worn by some dealers to shield their eyes from the glaring lights of the casino. But why would the woman need to wear it in the lobby? And if she worked in the casino, what was she doing out here?

There could be a reason for both, but the woman looked strangely out of place. As she turned slightly, Gemma noticed how poorly her clothes fit, as if she'd borrowed someone else's uniform. The blouse gapped across her ample chest, and the pants, worn without a belt, were partway unzipped over the rounded bulge of her belly. To Gemma's trained eye, she appeared to be . . . pregnant.

Gemma's pulse slammed. Turning away from the elevators, she walked back across the lobby, past the gift shop, and down the hall toward the women's restroom. A furtive glance behind her confirmed that the woman was moving in the same direction, holding her phone to her ear.

Could this really be Simone? Gemma had met her stepbrother's wife at Frank's memorial. It was hard to believe the woman slipping along behind her could be the elegant creature she remembered. But there were similarities in size and build, and Gemma knew about Simone's pregnancy.

Gemma wasn't afraid of Simone. She was concerned only because Sam Rafferty had warned Lila about Darrin's alleged plot. The fact that Lila had taken the warning seriously was even more of a cause for Gemma's worry—especially now, if she was really being shadowed by Simone.

The restroom, with its open entrance, was just ahead. Across the hall, a door that stood ajar was labeled STAIRS.

Maybe she should stop and confront the woman, Gemma thought. But that could prove dangerous, especially if she had a weapon. It might be safer to stay ahead and lead her away from Lila.

By now, Gemma had been gone from the hotel room for longer than thirty minutes. If she didn't check in soon, her mother would be worried. She needed a safe place to make a call. She could go into the restroom—but from there, there would be only one way out.

The woman had yet to enter the hallway. Making a split-second decision, Gemma tossed the bag of snacks into the restroom, then ducked into the stairwell and closed the door behind her.

The stairwell was stark and empty, its bare walls illuminated by bright fluorescent light. A flight of metal stairs led upward to a door on the next floor and continued all the way to the top of the hotel. If she could get higher without being seen, she should be able to exit the stairwell on any random floor and disappear into the maze of rooms.

She began to climb, each footstep echoing in the silent space. With luck, Simone—or whoever the woman might be—would check the restroom first, giving her precious seconds to get ahead.

But she'd calculated wrong. She was a few steps short of the first landing when the door opened and her pursuer stepped inside. Looking back down the stairs, Gemma could see her clearly. She had taken off the visor. It was Simone.

Gemma started to climb again, but Simone had clearly seen her. It was time to turn around and face the enemy.

"What do you want, Simone?" she called, her voice echoing up and down the stairwell. "Why are you following me in that ridiculous disguise?"

"Don't be afraid, Gemma." Simone spoke in a coaxing voice. "Come on down. I just want to talk to you."

"I'll stay where I am, thank you," Gemma said. "Just

answer my question. Why are you creeping around like a character in a bad spy movie?"

There was a silent pause, as if Simone was weighing her answer. "It's my . . . husband. I don't want him to see me." Her voice broke in a dramatic sob. "He's got this crazy plot against your mother, because of the house. I need to stop him before he breaks the law and ends up in jail."

"What does that have to do with me?" Gemma demanded. "Just tell me what you want."

"I have to talk to Lila, in person. She needs to know what Darrin is planning so she can protect herself. Please, he's mentally ill. He's capable of anything."

Gemma shook her head. "I don't believe a word you're saying, Simone. You can—"

Gemma's words ended in a gasp as an arm seized her from behind and yanked her off her feet. Something damp closed over her nose and mouth. She recognized the sweet smell of chloroform.

She struggled, trying not to inhale, but as fumes from the toxic liquid crept into her lungs, she could feel the blackness swirling and growing in her brain until she had to let go and give in. Then there was nothing left of thought or memory.

"You blithering fool!" Simone glared up at her husband, who was standing on the stair, holding the unconscious young woman in his arms. "What in heaven's name were you thinking?"

"I was thinking that she could ruin everything, and we had to take care of her."

"Take care of her? How? Should we drag her up the stairs and push her out of a window? Would that help to buy us the house? And what if we got caught? The charges would be kidnapping and murder—or attempted murder, at least. We'd spend the rest of our lives in prison."

"Can't we take her somewhere and force her to tell us where her mother is?"

"Not legally. I was doing fine until you showed up," Simone said. "I hadn't even broken any laws. All I did was follow her around and lie to her when she recognized me. But you—you've already committed a felony—felonious assault, I think it's called. But what do I know? You're the lawyer. I'm just a woman."

"What's this talk about you and me, Simone?" Darrin lugged the slender, long-limbed young woman down the stairs and laid her on the concrete floor. With one latex-gloved hand, he pulled off his black nylon mask. "We're in this together. You're as much to blame as I am. If she hadn't recognized you, you could've followed her all the way back to her mother. So, if you're so damned clever, tell me. What are we going to do with her now?"

"I'll tell you what we're going to do," Simone said. "Give her another dose of chloroform so she won't open her eyes and see us. Then we're going to walk out and leave her right here on the floor. With luck, when she wakes up, she won't remember what happened. Or if she does, nobody will believe her. Then I'm going to ditch these clothes. We'll drive back to the Excalibur and sneak into the movie theater in the middle of a film. As far as anybody who asks is concerned, we were there all the time. If you've got a better idea, speak up now."

Darrin glared at her. He hated it when Simone showed him up.

"Well?" she demanded.

Gemma was beginning to stir. He crouched next to her and held the chloroform-soaked cloth over her nose and mouth. Her body went limp again. For a moment, he gazed down at her—the stepsister whom he'd known since she was a skinny, bookish kid growing up on the ranch, the daughter of the woman he'd hated since the day she'd married his dad. Technically, Gemma was family. But he'd never felt the slightest brotherly affection toward her. He could strangle her now without a flicker of guilt.

"What about Lila?" he asked. "Could we force this girl to lead us to her?"

"I was working on that when you stepped in," Simone said. "But it's too late now. We're going to need a different plan. Come on, we need to get out of here."

Frustrated, Darrin followed his wife out of the hotel through the service entrance. Caught up in the plot to eliminate Lila, he'd almost forgotten about the mysterious call from the man claiming to be his brother. Now he remembered. What if the call had been real? What if the man was here, just out of sight, waiting for the right time to make a connection?

It was probably wishful thinking. But Darrin had longed for a better ally than Simone—someone who would have his back and wouldn't be always judging him, making demands, and putting him down. Someone like a brother.

But what was he thinking? He was stuck with what he had—and what he had was Simone. Nobody, especially a long-lost brother, was going to help him out of the mess he'd made.

Cheyenne sat in the stands of the main arena, sipping a Big Gulp and waiting for the cutting competition to begin. The seat next to her was empty. Roper had bought a ticket and promised to join her, but he had yet to show up. She was concerned about him. At a time when he needed food and rest, he was driving himself too hard, living on coffee and energy drinks, as if nothing mattered except winning the Run for a Million.

Although he refused to talk about it, Cheyenne knew that the pending murder charge weighed heavily on his mind. Maybe he viewed the competition as a final act of glory before the steel cuffs closed around his wrists and the fight to prove his innocence began.

She checked her phone, hoping for a text from him, but there was nothing. Nor was there any message from Hayden. Maybe he was busy with funeral arrangements and ranch business. Maybe he was consumed by grief. Or maybe he just didn't care enough to keep in touch with her.

Never mind. She was determined to enjoy the evening. Tomorrow her mother would be arriving, and her days of freedom would come to an end.

Her lunch with Buck Tolson, at a tiny Mexican restaurant with delicious food, had been a gold strike of information. Thanks to Buck, who'd done most of the talking, she knew the fine points of the sport, how a run was set up, the rider's job, the horse's job, and the reason there were four other cowboys in the arena. She knew how judges scored a two-and-a-half-minute run, the points and penalties. The more she heard, the more eager she was to get her own horse and start learning. She'd cut cattle as a teen on her family's Colorado ranch, but competitive cutting was a whole different world.

"In cutting, the show is all about the horse," Buck had told her. "Once the rider picks a cow and cuts it out of the herd, he—"

"Or she," Cheyenne had teased, drawing a smile from that serious mouth. "Girls can do it, too."

"He or she," he'd conceded. "After the rider lowers his—or her—rein hand to the horse's neck, then it's up to the horse to keep the cow under control. It's quite a show. I think you'll enjoy it."

"I don't just want to enjoy it. I want to do it," Cheyenne had said.

Buck had chuckled at her impatience. "Whoa, there. Something tells me you can do anything you put your mind to. But getting there is going to take more time and work than you can imagine—and the right horse."

Almost forgetting to eat, Cheyenne had hung on his every word. While he spoke, her eyes studied his face—not a handsome face, but strong, masculine, and trustworthy, with deep-set eyes, prominent cheekbones, a chiseled jaw, and a mouth that was firm but generous. His dark hair was lightly flecked with gray.

She knew next to nothing about the man—not even his age, which she guessed to be a little short of thirty. He wore no wedding ring, but that didn't rule out a woman in his life, or even children. His hands were callused and scarred—a workingman's hands. And he wore a workingman's clothes, without even a fancy buckle to show that he was a champion, maybe the best in the country or even the best in the world.

Watching him across the table, Cheyenne had found herself wondering how it would feel to be kissed by such a man. But she'd forced the thought away. She was here to learn about cutting, and this was a man who could teach her.

Last night, the draw party had been held to determine the order in which riders and horses would compete. Buck had drawn the second-to-last slot. Hayden would have been last if tragedy hadn't called him away. Now Cheyenne checked her phone again. There were no messages—not from Hayden and not from Roper. And the event was about to start.

She stood for the national anthem. Then the loudspeaker blared, and the four mounted helpers, there to contain the herd of cattle in the arena, took their places. When everything was in place, the first competing rider galloped his horse through the gate.

Cheyenne quickly lost herself in the beauty and intricacy of the sport. The cows—steers and heifers—were bunched in the center of the arena. The rider cut his chosen animal out of the herd. Once it was in the open, he lowered his hand to slacken the rein and let his horse take over.

Watching the beautiful bay horse work the cow, keeping it from running to the fence or back to the herd, was mesmerizing. Agile as a dancer, the horse wove, shifted, and dodged, blocking the cow at every turn, controlling the animal physically and mentally. The rider could give subtle cues with his knees but couldn't use the rein or his hands to guide the horse.

Perched on the edge of her seat, Cheyenne watched in rapt attention as the whistle sent the cow back to the herd and the rider chose a second animal to work. At the end of the run, the judges announced the score—76.2 points out of a possible 80. It was good, but not good enough to win. Other riders were bound to get higher scores as the competition continued.

The next rider was good but unlucky. The second cow he'd chosen broke away from the horse and made a beeline for the herd. The score, a disappointing 67.0.

More horses and riders exercised their skill as the leading score crept upward. At last, with the first place score at 78.2, it was Buck's turn.

Almost forgetting to breathe, Cheyenne leaned forward to get a better look at him. Dressed simply in a fresh denim shirt, jeans, well-worn leather chaps, and a battered Stetson, he sat his tall buckskin like a king. The horse, Chief, had been brushed until his hide gleamed like liquid bronze. His black mane and tail caught the air, flowing like silk as he loped into the herd, headed for the cow his master had chosen.

They made a splendid pair, the man and his mount—all the more because Buck was clearly out there to show off his horse, not himself.

The brindle steer was in the open now, expertly separated from the middle of the herd. Keeping it there would be up to Chief. With a grace that was almost dance-like, the big gelding blocked the steer's every move. The subtle guidance of Buck's knees was so slight it was almost invisible.

Cheyenne could sense the bond between the horse and the man—something so deep that it couldn't be acquired through training. It was as if the two of them communicated not just by word and touch but by instinct.

Did she have it in her—the empathy and the patience—to form that kind of bond with a special animal? The thought of the challenge made her blood race. Buck had been right. This was going to take more time and work than she'd ever imagined.

Buck's second choice, a feisty black heifer, was harder to control than the first one. But Cheyenne knew that managing a difficult animal added more points. When the heifer charged, Chief turned it deftly aside and kept it contained until the whistle. As Buck rode out of the arena, the judges' score was posted. A near-perfect 79.3 points had put Buck in first place for the win.

At least, that was what Cheyenne thought. But she was wrong. The contest wasn't over.

She was standing to cheer for the winner when a new announcement boomed from the loudspeaker. "Ladies and gentlemen, our final contestant will be Hayden Barr, riding Steely Dan."

For a moment, Cheyenne thought she might have misunderstood. *This was a mistake. It had to be.*

As the crowd stirred, Cheyenne sank back into her seat. It appeared that the announcer hadn't gotten the word, that was all. Someone needed to tell him that Hayden had been called away and wouldn't be competing.

She waited for the correction and the announcement that Buck had won the event. She was still waiting when a familiar-looking rider on a paint horse galloped into the arena.

Cheyenne stared, scarcely daring to believe her eyes. The rider was unmistakably Hayden.

She'd watched Hayden ride in the practice arena. She knew he was good. But tonight, he was on fire. Cheyenne knew that he was determined to beat Buck's near-perfect score. But where Buck had led with patience and precision, Hayden appeared to be almost angry, driving the horse with his voice and subtle jabs of his knees.

Steely Dan responded with bursts of amazing speed, pushing the cow into showy maneuvers meant to rack up points. Hayden was skating the edge of the rules, but the crowd was drawn in, even clapping at some of the flashier moves.

After the final whistle, a hush fell over the crowd as they waited for the score. Would Hayden be penalized for pushing the limits, or had his showmanship earned enough points to put him over the top?

At last, the score was posted and the winner announced. Hayden had earned a score of 79.5. He had beaten Buck Tolson, the national champion, by two tenths of a point.

The buckle and $250,000 prize money would be awarded later that night on the festival stage, to be followed by a party and concert. For now, the show was over. As the crowd flowed out of the stands, Cheyenne paused to check her phone. There was still no word from Roper. After sending him a short text, she headed for the area behind the arena. Hayden would be there, receiving congratulations and giving interviews to the press. He owed her an explanation. But right now, Hayden wasn't the man she wanted to find.

Making her way through the solid mob of well-wishers took time. At last, in the open space behind the arena, she could see Hayden talking to a TV crew. One of the stable hands was leading Steely Dan away. But Buck was nowhere in sight.

Maybe he'd taken his horse back to the stall. Cheyenne was about to go looking for him when Hayden broke away from the TV crew and called to her.

"Cheyenne! Wait up!"

Cheyenne kept walking. But she had no right to be angry with him, she reminded herself. She was just confused and needed answers. Slowing her step, she allowed him to catch up.

"Sorry," he said. "I know you must be upset with me."

"I'm not upset. I was concerned, that's all," she said. "I'm sure you had your hands full, but I would have appreciated a text—even a word or two."

"Again, I'm sorry," he said. "It's been a hell of a day."

"I can imagine. Don't apologize. Just tell me what you're doing here. I thought you'd be with your father."

Hayden took a deep breath. "I rented a plane at the airport and flew to Gallup. I got there too late. My dad had already passed. I knew how much he'd wanted to see me compete, so I decided to do it as a tribute. I made some calls—contacted a few friends and his lawyer and arranged for his transport to the funeral home in Wichita Falls. Then I turned around and flew back to Vegas. I got here just in time to saddle up for the competition."

"And you won. Congratulations, even though I'm sure your victory was bittersweet. I'm so sorry about your father. I never met the man, but I've heard good things about him." Cheynne remembered Roper's praise for Chet Barr—and she remembered that she needed to call her brother.

"The victory was more sweet than bitter. Wanting to beat Buck Tolson has driven me for as long as I've been competing. Now that buckle will finally be mine. The award ceremony will be starting soon, with a party and concert afterward. Are you coming?"

His question caught Cheyenne off guard. "I don't know," she said. "I hadn't even thought about it. Maybe I'd better—"

"You've got to come!" Hayden grabbed her hand. "I want you right there, front and center when I get that buckle and the check. Then, pretty lady, I want to show you off at the party. Come on, it's almost time to start!"

He swept her into the flowing crowd, the momentum carrying them toward the festival stage. Cheyenne had little choice except to grip Hayden's hand and follow his lead. She could only hope to make a fast escape after the award ceremony. She wasn't in the mood for the party that would follow, and she needed to connect with Roper.

As the throng moved her past the entrance to the barn, Cheyenne glimpsed a tall figure standing in a doorway, keeping clear of the crowd. For an instant, his gaze locked with hers across the distance. Then the river of people carried her past him. When she looked back, Buck was gone.

In the waiting room of the ER, Roper took a few minutes to check his phone. There were several voice messages from Cheyenne, clearly worried, asking why he hadn't shown up at the cutting event. He needed to call her.

Finding a quiet alcove, he scrolled to her number. She answered on the first ring.

"Roper! Thank heaven!" He could hear noisy music in the background. "Where are you? Are you all right?"

"I'm at the hospital. No—no, I'm fine. It's Lila's daughter, Gemma. She was found unconscious in a stairwell at the hotel. Somebody put her out with chloroform."

"What?" She spoke up to be heard over the music. "Oh, no! Will she be okay?"

"She's awake but still groggy. They've got her on oxygen and some kind of IV drip. The doctor says she'll be all right in a day or two. One of the cleaners found her. They got the room key off her and called her mother. Lila's with her now. You can imagine she's pretty upset."

"But who would do such a thing?"

"We've got our suspicions. Sam is on his way here to question her." Roper paused. "Where are you? What's all that noise I can hear?"

"I'm at the buckle ceremony for Hayden. He showed up at the last minute and won the cutting event. Now it's party time."

"But—Hayden? I thought he left. What about his father?"

"His father had already passed when Hayden got there. He decided to fly back here and compete as a tribute. Now that the award ceremony is done, I'm just getting out of here. The party's already getting too wild for me. Where can I find you?"

"I don't know how long I'll be here. Lila wants to stay with her daughter, and she's going to need some support. I can be here. There's nothing scheduled for tomorrow but the Shootout."

"I can look after One in a Million for you."

"Thanks, but I can manage that. You'll have your hands full when Mother gets here tomorrow."

She groaned. "Don't remind me. She said she planned to stay in the room, which is fine, except that she'll want me to stay with her."

"All the more reason to kick up your heels and have fun tonight. I know Hayden will be mourning his father, but the prestige that goes with winning a big event, along with the money, should at least give him something to celebrate."

"We'll see about that." Roper sensed the lack of excitement in her voice. Maybe things had cooled with Hayden.

"As long as I'm here, at least let me check on your horses tonight," she said. "That way you can spend all the time you need to with Lila."

"Thanks," Roper said. "Make sure they have feed and water. You can call me if you notice anything that seems off to you." Glancing back into the waiting room, he saw Sam walk in. "I've got to go. Have fun. That's an order."

Her laugh sounded strained. "You know how I feel about taking orders. Give my best to Lila and her daughter. Maybe we can meet when this mess is behind us—with or without Mother's approval."

"Thanks, Little Sis." Roper ended the call and hurried to meet Sam.

The party was ramping up. Hayden, surrounded by well-wishers, was already on his third Michelob. Cheyenne had seen enough rodeo parties to know that she didn't care to stay. The horses would give her an excuse to get away from the noise and the drinking.

When she failed to get Hayden's attention, she found a cowboy she knew and asked him to pass on the message that she was leaving to check on her brother's horses. Then she slipped out through a side door. Hayden wouldn't be pleased, but he had plenty of friends to keep him company. He might not even miss her.

The lights in the barn were low, the horses stirring and chuffing as they settled for the night. The familiar scent of fresh manure mellowed the machine-cooled air.

Cheyenne knew her way to One in a Million's stall. The great roan stallion nickered and peered over the gate as she approached.

"Hello, big boy," she said. "Are you lonesome?"

The stallion chuffed and lowered his head, allowing her to reach up and stroke his face. His skin was like warm satin. According to Roper, he was much calmer now. But it remained to be seen whether he'd be ready to perform in the Run for a Million on Saturday, two nights from now.

"Have you got hay and water, boy?"

A five-gallon plastic pail stood outside the stall. Cheyenne was petite. But by turning it over and standing on it, she could see over the gate. If the horse had needed anything, she wouldn't have been afraid to go into his stall. But she could see his water bucket and hay feeder. Roper had left him well supplied. She continued stroking him.

"Are you going to be our Saturday-night hero? Or is that too much to ask after what you've been through. How's your buddy next door doing, hmm?"

From Fire Dance's stall, there was nothing but silence. Cheyenne strained her ears and listened for the slightest movement, even the sound of breathing. She heard nothing.

She knew better than to open the gate. But she had to know whether the traumatized stallion was even alive. She moved the bucket and stood on it. Now she could see over the gate. But the stall was in full shadow. There was still no movement. No sound. She stretched on tiptoe, leaning a little over the top edge of the gate.

The dark silence exploded in screaming fury as Fire Dance lunged out of the shadows. Rearing, the powerful stallion leaped at the gate, his teeth catching the faint light, his front hooves kicking and flailing. Something skimmed Cheyenne's head. The pail toppled away beneath her feet. She pitched backward.

The arms that broke her fall were as unexpected as the stallion's attack had been.

"You're all right, Cheyenne. I've got you."

The voice that spoke, almost in her ear, was Buck's.

CHAPTER NINE

"What in blazes were you doing?" Buck lowered Cheyenne's feet, none too gently, to the sawdust-strewn concrete floor. "That stallion could've killed you—and don't think for a minute the gate would have stopped him! What got into your head?"

Turning to face him, Cheyenne found her voice. "I was checking Roper's horse, and Fire Dance was so quiet in his stall, I was afraid something was wrong—"

"Well, you found out, didn't you? You should have called somebody if you were worried. You work with horses. You know how dangerous they can be."

She glowered up at him. "Don't scold me, Buck. I'm not a child."

"Aren't you? Hell, girl, you're not even legal to drink." His eyes were in shadow, but Cheyenne could almost feel his gaze boring through her.

Behind the gate, the red stallion snorted and slammed his body against the rear of the stall. Cheyenne turned her attention back to the horse. "What's really wrong with him?" she asked. "I mean, I know what happened to him, and I know that he was high-strung even before the accident. But it's like he has PTSD. Can't something be done for him?"

"That decision will be up to your friend, Hayden. And right now he's busy celebrating."

"I know. And I'm sorry. I was hoping you'd win."

He shrugged. "There'll be other competitions."

"But we were talking about Fire Dance. What do you think is wrong with him?"

Buck fell silent for a moment. "He doesn't appear to have any visible injuries—although we can't rule out brain damage. That aside, he seems terrified. And he can't understand why. When somebody tries to approach him, he sees them as the thing that could be coming to hurt him again. So he lashes out. Does that make sense?"

"Yes. He's innocent, like a child," Cheyenne murmured, as if speaking to herself. "He doesn't understand. He only feels. And that wreck, with the trailer slamming him to one side, hurting him in ways we can only imagine, destroyed his trust in the people who were supposed to keep him safe. All he's ever done was obey, like a good horse. And now he's suffering for it. Oh, Buck, why does life have to be so unfair?"

"That's a question for the ages, Cheyenne." His fingertip traced the moist path of a tear down her cheek, then paused to lift her chin, tilting her face to the light. As if drawn by his touch, she strained upward. A muted groan rose in his throat as he lowered his head and claimed her mouth with his.

He smelled of horses and man-sweat, and his lips tasted faintly of beer. But the warmth that crept through Cheyenne's body was so powerful that it almost shattered her. As his arms clasped her, she melted against him. Her mouth softened and parted to let him in. She tasted his tongue, felt the gentle hunger in its probing. In the depths of her body a pulsing current woke and stirred, shimmering upward. As the kiss became more urgent, she gave herself to the powerful sensation. Her fingers raked the back of his hair. Her hips curled against his. She thought of her empty room upstairs in the hotel, and his room next door. It could happen. Heaven help her, did she want it to happen?

But she should have known better. Like a killing frost on a spring morning, the terror crept in. Her body tensed. Panic, driven by her pounding heart, surged through her limbs. Instinctively, she began to struggle. "No—don't—"

"Whoa, girl." He released her and stepped back. "Are you all right? Was it something I did?"

She shook her head vehemently. "No. I'm sorry, Buck. It wasn't you. It was me." A shudder passed through her body. "I was wrong to let things go this far."

In the faint light, emotions flickered over his rugged features—bitter amusement, wounded pride, a touch of concern.

"I won't stop you from leaving, Cheyenne," he said. "But that was a damned good kiss, and you liked it. I can tell when a woman is faking—and you weren't faking. What happened? Is there someone else? Like Hayden? Say the word. I'll understand."

Cheyenne hesitated. She barely knew Buck Tolson. Their shared kiss had shown her a hidden side of this tough, taciturn man. But did that entitle him to know her secret? Something in her wanted to trust him. But what if she was wrong?

Buck was waiting. In his calm patience, she found her answer.

The first painful words had to be forced. Then the story spilled out of her.

"When I was eighteen, I was raped—violently—by a man I thought was a friend. I was a virgin. It was my first time. I was so hurt and scared, I wanted to die. Since then, I haven't been able to . . . be intimate with a man. The memory comes back, and I freeze. All I want is to get away."

She forced herself to go on. "He took me home afterward as if nothing had happened. I never reported him—the shame would have killed my family. My brothers don't even know about it."

"Why the shame?" His voice was gentle. "It wasn't your fault."

"Wasn't it? I was there. I was alone with him, in his hotel room. Isn't it always the woman's fault?" Cheyenne turned away from him, suddenly cautious. Had she said too much?

"I can imagine what you're thinking," he said. "You've trusted me with something very personal. I promise to honor that. Your secret will be safe with me."

"Thanks." She arranged her face into a smile. "I'm still wondering whether I just made a fool of myself."

"Hear this, Cheyenne," he said. "I had a sister, a bit younger than you. She's gone now. That's a story for another time. But I wish I'd told her what I'm telling you now. Someday you'll meet the person who'll make everything all right, and you'll know it was worth the wait. He won't be some down-at-the-heels cowboy like me. He'll be worthy of you. And when it happens, maybe in your head, you'll hear me saying, *I told you so*. Remember that, all right?"

"All right." There were tears in Cheyenne's voice. She battled the urge to fling herself into his arms again, if only for comfort. But that wasn't going to happen.

The tension was broken by a voice calling her name. Hayden was striding down the row of stalls toward them.

"Hey, there you are, pretty lady." Hayden reached her side. "I've been waiting for you to come back to the party."

He'd been drinking when she left, but he appeared sober enough now. "I wasn't sure you wanted me to come back," she said. "You seemed to be having a great time without me."

"Hey, it was my party. I owed it to the presenters to kick up my heels. But I missed you enough to leave and come looking for you. How long does it take to check on a couple of horses, anyway? I'd begun to wonder if you had company."

Cheyenne was grateful for the dim light, which hid the rush of heat to her face. "I did. Buck was here. I was asking him about Fire Dance."

"Well, I don't see him now. Maybe he's off licking his wounds. I finally beat him, Cheyenne, fair and square!"

Cheyenne glanced around. Buck had indeed made a discreet exit.

"About Fire Dance," she said, "he's your horse, Hayden. He won't be allowed to stay here past the weekend. You've got to decide what to do with him."

Frowning, Hayden gazed toward the stall, where Fire Dance had finally settled into silence. "What would you do if he was your horse?" he asked Cheyenne. "Would you try to load him and haul him home or save yourself the trouble and put him down right here?"

The question triggered a chill. "That isn't my decision," Cheyenne said. "He's a beautiful horse, and he doesn't deserve what happened to him. If there's any way to save him—"

"You didn't answer my question."

"But I did. I said it wasn't my decision. So what will you do with him?"

Hayden's expression hardened. "It's a no-brainer. That damned hundred-thousand-dollar horse is worthless the way he is. And even if he can eventually be handled, he'll never compete again. When I get home, I'll have my father's funeral to arrange and a ranch to take over, to say nothing of the legal issues I'll be dealing with. I won't have time to waste on a useless horse. Tomorrow I'll arrange with the vet to put him out of his misery."

"No! What if he can still be saved? What if he just needs time, and maybe some therapy?"

"I won't have time or patience—or money to pay some so-called horse whisperer to work with him. The vet here is paid by the arena. He'll euthanize the horse for free and call somebody to haul away the carcass."

"But that would be such a waste," Cheyenne argued. "And to do it before you even know what's wrong with him—"

Hayden cut her off with an impatient gesture. "You say you want to save the damned horse? Fine. Have it your way. Fire Dance is yours. I'll have my lawyer fax his pedigree and ownership papers, dated from tonight, to the hotel in the morning. You can do whatever the hell you want with him. Just leave me out of it."

Cheyenne stared at him. "You're joking. You can't just give him to me."

"I certainly can. And if you don't accept him, he'll be euthanized tomorrow. It's your choice. Make it now."

"But what would I do with him? How would I even get him home? He can't ride back in the trailer with One in a Million."

"That, sweetheart, is your problem. If you can't figure out what to do, you can always have him put down—but it'll be your decision, not mine."

Cheyenne glared up at his sardonic grin. She was trapped, and Hayden was enjoying his victory. His gift, which she couldn't refuse without sentencing Fire Dance to death, had relieved him of all responsibility.

Hayden raised an eyebrow. "Maybe you could get your friend, Buck, to help you. He's supposed to be some kind of horse whisperer. And I've seen how he looks at you. I'll bet he'd do anything for you, even take on a crazy, killer horse. Go ahead and ask him. I won't be jealous. If I can beat him in the arena, I can for sure keep him from stealing my girl."

"I'm not your girl, Hayden. I'm nobody's girl except my own."

"That's not what you say to a man who just gave you a stallion with a pedigree as long as your arm." He chuckled. It appeared he was drunker than Cheyenne had first thought. Maybe in the morning, when he'd sobered up, he would change his mind about giving her Fire Dance. But she'd made up her mind about one thing. She couldn't turn her back and let him kill that beautiful horse.

"Come on, baby," he said, reaching for her arm. "Let's go back to the party. The night's just getting started, and I know how I want it to end. You've kept me at arms' length too long." He whipped her against him, his mouth finding hers in a forceful but sloppy kiss.

Summoning her strength, she shoved him away from her. He staggered, then righted himself and stood wiping his mouth. "What's wrong, honey? I could've had my choice of women tonight, and I chose you. You ought to be grateful."

"Ask me out when you're sober," she said. "Tonight I'm not going anyplace with you. Enjoy the party without me, Hayden. I'm exhausted. All I want is to go back to my room and sleep."

"But you said your mother would be showing up tomorrow. This will be your last night to have fun." The implication was clear.

"Go on," she said. "There are plenty of girls at the party who'd be thrilled to share your company."

"I was hoping for something classier than a buckle bunny," Hayden said. "And, hey, I just gave you a horse."

"Good night, Hayden. If you're serious about the horse, talk to me in the morning." She turned away and started walking.

"No need," he said. "The paperwork, with my signature, will be waiting for you at the front desk by tomorrow. Consider him yours."

"Have a good time." She kept on walking down the row of stalls toward the hotel lobby. She didn't look around, but at some point she sensed that Hayden had headed back to the Arena Stage and rejoined the party.

Cheyenne felt vaguely ill as she crossed the lobby. She'd fended off her share of drunken cowboys, but Hayden was different. He was her friend. She'd liked him. But what had passed between them tonight was ugly. She wanted to blot it from her memory.

As she rode the elevator alone, up to her floor, a shadow of disbelief crept over her. Had the past forty-five minutes been real? Had Hayden actually given her Fire Dance—a horse so traumatized that no one could approach him, a horse that would be a nightmare to load and transport and who would most likely be too dangerous to keep? Now the stallion's life was in her hands—a burden she'd never expected.

As she left the elevator and walked down the hall, she passed Buck's room. His kiss had left her weak and quivering—a feeling that returned as she paused outside his closed door.

She remembered Hayden's words—"*I've seen how he looks at you. I'll bet he'd do anything for you.*"

But Hayden was wrong, Cheyenne told herself. Buck was older than she was in years and experience. He saw her as an amusing child—maybe like the younger sister he'd mentioned. Even that soul-shattering kiss had been no more than an impulse—deeply felt but without promise.

Tomorrow, with the cutting competition ended, Buck would load his superb buckskin horse in the trailer and leave for home. And her mother would be arriving later that morning to take over her life.

What were the chances she would ever see Buck again?

She stood in front of his door, daring herself to knock. She wanted more time with the man who had so much to teach her. She wanted to ask him about training and hear his wise advice about Fire Dance.

And, fool that she was, she wanted to share one more heart-stopping kiss, even if it was only to say goodbye.

Summoning her courage, Cheyenne rapped lightly on the door and waited. There was no reply and no sound from the other side. Maybe he was asleep. She tried again, knocking harder this time and waiting even longer.

Was he downstairs having a drink at the bar, maybe trying his luck in the casino? Or had he found a woman willing and able to give him what Cheyenne couldn't?

Never mind, she told herself as she fished out her key card and opened her own door. Buck was his own man. What he did for pleasure shouldn't matter.

But it did matter. It mattered enough to hurt.

At 2:17, Darrin's cell phone rang. He rolled over in bed and groped for it where it lay on the nightstand.

Beside him, Simone lay deep in slumber. She'd taken one

of her prescription sleeping pills that tended to knock her out like a dose of chloroform.

Chloroform. The word jarred him fully awake. He grabbed for the jangling phone, knocking it to the floor. What if it was the police calling? What if Lila's daughter had died or awakened with a vivid memory of the incident in the stairwell?

Scrambling to his feet, he located the phone partway under the bed. It was still ringing. The caller was unknown.

"Hello?" he muttered.

"Hello, Brother. Remember me?"

The disguised voice raised the hair on the back of Darrin's neck. With a glance at his sleeping wife, he carried the phone into the bathroom, closed the door, and turned on the water in the basin. Until he knew more about this new development, he didn't want to involve Simone.

"Who is this? What do you want?" he demanded, speaking into the phone.

"As I said, I'm your brother—actually your half brother. As for what I want, you'll find out in time, when we get to know each other better."

"But how can I trust you? How do I know whether you're telling the truth?"

"We have the same father—Frank Culhane. His name isn't on my birth certificate because my mother was married and so was Frank. But she told me the truth before she died. And I have the DNA test results to prove it. I can show you when we meet."

"I know my father was no saint. But before I accept your story, I'll want to have those DNA results examined by an expert."

"That's no problem. I've already prepared a copy. I'll give it to you when we meet."

"Not so fast. Before I agree to meet you, I need to know why you're calling me now, in secret, in the middle of the night. Tell me what you want, or this stops now."

"What I want is to help you. I know about your legal fight with Lila Culhane over the house and stables. Lila's got the will. That gives her the upper hand. I can fix that for you—something you've had no luck doing yourself."

"You mean—?" Darrin's pulse lurched.

"I hope I don't need to draw you a picture."

"So what's in this for you?"

"As someone who shares your Culhane blood, I think I'm entitled to a piece of the pie. Say, a partnership?"

Darrin had begun to perspire. Sweat oozed between his shoulder blades and trickled down his back. "What if I'm not interested?" he asked.

"Oh, but I think you will be. Especially when I tell you that I've looked into your business affairs and know enough about your tax evasion and investment scams to put you behind bars. We can talk more when we meet. But we'll have to be careful. For now, we mustn't be seen together."

"Do you have someplace in mind?" Darrin could scarcely believe he was getting pulled into this scheme. The man was probably a con artist. But he needed to know more.

"Yes, a place and a time. If we go now, we'll have the place to ourselves."

"Now? But it's after two in the morning!"

"So much the better." The mysterious caller gave Darrin directions, which sounded simple enough. "Call me at this number when you get there. I'll be close by. What about your wife?"

"She's not part of this."

"You've got the directions?"

"I've got them." Darrin repeated the ones he'd been given. "One question. Why all the secrecy?"

"You'll understand when you meet me. All right?"

"Fine. I should be there in about twenty minutes." Darrin ended the call, turned off the tap, and flushed the toilet for good measure.

Simone had gotten out of bed to pee, only to find the bathroom door locked. From the other side, she could hear running water and her husband's voice, evidently talking on his phone. At first, the one-sided conversation made no sense. But as she pressed closer to the door, she could hear enough to discern what was being said. Darrin was arranging to meet someone in the barn of the South Point complex, outside the stall where the Culhane horses were kept.

Was it a woman? She wouldn't put it past Darrin to cheat, but his tone suggested he was speaking to a man. So why the closed door and the running faucet—unless he was keeping something from her?

Simone would make it her business to find out.

The water had stopped running, and now she heard the toilet flush. She raced back to the bed, burrowed under the covers, and pretended to be asleep while Darrin dressed and left the room.

As soon as he was safely gone, Simone sprang out of bed, threw on her sweats and shoes, grabbed her purse, and followed him.

Several taxis were lined up outside the main entrance to the Excalibur. Darrin took one to South Point. By the time he arrived, the sweat was dripping down his body. His pulse was a loud drumming in his ears. What if he was making a dangerous mistake?

Though he hadn't been here before, the barn was easy to find, and he knew the stall number. The security guard recognized the Culhane name and let him in the gate. The earthy smell of horses assaulted his senses as he walked past the rows, looking for the right number in the dim glow of the security lights. Darrin hated horses and wanted nothing to do with them. The hours his father had forced him to spend in the saddle were among the worst memories of his life. Had his mysterious so-called brother known that when he chose the barn for a meeting place?

After a couple of wrong turns, Darrin found the correct row and headed down it, following the stall numbers in the dim glow of the security lights.

The three stalls leased to the Culhanes were just ahead. Darrin had half-expected to see someone waiting for him. But he appeared to be alone. A nervous shiver ran like an icy finger down his spine. Was this a trap? Was he about to be beaten and robbed?

His cell phone was in his pocket. Standing in front of the stalls, he pulled it out. He was about to enter the number he'd been given when a short, lumpy figure stepped out of the shadows.

"What's going on here, Darrin?" Simone demanded. "Why are you sneaking around, keeping secrets from me?"

Darrin bit back a curse. Why hadn't he checked to make sure he wasn't being followed? Now Simone could ruin everything. All he could do now was hope to get her on his side.

"I want the truth," she said, placing her hands on her hips. "Now."

With no time to think of a good lie, Darrin spilled a condensed version of his story. Simone listened, shaking her head in disbelief.

"Some stranger calls, claiming to be your long-lost brother? That sounds like a scam to me, or worse. Why does he want to meet in a place like this? He could rob you and leave you with your throat slit!"

"I didn't ask you to come, Simone," Darrin said. "Now that you're here, just be quiet and stay back. Meeting this man and hearing his offer is my decision."

"Then you're an idiot!" Simone sputtered. "What are you doing with that phone?"

"Calling to let him know I'm here—and now I'll have to warn him that you're here, too." Darrin started to enter the number he'd been given."

"You're crazy! He'll come with his friends and kill us both! Give me that phone!"

"Get back! This is my business, not yours!" Darrin had mis-entered the number. He deleted it and started over.

"*You're* my business! I'm your wife!" She sprang at him. Darrin tried to hold the phone out of reach, but she was too fast for him. Before he could stop her, she had snatched the phone from his hand and tossed it over the gate, into the nearest stall.

Darrin stared at her, horrified.

"You'll thank me later," she said calmly. "Maybe by the time you find your phone, you will have come to your senses."

White-hot rage sizzled through Darrin's veins. "Damn you, woman, this mess is all your fault. You're the one who had to have that house. You've pushed me, bullied me, treated me like I was no better than a dog. I'm sick and tired of it!"

Driven by anger, he doubled his fist and swung hard, slamming her in the jaw. She doubled over and collapsed, whimpering like a kicked puppy.

Leaving her, Darrin strode to the stall gate, which was latched but surprisingly wasn't locked. Slipping through the gate, he clicked the latch shut behind him. Even with the night lights, the interior of the stall was in deep shadow, and his only flashlight was on his phone. To find it, he would have to grope his way over the layer of dirty straw that covered the floor of the stall.

Damn Simone to hell for putting him through this.

He could smell the horse and hear it breathing in the shadows. A shudder of revulsion passed through his body. He would need to make sure he didn't get too close to the beast or crawl through its droppings. But never mind that. All that really mattered was finding his phone and connecting with the man who claimed to be his brother.

He had dropped to his knees and was feeling for the phone when a dark shape rose from the corner of the stall. A shriek of animal fury rang out as the creature loomed over him—eyes flashing white rims, teeth bared, steel-shod hooves flailing like deadly clubs.

Outside the stall, Simone screamed. Her voice was the last thing Darrin heard.

Sam got the call toward morning. By the time he arrived at the stable, the police were there. Darrin Culhane's body had been bagged and taken away. His hysterical wife had been transported to the hospital, and the wild-eyed stallion had been lassoed and immobilized with ropes. Horses in the nearby stalls, including One in a Million, had been moved out of the way.

Sam had been called, almost as an afterthought, when one of the officers had remembered the FBI agent's connection to the Culhanes. After the initial shock, Sam's first thought had been for Jasmine. She'd never gotten along with Darrin, but they were brother and sister. He would call her as soon as he found out more. It would be up to her to contact her mother.

Roper was here. He stood back, watching while the officers and crime-scene crew did their work and gathered their gear.

Sam moved to his side. "What the hell happened here?" he asked.

"Nobody knows for sure. One of the security guards found Darrin dead in Fire Dance's stall. His phone was a few steps away, like he might have dropped it. Simone was huddled on the floor outside the stall—she was rocking back and forth, saying she'd killed him."

"Do the police think that's true?" Sam asked.

"It doesn't look that way. But we won't know what really happened until she's able to tell her story."

Sam made a mental note to arrange an interview with Simone in the hospital. This wasn't his case, but he was looking for connections. The fact that a father and son had both died in a stall with a stallion could be a coincidence. If so, it was an odd one.

Sam had spoken last night with Lila's daughter, Gemma, in the hospital. She'd claimed that Simone was following her, but she hadn't seen the assailant who'd drugged her with chloroform. It would have almost certainly been Darrin, but there was no proof.

And now this.

"What about the horses?" he asked.

"You've seen Fire Dance," Roper said. "It took four strong men to get him roped and tied so we could get Darrin's body out of the stall. The poor bastard doesn't understand what he's done. He was only trying to be safe."

"Is One in a Million all right?"

"I hope so. I moved him to a quiet stall. But what he heard in the night could have affected him—especially since he's already witnessed one death."

Roper's jaw tightened. Both men were aware that tomorrow night the week would end with the Run for a Million. And if no new evidence turned up, Sam would have a heartbreaking decision to make.

"Blast it, Sam," Roper said, "I know you've got a job to do, but I didn't kill Frank. You have to believe that."

"I want to believe it," Sam said. "But let's put that aside while I focus on what happened here. If something important shows up, I don't want to miss it."

Sam forced himself to concentrate on what he already knew. Maybe he'd been wrong, dismissing Darrin as Frank's killer. Darrin could've had any number of motives to kill his father. His only alibi had been his wife—and he could have tossed the murder weapon in the creek on his way back to town.

Now, with Darrin dead, it would be easy to hang the murder on him—especially if Simone were to admit that she'd slept soundly through the night. The case would be closed to everyone's satisfaction. At the very least, having a second suspect would help Roper's chances at trial.

"What the hell—?" Hayden had come around the end of the row. He looked hungover, probably from last night's celebration of his win. His bewildered gaze took in the trussed horse and the crew of police technicians who were still bagging their gear. Sam caught his attention and beckoned him over.

"What's going on?" Hayden demanded.

"There's been a death," Sam said. "A man—Darrin Culhane—was killed in the night when he wandered into your horse's stall. It appeared he was attacked by the horse. Did you know him?"

"I know he's—was—a Culhane, but we never met. And that horse isn't mine."

"I was given to understand you were the owner. That's what Roper McKenna told me."

"Roper doesn't know yet," Hayden said. "That horse isn't mine anymore. As of last night, he belongs to Miss Cheyenne McKenna."

Chapter Ten

Cheyenne had awakened before dawn. Too restless to go back to sleep, she had showered and shampooed her hair, dressed, and tidied the room for her mother's impending arrival. Now she stood at the window, watching the sky fade above the glittering streets below.

Stetson, her older brother, had texted her last night from somewhere in New Mexico. He and their mother would be getting into Las Vegas by midmorning. Stetson would be dropping Rachel off with Cheyenne, after which he'd be free to make his own plans. Cheyenne suspected he'd be spending time with a girl he'd met at a rodeo here. But she wouldn't ask. She respected her brother's right to privacy—especially since she had so little of her own. In this capital of sin, surrounded by lustful cowboys, Rachel McKenna would be watching her daughter's every move.

Cheyenne would need to make the most of the few hours that remained. Checking on Fire Dance would be at the top of her list. She would find Roper and get his suggestions on how to move the stallion out of South Point and into an open place like a paddock, where he could have room to run off his fear—a place where he might begin to heal.

Buck's advice would be useful, too. Even though he'd suggested putting Fire Dance down, she respected his judgment. But Buck would likely be leaving today. Earlier, she'd heard water running and the sound of movement in his room. Afraid of making a fool of herself, she'd resisted the urge to knock on his door. Now the room was quiet. He could already be down at the trailer dock loading Chief for the long drive back to Ten Sleep, Wyoming, wherever that was. Maybe she could catch up with him before he left.

Torn, she picked up her purse and swung toward the door, then hesitated as she heard a knock. That it might be Buck was too much to hope. But maybe it was Roper. She flew to open the door.

Hayden stood in the doorway, a manila envelope in his hand and a sheepish expression on his face. "You don't look happy to see me," he said. "May I come in?"

"Of course." Cheyenne stepped back. "At this hour, I take it this isn't a social visit. What's on your mind?"

Hayden closed the door behind him as he came inside. "First of all, I want to apologize," he said. "I was a jerk last night. Blame it on a few too many beers. I'm sorry."

"It's forgotten," Cheyenne said.

"Then how about a hug—between friends?" He opened his arms. Cheyenne allowed herself to be drawn close for a moment, but she could feel her nerves tingling. Something about him—perhaps the sound of his breathing or the scent of his body—triggered an unexplained chill.

She eased away from him. "Is there something else? Have you changed your mind about giving me Fire Dance?"

"No, the horse is yours. I've got the transfer papers right here. I called my lawyer in the night to get them drawn up and faxed." He thrust the manila envelope toward her. Cheyenne's hands shook as she accepted it. She'd owned other horses, but none that came with Fire Dance's challenges. She would do her best to save him. That was all she could promise.

"I suppose I should thank you," she said. "Or maybe you should thank me for taking him off your hands."

"No thanks necessary," Hayden said. "But now that he's yours, there's something you need to hear. If I'd known about it, I would never have offered you the horse."

His tone startled her. She glanced up at him, her instincts braced. "Tell me," she said.

He swallowed. "A man was found dead this morning—in Fire Dance's stall. The Clark County sheriff has taken charge. He'll probably order your horse put down."

"A man? Who was he?" The floor seemed to be buckling under her feet.

"His name was Darrin Culhane—a neighbor of yours, I take it."

"Frank Culhane's son?" The news—and the name—hit her like a shotgun blast. "What was he doing in the stall?"

"Evidently, he was looking for a phone his wife had thrown over the gate. Neither of them knew the horse was dangerous."

"Then it wasn't Fire Dance's fault! He was scared. He was just protecting himself."

"We don't know that, Cheyenne. All we know for sure is that the horse is a killer."

"I've got to get down there!" Still clutching the envelope with the ownership papers, she flung open the door, grabbed Hayden's arm, and pulled him out into the hall—where Buck, carrying a canvas duffel, was just coming out of his room.

Buck tried not to look dismayed when he saw Cheyenne come out of her room with Hayden. He'd hoped she might have better judgment, but there was no accounting for a woman's taste.

He knew better than to hope she might have chosen him. But the thought of her with Hayden, responding despite the secret she'd shared, sharpened the ache in his throat. Maybe she reminded him of the innocent sister he'd failed to guard. But no, Buck knew better. His feelings for Cheyenne were anything but brotherly.

He was about to give the pair a polite nod and head for the elevator when he noticed her desperate look and the glint of tears in her eyes. His protective instincts surged. *If the bastard had hurt her, so help him . . .*

"Are you all right, Cheyenne?" he asked.

"Not really. I could use your advice if you've got a minute to listen."

Buck lowered his duffel to the floor. As Cheyenne poured out her story, his anger seethed. Hayden had used her compassion to rid himself of any liability for damages and expense caused by the stallion.

Hayden Barr was everything Buck had judged him to be, maybe worse.

"Of all the dirty, underhanded—" He'd meant the words for Hayden, but he spoke them to thin air. Hayden was gone.

"Does your brother know about this?" he asked her.

"Probably. But he's getting ready for the Run for a Million tomorrow night. I don't want to distract him." Her sigh was almost a sob. "Buck, I don't want to kill that beautiful horse. Can you take a look at him and help me decide what to do?"

"You already know what I'd recommend," Buck said. "The horse is miserable—and he's dangerous."

"Please. We may already be too late." The heartbreak in her velvety eyes would have broken the will of any man.

Buck opened the door of his room, tossed the duffel inside, and closed the door again. "Come on," he said. "I'll look at him, but he's your horse. The final decision will have to be yours."

Dressed in a faded hospital gown, Simone huddled in the bed like a child awakened from a nightmare. Her blond curls clung to her tear-blotched face. A fist-sized bruise purpled the left side of her jaw. She was able to talk, but the story she'd told Sam was so strange that he was tempted to dismiss it.

"You say you killed your husband, Simone. Why do you say that?"

"Don't you understand? I threw his phone into the horse stall. I thought I was saving him from a foolish mistake—Darrin wasn't really smart, you know, even if he was a lawyer. He was going to call this man who claimed to be his brother. I could tell it was a scam—or worse. If Darrin had met with the man, he could've been blackmailed or even robbed and killed."

"And you heard their conversation in your hotel room?"

"Through the bathroom door—and only Darrin's side of the call. But that was enough." She choked back a sob. "If only I'd stopped him then, he'd still be alive. But no, I was curious. I had to follow him."

"And when did he tell you the man was claiming to be his brother? Did you hear that on the phone?"

"Yes, and I heard it again from Darrin in the barn. He mentioned wanting to see a DNA test."

"And did Darrin mention a name, an age, anything that might tell us more?"

Simone shook her head. "I've told you—and the police—everything I know. Now, please leave me alone. I've just become a widow, with a baby that will never know his father. I need a chance to grieve."

Sam might have asked her about the bruise on her face. But he'd seen other such bruises, and he knew where they came from. For now, he would spare her the humiliation.

His thoughts churned as he left the hospital and drove back to the hotel. If Simone's story could be believed, the FBI murder case had a new suspect—Frank Culhane's illegitimate son. But what were the odds that such a person even existed? The story could be a dead end—a staged prank or a scheme to extort something from Darrin.

Or the phone call to Darrin could have been the real thing, in which case, the caller had to be found. Since he'd requested a meeting, he was likely close by. With so many people here for the big event, searching the crowds would be a waste of time—and time was running out. If Frank's son existed, there had to be a way to lure him into the open.

Sam took the elevator back to his room and prepared to call Jasmine. She'd been hurt and angry when they'd last parted. He wanted to set things right. But that might have to happen later.

He placed the call. The phone rang once, twice, then a third time. She probably didn't want to talk to him. But if she didn't pick up, the next call would be from the sheriff.

He was composing a voicemail in his head when she answered. "If you're calling to apologize, Sam, you can save your breath. I'm not ready to listen to your excuses."

"This is something else, Jasmine. Something hard, but I wanted to be the one to tell you."

"This had better be good."

"I'm sorry, Jasmine. Darrin's dead. He was killed in the night—killed by a horse."

"Darrin always hated horses." She spoke in a flat voice, as if reading a line from a book.

He gave her the facts in a few short sentences. She listened without a word, but he could hear her breathing. "Are you all right?" he asked her.

"You know I never got along with Darrin," she said. "But he was my brother—the only one who understood about our crazy parents. It's like . . . like part of me is missing. Oh, Sam."

He could sense her crumbling. If he could, he would have taken her in his arms. "Your mother will need to know," he said. "I'll call her if you want me to. Or you can call her yourself."

"My mother has gone off the radar, Sam. You know she was involved with Louis Divino."

"I suspected it. I didn't know for sure. Maybe I didn't want to know. But Divino's dead. His body was found in Lake Travis."

"I know. I can't tell you the story now; but after Divino died, things got dangerous for her. She sent me away and disappeared. I'm hoping she was able to leave the country—or at least that she's alive."

"So you can't even reach her to tell her about Darrin."

"Mother wanted it that way. For our safety. She always liked you, Sam."

He could feel the emotion in her voice. "I liked her, too," Sam said, meaning it. He had liked Madeleine Culhane even while he was arresting her for murder, a charge that was later dropped.

"I've lost them all," Jasmine said. "My father, my mother, and now my brother. At least Lila will get to keep that blasted house. I've never wanted the place. Too many memories." She stifled a sob. "How is Simone, by the way?"

"She's had a bad shock. But her doctor says the baby's all right. I'm guessing once the funeral's over, she'll go home to her family." Sam took a breath and changed the subject. "Jasmine, I'm sorry, but I need to ask you some questions."

"Go ahead, Mr. FBI man. I expected this." Sam couldn't have missed the edge in her voice.

"This is about Frank," he said. "Do you know of any children he might have fathered besides you and Darrin?"

"He never mentioned any. Neither did Mother. But Dad did get around, bless his heart. I like to think he was smart enough to use protection. But you know, things happen. He might not even have known. Why are you asking?"

"Simone said that Darrin got a call from a man claiming to be his half brother. Darrin was waiting to meet him when Simone threw his phone in the stall."

"And you think that man may have killed my father?"

"Anything's possible. I'm grasping at straws here."

"Maybe it was a scam. That would be my guess. I'm sorry, Sam, there's nothing I can tell you."

He sensed that she was about to end the call. Suddenly he didn't want to let her go. "Where are you?" he asked. "California?"

"I'm right here in Las Vegas. I couldn't get a flight out until Sunday." In the silent pause that passed between them, she seemed to read Sam's thoughts.

"Don't come to me now, Sam. I don't want you with me if your mind is somewhere else. Get this case behind you. Then you can decide how much of yourself you can spare for me. If it isn't enough, I'll feel free to move on."

Her words tore through him like bullets. But he knew she was right—this wise, strong, compassionate woman. Whatever happened, he couldn't allow himself to lose her.

"I love you, Jasmine," he said. "I'm not going anywhere. Whatever happens, I'll be here for you. Just give me a chance to prove it."

He waited for a reply, but Jasmine had ended the call. Sam knew better than to call her back. That would only push her to say things he didn't want to hear. And he had a murder to solve.

With the reining Shootout scheduled to run all day, the barn was a busy place. As the riders prepared their mounts for a chance at next year's Run for a Million, emotions were running high. Even the horses caught the tension, dancing nervously as they were saddled and led out of the barn. Cheers and groans from the fans rose from the arena.

Buck willed himself to ignore the hubbub as he studied the immobilized stallion over the stall gate. He'd seen Fire Dance before, but he hadn't taken the time to study him closely. The horse was magnificent—that was a given. And he appeared to have no visible injuries. But what Buck saw in the wild eyes and straining limbs was misery and terror.

This horse had killed a man. That was beyond dispute. The question Buck asked himself now was why. As a trainer with a reputation for healing troubled horses—he'd been called a horse whisperer, though he disliked the term—he knew that horses in their natural state were prey for animals like wolves, bears, and cougars. Fire Dance had probably never seen anything bigger than a coyote. But the fight-or-flight instincts, buried over generations, would still be there. When Cheyenne had climbed on a bucket to look over the gate, the distressed horse had seen her as a predator ready to leap from above. And a man on all fours, groping through the sawdust for his phone, would take on the shape of a wolf or bear, about to lunge at the horse's throat. Fire Dance had fought for his life with the strength of imagined terror.

Now, with his legs hobbled, his head cross-tied, and a canvas sling holding his body in place, Fire Dance was helpless.

"What do you think?" Cheyenne waited next to him.

"I think he's terrified—which makes him dangerous.

Get way back and don't move. I'm going to try something."

After Cheyenne had moved to a safe distance, Buck opened the gate of the stall and stepped inside. The stallion's ears flattened. An exhausted snort rose from his throat, but the rigged restraints held him prisoner. His mane and tail were tangled, and he smelled of urine, manure, and sweat. A bucket of water stood within reach, but it was almost full. If he didn't get out of this situation soon, the horse would die a miserable death. Euthanasia would be kinder.

That's what he would tell Cheyenne.

Speaking softly, he took plenty of time to approach the stallion, trying to reassure him that he wasn't a predator. The horse's ears pricked, a sign he was listening. That was good. But it was his eyes, the most evident place to spot a sign of a brain injury, that Buck wanted to check. Still talking, he reached out and stroked the stallion's sweat-encrusted neck. A shudder passed through the powerful body, but he was too spent to struggle. "Good boy," Buck murmured. "Now, let's have a look."

He moved in closer, aware that the stallion could still hurt him. Murmuring and stroking with his free hand, he aimed his phone light into each of the horse's large eyes. The pupils reacted, contracting to black dots. Good. No obvious sign of brain damage. Or maybe not so good in terms of the work it would take to rehabilitate this animal. Euthanasia would have been a simpler solution, but he knew that Cheyenne would never choose that. She would want to save Fire Dance—and she lacked the experience to do it alone.

Moving slowly, he backed out of the stall and latched the gate behind him. When he turned, Cheyenne was watching him, her face shining with hope.

Heaven help him, what was he getting himself into?

"I didn't see any obvious injuries," he said, speaking before she could ask. "But he's a sensitive horse, and he's in bad shape. If you can't get him out of here soon, you might as well put an end to his misery."

"I'll do anything—pay anything!" She clasped his forearm with a horsewoman's grip. "I've got cash from my rodeo winnings and a check from the fashion shoot I just did for *Vogue*. I was saving the money for a cutting horse, but—"

"This isn't about money, Cheyenne, and if you take him, you won't be getting a cutting horse. I can't even promise that you'll be able to ride him."

"But you'll try to help him?"

Buck sighed, knowing he was roped in. "Here's what I'm thinking," he said. "I can't trailer him with Chief, and sedating him for that distance could kill him—especially if he has brain damage. But I've got a friend in Henderson—that's the next town over—who does stock hauling with the kind of rig you'll need to keep him stable. He owes me some favors. If he's available, I can have him pick up Fire Dance today and drive him to my ranch in Ten Sleep. My cowboys can turn the horse loose in the corral with food and water and leave him till I get there."

"You'd do that? You'd take him home and work with him for me?" She gazed at him as if he'd hung the moon.

"Not so fast. If my friend can't drive him, we'll have to make other arrangements. That could take time—time we don't have. Also, if I take him on, you'll have to agree to one thing."

"I'll pay whatever you need."

"We can work that out later," Buck said. "But here's what you've got to understand up front. If your horse is suffering, or if he turns out to be an ongoing danger to people or other animals, I'll make the decision to put him down. It will be my decision, and I'll see it done. Is that clear?"

"Is that your policy with all your clients, Buck?"

"Not all. But some. I don't want to give you false hope. Fire Dance is going to be a challenge. Do you trust me to make the right choice?"

She hesitated, her eyes brimming with tears. "I trust you," she said. "And don't worry about me. I know how to be a big girl."

The urge to take her in his arms and kiss away her tears swept through Buck like a fever. He knew better than to try, especially with people and horses moving around them. But the temptation was there.

He was saved from making a fool of himself by the sound of Cheyenne's phone. She answered, cupping her ear to hear over the background noise. After a few words, she ended the call and turned to Buck. "That was my brother, Stetson. He'll be out front with our mother in about twenty minutes. I'll need to meet them there and take her up to our room. Can you wait?"

"No need," Buck said. "I'll call my friend and hopefully arrange to have him pick up Fire Dance. You'll want to leave the paperwork with me—that needs to go with the horse. Go and meet your mother. I've got your phone number. I'll keep you posted by text. All right?"

"Yes. Thank you, Buck. I can't believe you're doing this for me."

"Don't thank me yet. We'll see how things go. Now get moving, and don't worry. I've got this."

She strode off in the direction of the hotel lobby. For an instant, she paused, glancing back as if to see if he was watching her. Then she moved on.

Buck stood looking in the direction she'd gone, cursing himself for the way she made him feel. He knew it would be useless to want her. He was a good eight or nine years her senior, with more mistakes behind him than he cared to remember—not the sort of man she'd choose for anything more than a friend. And then there was the sight of her stepping out of her room this morning with Hayden in tow. Seeing them together like that, and guessing what must've happened, had gnawed at his gut.

So why was he knocking himself out to save a damaged horse that ought to be put down for its own good?

It was because he cared for the horse and the woman. He cared too damn much.

And it scared him.

With the Shootout going on in the arena, the hotel lobby was crowded and noisy. Cheyenne picked up a local paper at a newsstand and sat down in a quiet corner to read and wait.

There wasn't much in the way of news—mostly just event scores and interviews. Anything about Darrin Culhane's death would have to be covered in a future issue. But on page 2, an article caught her interest.

> *TEXAS HORSE BREEDER DIES IN CRASH*
> *Chester (Chet) Barr, a well-known breeder of champion horses, died Tuesday morning after the crash of his small plane near Gallup, New Mexico. Also killed in the crash was his fiancée, Eva Marconi, who perished along with their unborn child. Mr. Barr was piloting his own plane en route to Las Vegas, where his son, Hayden, was scheduled to compete for the Cutting Horse championship in the Run for a Million. Funeral arrangements are pending.*

The accompanying photo, a business-style portrait, showed a balding, middle-aged Chet Barr in a western shirt and a bolo tie. Pale-eyed, with a double chin and an affable smile, he bore no resemblance to Hayden.

There was no photo of Eva Marconi. Hayden had claimed not to know her—his father's pregnant fiancée. There had to be a story behind that—sadly, never to be finished. It would be up to Hayden to write his own version of the story.

Where was Stetson? He should have been there, with their mother, by now. Laying the newspaper on a coffee table, she checked her phone again. There was a voicemail from Stetson. A semi accident on the freeway had brought traffic to a standstill. He would let her know when they were moving again.

Cheyenne slid the phone back into her purse. At least, with extra time to wait, she could go back to the barn and check on Buck's progress with Fire Dance. Roper might be there, too.

The walkway to the arena was jammed with people. But off to Cheyenne's right was a hallway that led past offices, a mailroom, and a workout area. If she followed it to the end, it should take her back to the barn.

She had gone partway down the hall, which was long and straight, with doors on one side and a row of framed photos on the other, when she heard a familiar voice calling from behind. "Cheyenne! Wait!"

She paused long enough for Hayden to catch up with her. He was slightly out of breath, but grinning as if nothing had taken place between them earlier. Cheyenne resolved to be friendly but cautious.

"I assumed you'd be gone by now," she said. "You've won your prize, and now you've got a funeral to plan."

"I'm handling the funeral arrangements via long distance. Between the funeral home and the caterer, the planning's pretty much done. Dad will be laid to rest in the family plot, next to my mother."

"What about Eva—his fiancée—and her baby?"

He looked surprised. "How did you know about her?"

"She's mentioned in the news article I read. Where will she be buried?"

Hayden shrugged. "That's up to her parents, I guess. She's got nothing to do with our family."

Cheyenne began to walk again. The short hairs on the back of her neck prickled as Hayden fell into step beside her. Something about him wasn't right. But maybe he was simply in denial about his father's death.

"I'm surprised that you're still here," she said. "What about your horse? Don't you need to get him home?"

"Steely Dan's already on his way. I paid a friend to take him in his trailer. By now he's probably halfway back to Texas."

"And what about you? Why are you still here?"

"Why not? As long as I'm in Vegas, I figured I might as well put the funeral off and stay for the big event. Maybe I'll do some business for the ranch—*my* ranch now. I'm still getting used to that."

"For heaven's sake, Hayden!" Cheyenne's frustration boiled over. "Your father just died—suddenly and tragically. Why aren't you on your way home? Why aren't you grieving?"

He gave her a contemptuous look. "Why should I be? Chet Barr wasn't my father. I've got the DNA test results to prove it."

She stared at him. "I don't understand."

"Then maybe you're not as smart as you think you are. Figure it out."

"I saw his photo," she said. "I noticed that he didn't look like you. Were you adopted?"

"No need. Chet was already married to my mother when I was born. You should have seen her. She was beautiful. Big, dark eyes. She looked a little like you."

"So, who was your father? Did he know about you?"

"Oh, he knew. But because my mother was married and so was he, they agreed to keep it quiet. My mother told me the truth before she died, but as far as I know, my father took his secret to his grave."

"And Chet?"

"He raised me to be a good cowboy. But I wasn't the blood son he wanted. I always wondered why he never showed me much affection. Then I found out. So forgive me if I'm not prostrate with grief. Like I said, Chet Barr wasn't my father."

"So who was your father? Was he someone you knew?"

"Only from a distance. That's his picture, on the wall, right behind you."

Cheyenne turned around. Her chest contracted, shutting off her breath.

The handsome, silver-haired man in the framed photo was Frank Culhane.

Chapter Eleven

Cheyenne was staring at the framed photo, struggling for words, when her phone rang. She yanked it out of her purse.

The call was from Stetson. The traffic backup had cleared. He and their mother would be arriving in the next ten or fifteen minutes.

"I've got to go, Hayden," she said. "You shouldn't be here. Go home to Texas, and do what needs to be done."

"Can I call you?" he asked, ignoring her words.

"Only if you have a good reason. I'll keep you posted about Fire Dance, if you care to know."

His indifferent look told her that he'd moved on from any concern about the stallion. Slipping the phone back into her purse, she turned around and raced back to the hotel lobby. Her mind was still processing what she'd just learned. If Hayden's claim was true—and his resemblance to Frank bore that out—Frank's affairs had fathered at least one child. If she believed him, the question was what she should do with that information.

Hayden had shown her one symptom of a toxic personality—a lack of concern for anything but himself. Common sense told her to walk away and forget him. But what if Hayden had played some part in Frank's death? He could have confronted his biological father that night in the stable. When Frank rejected him, he could have had the hypodermic ready and used it. The story was far-fetched. But Cheyenne's beloved brother was about to be arrested for Frank's murder. The smallest scrap of information might be the one that would clear him.

Decision made, she stopped at the entrance to the lobby, fished her phone out of her purse, and scrolled to Agent Sam Rafferty's number.

Sam took the phone call in his room, where he'd been working on a report for Nick. Not that he had much to report. The discoveries he'd made were like pieces from random jigsaw puzzles tossed into the same box. No two of them fit together. And time was running out.

By the time the call with Cheyenne had ended, Sam was pacing the floor with excitement. What if Hayden Barr turned out to be the key to the whole mystery—not only as Frank's son, but as his murderer?

Hayden could have done it—shadowed Frank from a distance, arranged a secret meeting in the stable, and confronted his father with the demand that he be recognized and given his share of the Culhane dynasty. Rejected, he could have killed Frank and tossed the syringe away as he was passing the creek. Later, here in Las Vegas, he could have tried the same approach with Darrin. But he hadn't counted on Simone or a maddened horse.

The pieces were sliding into place, but not all of them fit. Hayden was the sole heir of a wealthy rancher. He didn't need money. Why would he seek out his natural father and then kill him?

Cheyenne had mentioned a newspaper article. Sam had

picked up a paper earlier, after breakfast. The paper lay folded on the bed. Opening it, he read the news item about Chet Barr's fatal crash.

The pregnant fiancée. That could be another piece of the puzzle. Did Hayden feel that he was about to be replaced by a child of Chet's own blood? Did he feel threatened enough to kill?

The puzzle was coming together, but every piece of it was conjecture. Before he took any action, he would need something solid. At least, before questioning Hayden, he should try to find out more about where he might have been on the night of the murder. If he had an ironclad alibi, everything else would be out the window.

The Barr ranch was near Wichita Falls, a couple of hours from the Culhane spread. A call to the sheriff there might be a good place to start.

Roper had promised not to see Lila until after the Run for a Million. He'd broken that promise once to sit with her at the hospital when her daughter was drugged with chloroform. Now he was about to break it again.

He knocked on the door of her hotel room, giving his name before Gemma would open it. The young woman was nothing if not protective. At least, by now, she was getting to know him.

"How's your mother, Gemma?" he asked. "Is she awake?"

"I'm in here," Lila called from the bedroom. "Just resting. With my good nurse to do everything for me, I've become a lazybones. Hang on, I'll get up."

"No, stay where you are. I'll come in," Roper said. "I'm just here to give you some news. Then I'll be on my way."

He walked into the bedroom. Lila, dressed in blue sweats, reclined on one of the two queen-sized beds. She was propped against a heap of pillows with her e-reader in her hand. Fresh from her shower, with no makeup and her hair twisted up in a scrunchie, she looked like a young girl. Roper's pulse skipped at the sight of her. But he wasn't sure how she would react to what he was about to tell her.

"I'll give you some privacy." Gemma backed away from the doorway.

"No, come on in, Gemma," Roper said. "This news concerns you, too?"

As they waited for Gemma, he saw the slight change in Lila—the narrowing of her eyes, the tightening of her lips—as if she were preparing herself for a blow. Gemma sank onto the foot of the bed. Roper remained on his feet.

"Darrin Culhane died last night," he said. "He was killed by a horse when he went into its stall."

Lila stifled a gasp, her face paling as the news sank in. "What about Simone? What about the baby? Are they all right?"

"Simone was there. Once she gets over the shock, she and the baby should be fine. The important thing is, with Darrin gone, the danger to both of you should be over."

Lila shook her head. "Darrin was my stepson. The baby will be my grandchild—in a way. I know how they hated me and what they tried to do, but I wouldn't wish this tragedy on anyone."

Roper held out his hand. She reached up and clasped it. Her fingers were cold. "You know that without Darrin, the legal battle for the ranch goes away," he said.

"Simone could still contest the will for her baby. Jasmine, too, although I know she's never wanted the property."

"Don't worry about it," Roper said. "For now, you've got the upper hand. When you get home, you can take legal steps to protect your ownership."

Roper knew better than to mention Darrin's mysterious

caller. Lila didn't need that kind of stress. Hopefully, with Darrin gone, the man would give up on his scheme and disappear.

"I'll be going," he said. "Get some rest, both of you."

"Don't worry," Lila said. "We'll be front and center to watch you show One in a Million tomorrow night."

He gave her a light kiss and headed for the elevator. It was time to focus entirely on getting the big bay roan ready for the performance of his life. But on the way down to the lobby, he couldn't stop wondering about the caller who'd claimed to be Frank's illegitimate son.

What if his claim was true?

What if he'd meant to kill Darrin and take over the fight for Lila's ranch?

What if he was the one who'd murdered Frank?

Who was he?

Cheyenne checked her phone again as she waited in the lobby. There was a text message from Buck. His friend had agreed to load Fire Dance and take him to Ten Sleep.

The sheriff came by with a deputy, ready to put Fire Dance down. It took some fast talking to convince him that the horse would be gone within the hour. I hear Fergus's truck outside now. I'll keep you posted if I don't see you later.

Cheyenne tapped out a quick reply.

Thank you, thank you, thank you. Let me know how much I will owe your friend, and I will double it. As for you, I will owe you forever. I love you for this, Buck.

She reread the message. No, the love part was too much. That might make him uncomfortable. She deleted the final sentence before sending the reply. It was done. She'd saved herself from looking like a fool. But a stab at her heart told her that if ever there was a man she could love, it was Buck Tolson.

As she tucked the phone into her purse, she could see her brother coming through the revolving door into the crowded lobby. Stetson was tall for a bull rider and beanpole skinny, but everywhere he went, his lanky charm was a magnet for girls.

Rachel, their mother, walked a half step ahead of him, ramrod straight in a white blouse and gray slacks, with the light blue blazer she wore to church. Her head, crowned with graying hair pulled into a neat bun, came even with her tall son's ear.

She wore no makeup and no jewelry except for a practical Timex watch and her thin gold wedding band. But even in her mid-fifties, she was striking, with classic features she'd passed on to her four handsome sons and a daughter who'd turned down movie offers. Her work-worn hands testified to decades of hard toil, scrubbing, gardening, childbearing, tending cows, chickens, and children, making nutritious meals out of whatever was at hand, and nursing a bitter, disabled husband night and day.

Rachel was the embodiment of a favorite piece of Scripture—*Who can find a virtuous woman, for her price is above rubies.*

As their gazes met across the crowded lobby, Cheyenne stifled a groan. Her mother possessed the attitude of a saint walking through the gates of hell, ready to overturn the gaming tables and drive out the money changers.

"Hang in there, Little Sis. It's only for a couple of days."

Roper stood behind her. Cheyenne's heart warmed as she turned to meet his understanding smile. What would she do without him? Her other brothers were self-absorbed louts. Her father ignored her, and her mother controlled her with an iron hand. Only Roper gave her unconditional love and support.

It was too bad they didn't have time to talk. She wanted

to tell him what she'd learned about Hayden. But at least she'd told Sam.

Rachel and Stetson made their way across the lobby toward them. Stetson shoved the small suitcase he was carrying into Roper's hands. "Mom's all yours," he said. "I'll see you tomorrow night at the big show. Good luck, man." He rushed off as if he couldn't wait to make his escape.

"I need to go, too," Roper said. "I just wanted to be here when you arrived, Mother." He brushed a kiss on her cheek. "I'll see you later. Maybe tonight we can go out for a nice dinner."

"You can join us in our room, if you like. I don't plan to eat out. It's too expensive—what with all the noise and the people." Rachel sniffed the air, an expression of distaste on her face. "It smells like cigarettes in here," she said. "And how does anybody stand that hellish noise from the casino? Get me up to the room, Cheyenne. We drove all night to get here. What I need now is a nice, long nap."

Cheyenne took the suitcase from Roper and escorted her mother to the elevators. Since most people were coming down at this hour, they had a car going up to themselves. No sooner had the doors closed than Rachel impaled Cheyenne with her laser-like gaze.

"Have you been all right here? Has Roper been looking out for you?"

"I've been fine," Cheyenne said. "And Roper's been keeping a sharp eye on me. His room is right across the hall. You'll see when we get there."

"What about that young man? The one who owns the red horse? Is he behaving like a gentleman—and are you making sure he does?"

"Hayden? We're just friends—barely that. Please, Mother, I'm not fifteen anymore. Can't you please stop hovering over me?"

"If I'd done more hovering when you were eighteen, you wouldn't have been allowed to go to that big horse show in Scottsdale with that . . . that devil. You told me he could be trusted."

Cheyenne shook her head. "Please, let's not do this. It was in the past. I've moved on. I should never have told you what happened."

"You shouldn't have kept it from me for so long. Almost two years, and then you tell me."

Cheyenne would never forget the fight they'd had earlier that summer. It had started in the kitchen, after supper, when Rachel had been giving her yet another sermon on the importance of remaining a virgin until her wedding night. "Your purity is the most precious gift you can give your husband—anything less is second-rate, like settling for a used car instead of a new one. A worthy man, one who respects you, will want the best. And when he sees you walk down the aisle in that perfect white dress, he'll know that you've kept yourself just for—"

Cheyenne's self-control had exploded. "Stop it, Mother! You're too late! I'm not a virgin! I'll never be a virgin again!"

While Rachel had gazed at her in shocked disbelief, Cheyenne had poured out the whole story in brutal detail, sparing her nothing. By the end of it, Rachel's pale face had been streaked with tears.

"You poor, poor girl," she'd said. "This was my fault. I should never have let you go with him."

"You couldn't have stopped me. I wanted to learn about reining, and he'd offered to teach me. Then I found out what he really wanted."

Cheyenne had left with her brothers on the rodeo circuit the next day. When she came home days later, Rachel had treated her as always, except that the words *virgin* and *pure* had disappeared from her lectures.

The elevator had stopped on the fourteenth floor. Cheyenne ushered her mother out through the doors and down the long hallway. As they passed the door to Buck's room, she couldn't help wondering if he was still in town. She wanted to see him one more time, to thank him and wish him good luck with Fire Dance. At least with her horse on his ranch, they'd have a reason to keep in touch.

She unlocked the door, carried Rachel's suitcase inside, and set it on the luggage rack. Housekeeping had cleaned the room in her absence. Everything was in order. Rachel made a beeline for the bathroom. While she was inside, Cheyenne took a moment to check her phone. In the short time since she'd last checked, there were three new texts. The first one was from Hayden.

Hey, I didn't mean to scare you off. I hope we can get together again while you're still here. What are you doing tonight?

Dismissing the message until later, she scrolled to the next one. It was from Sam Rafferty.

Cheyenne, I need your mother to refresh my memory of what she recalls from the night of the crime. Please let me know when she's available, the sooner the better.

Cheyenne hesitated, suddenly uneasy. Was Sam already putting a case together? Would her mother's testimony help Roper or hurt him?

Mother is here but she's tired, she texted back. **I'll ask her and let you know.**

She left Buck's message for last, hoping it was good news. She needed that today, and she needed to hear from him.

Fergus just left with Fire Dance in his trailer. The stallion was so tired he didn't put up much of a fight. We even got some water down him. I'll be staying here tonight, maybe leave with Chief tomorrow. Enjoy your family. Good luck to Roper.

Thank you, Buck. I love you.

She deleted the last sentence and sent the message as her mother walked out of the bathroom, wiping her hands.

"How much is this room costing you?" Rachel demanded. "There have to be cheaper places around."

Cheyenne sighed, reminding herself that her mother's frugality had gotten the family through some rough times. "There are cheaper places. But trust me, you don't want to stay there."

"Hmmph. I can imagine." She sat down on the bed.

"I got a text from Sam Rafferty, the FBI man," Cheyenne said. "He needs to come up and talk to you again about the night Frank died."

"I've told him all I know. Do I really need to do it again?" she asked. "Can't I just say no?"

"This man is FBI, Mother. If he wants to talk to you, he can."

"I was going to read my Bible and take a nap. But all right. I might as well get it over with. Tell him to come up. But I want you in the room while he's questioning me. I don't want him twisting my words around."

Cheyenne sent the text. Sam replied immediately. He was on his way. A few minutes later, Cheyenne answered his knock on the door of their room.

All morning, as he weighed Darrin's death against Hayden's secret revelation, Sam had sensed that he was missing something—something simple and true that was right in front of him.

Desperate for answers, he decided to go back to back to the early interview that stood between Roper and his arrest for murder—his mother's sworn testimony that, on the night in question, he'd been at home and never left.

Now, Rachel McKenna sat facing him in a high-backed, overstuffed chair, while Cheyenne hovered behind her.

"Thank you for seeing me, Mrs. McKenna," he said. "I'll try not to take too much of your time."

"I can't see as I had much choice about seeing you, Agent," Rachel said. "Now, let's get this over with."

"Fine." Sam cleared his throat and switched on his miniature recorder. After the introduction, he began. "Mrs. McKenna, will you tell us, in your own words, what happened on the night in question?"

"Like I said, it was after midnight. My husband, my son, Roper, and I were home. My other four children were away at a rodeo." Rachel paused, thinking. "We were all in bed. I'd seen my son go to bed. He slept in the next room, so I knew he was there. I'm a light sleeper, and I never heard him leave the ranch, never even heard his truck."

"What about your husband?"

"Kirby was snoring. The man could sleep through a train wreck. He wouldn't remember anything about this."

"Can you tell us what happened next? What time was it?"

"I didn't look at the clock. Maybe about two. I heard our dog barking outside. Big old mutt, just a ranch dog. He sleeps on the porch. Anyway, there's this skunk that tries to eat his food. I figured he must be barking at it, so I thought I'd get up and run the critter off before it sprayed.

"I was about to get out of bed when I heard Roper moving in the next room, like he was putting on his boots to go outside and take care of the skunk himself. The screen door slammed shut, and the dog quit barking. I decided to wait for Roper in the kitchen to make sure everything was all right. So I got up, put on my bathrobe, and sat down at the table.

"A few minutes later, I heard him come back inside through the kitchen door. I asked him what happened. He said the skunk ran off and he had to put the dog in the barn to keep him from going after it. After that, we both went back to bed. I lay awake for the rest of the night. If Roper had left after that, I'd have heard him." She frowned at Sam. "See? The same as I told you before. And it's God's truth. My son is innocent, Mr. Rafferty. Now, are we finished?"

"Just a couple more questions," Sam said, remembering something Roper mentioned. "When Roper came back into the kitchen, do you remember what was he wearing?"

"He sleeps in his skivvies, but he had to pull on his boots to rush outside and grab the dog. He was wearing skivvies with boots to protect his feet. The kitchen was dark, but not that dark. I could see well enough to tell. That's another reason why I know he hadn't gone anywhere else. He wasn't dressed."

"And what were you wearing?"

"I told you, my bathrobe." Rachel sounded annoyed and impatient to be done. "It's the old-fashioned kind, blue chenille and long, with ties around the waist. I got it from my children last Christmas. And for the record, my son's briefs were white Fruit of the Loom. Any more questions?"

"I believe that's all." Sam switched off the recorder and stood. "Thank you, Mrs. McKenna. I won't trouble you any more today. Enjoy the Run for a Million tomorrow night."

Sam rode the elevator back to the lobby. Rachel's story matched Roper's version to the letter. If it was true, and it was at least plausible, then Roper had to be innocent. But what about motive? What about the murder weapon, found in the creek by two young boys with traces of fentanyl but no prints or DNA? Without solid evidence, one way or another, how could he clear a man based on two matching stories that could easily have been rehearsed?

There was no simple answer to that question. Either he could arrest Roper and leave the final outcome to the jury. Or, if Roper was truly innocent, he could find the real killer.

Lost in thought, he passed through the hotel lobby and wandered back to the practice arena, where some of the reining contestants were drilling for tomorrow's big event. Watchers were scattered among the seats. Slipping onto a bench seat along the side, he let his mind work while his eyes watched some of the most magnificent horses and riders in the world.

Roper was at the far end of the arena with One in a Million. Sam made no effort to catch his eye. He'd resolved to leave him alone until the competition was over. Roper deserved that much respect, at least. And the man was innocent until proven guilty.

The stallion was in top form, head alert, muscles rippling beneath his silvery bay roan coat. His moves were flawless, beautifully done. One in a Million had earned the right to be here—but at such a tragic price.

Earlier, Sam had watched Buck Tolson and his friend maneuver Fire Dance into a trailer that was fitted with a supporting rack for medical transport. The fiery young stallion had looked utterly beaten. But at least he was alive and not lying cold on a concrete slab.

One in a Million had experienced a tragedy of his own. As the single eyewitness to Frank's murder, the big roan's memory held the answer to Sam's most vital question. What a shame the horse couldn't communicate.

For a few minutes, he watched Roper take the stallion through his paces. The connection between horse and rider was smooth and subtle, almost poetic. He could imagine the pair winning the million-dollar prize.

And then what?

At first, Sam hadn't paid much attention to the lanky cowboy seated at the far end of the row, his black hat shading his face. Only when the man turned at an unexpected sound did Sam realize he'd hit the jackpot. He was looking at Hayden Barr.

Putting his phone on silent, Sam moved down the row to sit beside him, showed his ID, and introduced himself. Hayden stirred as if to get up, then appeared to think the better of it. "I know who you are," he said. "And I know you're investigating Frank Culhane's murder. But I didn't have anything to do with it. I didn't even know him. And I sure as hell didn't kill him."

"But you knew he was your father," Sam said.

In the silence that followed, cheers could be heard from the Shootout in the main arena. "You've been talking to Cheyenne, haven't you?" Hayden said at last. "Never trust a woman."

"Who else knew?" Sam asked.

"My father, and my mother, of course—both of them gone now—Cheyenne, and now you. That's about the size of it."

"And did Frank Culhane know about you?"

"My mother said she told him, but he was married and so was she, so he never came around. What's this all about? I told you I didn't kill the man. I never met him."

"Can you tell me where you were on the night Frank was murdered?"

"Hell, I don't even remember what night it was or what I was doing. But I know that I was nowhere near Frank's place."

"Have you ever telephoned Darrin Culhane?"

"That's Frank's son, isn't it? I don't even know him. But I know how he died. A story like that gets around fast."

"Somebody called him late last night, claiming to be

his brother and wanting to meet by the horse stalls. Was that you?"

"No way. If I'd wanted to meet him, I'd have invited him to lunch in broad daylight. Check my phone. I never called him."

"Records indicate that the calls to his number came from a burner," Sam said.

"Well, it wasn't me. None of this has anything to do with Frank's death. Don't I have rights or something?" Hayden was getting defensive. Time to back off.

"Just a couple more questions," Sam said. "Have you had any contact with Simone Culhane, Darrin's wife, or with Jasmine Culhane, his sister?"

When Hayden hesitated, Sam felt his heart drop. Could there be some connection between Jasmine and this attractive but highly suspect young man? Could they have been scheming together to take Darrin out of the picture? But what was he thinking? He loved Jasmine. He trusted her. But then again, she was her mother's daughter.

"Oh, yeah, Jasmine Culhane. It took me a minute to place her," Hayden said. "A few years ago, she was with a movie company that came to shoot a TV western on our ranch. Hottest woman on the set. I had a crush on her, but I was just a horny teenage kid. Even with her name, how was I to know she was my half sister?"

Sam began to breathe again. "One final question for the record. Did you kill Frank Culhane?"

"Hell no. I'd always wanted to connect with Frank. Darrin was nothing but a little wuss—a *lawyer*, for Pete's sake. I was the son Frank would have wanted—a champion cowboy. And I proved it last night. But by then it was too late. When Frank died, it broke my heart."

Walking back to the hotel, Sam mulled over what he'd learned from the interview. Hayden's words about wanting to meet Frank had the ring of truth. He'd wanted Frank to recognize and accept him. He'd had no reason to wish the man dead. But the late-night phone call to Darrin was another matter. That sounded like something Hayden might do. He could have planned to extort Darrin or even to kill him. But the ghastly accident in the stall had put an end to any intention he might've had. Since no crime had been committed, there was no case.

Sam planned to follow up on Hayden's whereabouts on the night of the murder. If he had an alibi, Sam would forget him and focus on his remaining mental list, with Roper at the top, then Darrin, then Lila, Jasmine, and Mariah as wild cards, and, finally, his latest entry—an unknown, unnamed stranger.

He checked his phone. The sheriff in Wichita Falls had left a voice message. Sam found a quiet corner and returned the call. Maybe the sheriff had learned something about Hayden's whereabouts on the night of the murder.

"I'm afraid we weren't much help," the sheriff said. "We did some asking. But nobody around the ranch or in town remembers seeing Hayden that night. He could've been home or out of town. His dad would've known. But now . . ." His voice trailed off. Sam could hear the sound of a police radio in the background. "Do you happen to know what time he's heading home? Folks 'round here thought a lot of Chet and want to show their support at his funeral. But they don't even know when to order flowers or bring food around to the house."

"The Run for a Million will be over Saturday night," Sam said. "After that, there'll be no more reason for Hayden to be here. Sorry, but that's all I know. Can't you call him?"

"We've tried. He's not picking up. I know his father's death was a shock. Maybe he's just in denial." The sheriff paused, as if weighing what he was about to say. "We're still not sure why Chet's plane went down in clear weather.

There was no sign of a collision with, say, a drone or even a bird. The plane was new, and Chet wouldn't go anywhere without filling the tank and checking the oil. The FAA is going over the wreckage now. They'll let us know what they find."

"Would it be an imposition for you to keep me in the loop?" Sam asked.

"No problem, if you'll do us the same favor," the sheriff said. "I've learned not to jump to conclusions. But I figure that since Hayden's already on your radar, you'll want to know."

CHAPTER TWELVE

Sam found Roper in the barn, giving the stallion a rub-down after their workout. For the space of a long breath, Sam stood back, watching as the towel burnished the big roan's coat to a sheen. At last, he ventured to speak.

"I'm no horse expert, but I'd say that's one magnificent animal. He deserves to win on looks alone."

Roper paused and turned his head. "So you've found me. I had a feeling my turn would come. Have you made a decision?" He was clearly trying not to sound like a man with his freedom hanging in the balance.

Sam's gut told him that Roper was innocent. But he knew better than to give the man what might be false hope. That would be cruel. His final conclusion would have to be based on evidence, not intuition.

"The jury's still out," he said. "Meanwhile, I'm just doing my job. I spoke with your mother in her room. Her story hasn't changed. It still matches yours to the letter."

"My mother doesn't lie. Neither do I." He shook out the towel, laid it aside, and picked up a fresh one. "Was Cheyenne with her?"

"She was. She didn't say much, but I'd spoken with her earlier. Did she tell you what she'd learned about Hayden?"

"Hayden?" Roper raised an eyebrow. "No, but she and I haven't talked much since we got here. I have the feeling she's trying not to distract me. What's this about Hayden?"

"I don't know Hayden very well," Sam said. "Tell me, what do you think of him?"

Roper shrugged. "As far as I know, he's a damned boy scout. Cheyenne seems to like him. Why are you asking me?"

"According to Cheyenne, Hayden claims to be the illegitimate son of Frank Culhane. What's your take on that?"

Roper looked startled, then went back to rubbing down the horse. "Frank was known to be a womanizer, and Hayden didn't look much like Chet. So I guess it could be true. What's that got to do with me?"

"Maybe nothing—unless you think Hayden could have killed Frank."

Roper's hand froze in mid-motion. "Why should he do that? Did you ask him?"

"Yes. He denied it, of course—claimed he was hoping to connect with Frank as a son but never got the chance. He also denied being Darrin's mystery caller. As you say, he's a boy scout, but only if you choose to believe him."

"So, why are you telling me this?" Roper asked.

"No special reason. I just wanted to pick your brain. And I'm hoping that, if you happen to see him, you'll let me know."

"I might." A note of mistrust had crept into Roper's voice. "Have you heard how Simone is doing?" he asked.

"Her parents flew in and took her home to Dallas this morning," Sam said. "They'll have a funeral to plan, but that's not our problem. What happened to that red stallion? I saw that his stall was empty. I hope he wasn't put down."

"Buck Tolson had Fire Dance shipped to his ranch in Wyoming. He's going to try and work with him. I get the impression he's doing it as a favor to Cheyenne."

"That sounds like a big favor. That horse is going to be a handful. I wish him luck. And you, too. One in a Million deserves to win tomorrow night."

Sam took his leave and walked back through the barn to the hotel. He could hear the cheers and whoops from the nearby arena as the Shootout continued. He was tempted to go and watch. But he had a report to prepare for Nick, and avoidance wasn't on his agenda today. He could feel the pressure of time running out.

Unless she'd found a flight, Jasmine should still be in town. Sam checked the urge to call her, just to hear her voice. She'd been right to break off with him while he was working this accursed case. She deserved better than the time he'd given her. When the Culhane murder case was put to rest, he would do everything in his power to make up for lost time. Jasmine was the love of his life. He could no longer imagine that life without her.

For Cheyenne, the afternoon had dragged on like a prison sentence. She'd tried to talk her mother into going downstairs to explore the shops, enjoy some ice cream, or watch the Shootout in the arena. Rachel had responded as if she'd been invited to visit the fleshpots of hell. "When I walked through the lobby, I could smell the stink of greed and lust," she said. "I came here to watch my son ride. The devil can keep the rest."

They'd ordered lunch, then later a light dinner, from room service. The food had been all right, but Rachel had been aghast at the prices. "For the cost of a sandwich here, I could feed a family for a week," she'd complained.

Cheyenne had done her best to remain calm and respectful. Her mother was a good woman, a strong woman, who believed in living a life unsullied by worldly sins. That her children hadn't followed her belief was source of deep pain.

As the youngest child and only daughter, Cheyenne had grown up with Rachel's faith. She had watched it work small miracles in the circle of her family—survival in the hardest of times, a sick child healed, a lost animal found, a brushfire stopped practically at their doorstep. Cheyenne admired her mother's steadfastness, but she'd never wanted it for herself. Like her brothers, she had long since embraced the ways of the world.

Now, after a long and dreary afternoon, it was night. While Rachel studied her Bible, Cheyenne had watched a string of old-time films on the hotel's Family Movie Channel. Through the wall, she could hear the faint sounds of Buck coming and going. She was grateful he'd decided to stay another night. His presence in the next room was strangely comforting. But with her family here, she probably wouldn't get more time with him.

She'd checked her phone for messages, but so far, there'd been no word from him. His friend must still be on the road with Fire Dance, or he would have let her know.

Her family would be leaving after the competition tomorrow night, with Cheyenne and Rachel in the pickup and Stetson staying behind to help Roper load the stallion into the new trailer. After an all-night drive, they planned to reach home sometime in the morning.

There was always the chance that Roper wouldn't be with them. Cheyenne had tried not to think about that. But the worries were seeping in like a murky fog through the cracks of her mind.

What was going to happen to the family now, with Roper facing arrest, the younger siblings itching to strike out on their own, and their father's issues getting harder to manage? For as long as Cheyenne could remember, Rachel had been the strong link that held them all together. Was that link about to be broken?

"You look troubled, child." Rachel had closed her Bible and taken up the baby blanket she was knitting for a woman at her church. The soft, blue yarn passed back and forth between her flying needles as she spoke. "I've been watching you all day. I can tell that something's bothering you. Do you want to tell me about it?"

Cheyenne had been expecting this. "I'm not a child, Mother. I have worries like anybody else, mostly about Roper."

"Well, you can stop worrying," Rachel said. "Your brother is innocent, and I believe in the Lord's justice. Everything will come right in the end. You'll see."

"I wish I had your faith," Cheyenne said. "But justice isn't always served. There are plenty of wrongly convicted people behind bars. The fact that Roper is innocent might not be enough to save him."

Rachel put her knitting aside and fixed Jasmine with a riveting gaze. "Answer me this. Do you believe that God wanted Frank Culhane to pay for what he did to you—and for whatever he might have done to other women?"

Something clenched and hardened below Cheyenne's rib cage. A bitter taste crept upward into her throat. "I'm not in a position to judge," she said. "And it's certainly not my place to know what God would want."

"Are you saying that Frank didn't deserve to die? What if the real killer was doing God's will? Mayhe he'll never be found."

Cheyenne stood, fighting to control her temper. "How many times have we had this discussion? I'm done with it.

It only stirs up ugly memories. I wish I'd never mentioned it to you. Please, just let it go!"

"I'll let it go when your innocent brother is cleared of all wrongdoing. Meanwhile, at least we can pray."

"Mother, I . . . Never mind." Cheyenne exhaled and turned away. What was the use? Her mother would never change. "I need a break," she said. "Why don't I go down to the lobby and buy a paperback to read later? I won't be gone long. Maybe I could bring us some snacks. How about some popcorn? We could eat it while we watch a movie—a good one. And some chocolate-chip cookies—oh, I know they won't be as good as yours. And I know you don't like sodas, but they have those little cartons of milk—"

"Oh, don't bother, dear. I've had plenty to eat. Maybe we could call Roper and invite him for a visit."

"Roper's going to be busy. I don't want to disturb him," Cheyenne said, dismissing the idea. This would be Roper's last night before the Run for a Million, and possibly his last night of freedom. If he chose to be anywhere, it would be with Lila. Now that the threat of Darrin was gone, if she was feeling strong enough, they might even choose to go out.

"Anyway, dear, I'd rather you didn't leave me alone," Rachel said. "This place makes me nervous—all the creepy people and the spooky noises. Anybody could force that door and come in."

"That isn't going to happen." It was hard for Cheyenne to believe that her mother, who'd faced charging cattle, wildfires, and raging blizzards, shot coyotes, set broken bones, nursed fevers, and delivered babies, would feel spooked in a Las Vegas hotel room.

"Will you be all right going to the Run for a Million tomorrow night?" she asked. "There'll be a huge, noisy crowd. The stands will be packed."

"Oh, I won't mind the crowds. Nothing could stop me from watching Roper ride. It's just this room, this place, so high up and strange with the ground so far away. I know it's perfectly safe, but it doesn't feel that way."

"Will you be able to sleep?"

"I hope so. I chose not to nap this afternoon, so I'd be tired. And I brought along some of the tea I give your father at night. I'll brew and drink it now. That'll give it time to work."

There was an alcove with a coffee maker in the room. Rachel used it to brew a cup of the bitter-tasting tea she made from wild plants. She sat back in the armchair and sipped it thoughtfully. "I was hoping to meet your friend Hayden," she said. "I had the impression you like him. Is it serious?"

"Not anymore, if it ever was. I was thrilled when he gave me that poor traumatized stallion—until I realized that it was his way of getting off the responsibility hook."

"But you were able to save the horse, weren't you?"

"I hope so. I'm still waiting to hear about that." Cheyenne stretched and yawned. "While you drink your tea, I'll take a quick shower and get ready for bed. After that, the bathroom will be all yours."

She gathered up the leggings and oversized tee she wore for sleep, carried them into the bathroom, and closed the door. After stripping down, she turned on the water. At last, the endless day was almost over. Sleep, when it came, would be a welcome release.

"I know you want this, girl. They all do."

In the red neon light that filtered through the blinds, his devilishly handsome face grinned down at her. One powerful hand pinned her wrists above her head. He had booked them adjoining rooms in the hotel across from the reining competition. Now she knew why.

"Don't! Please . . . for love of God . . ." She twisted and thrashed beneath him, her strong, young legs no match for his muscular weight. His free hand bunched the fabric of her pajama bottoms and ripped them down, leaving her naked below the waist. As he groped between her thighs, she worked a knee loose. With all her strength, she jabbed upward. Her blow missed the target but struck his gut hard enough to trigger a grunt of surprise.

His palm cracked against the side of her head. The flash of pain blurred her vision and made her ears ring like fire alarms. "Try that again and you won't walk out of here," he growled.

Beaten and helpless, she lay unresisting as he yanked her legs apart and entered her with the force of a doubled-up fist—shoving, tearing, bruising, again and again . . . "No . . ." she pleaded. "Stop, please stop . . ."

Cheyenne woke with a jerk. She lay in the darkness of the hotel room, her limbs rigid and trembling, her face wet with tears. It was only a nightmare, she told herself, the same nightmare she'd relived more times that she cared to remember—the nightmare that had still left her frozen at the rare times when she'd tried to be intimate with a man.

Her humiliation had continued the next day when she had to ride home with Frank in his Cadillac. By then, she'd understood that if she told anyone what he'd done, he would make trouble for her family. She'd kept the story to herself until a few weeks ago when her mother had forced it out of her—and then again two days ago when she'd mentioned it to Buck.

The thought of Buck brought her fully awake. She sat up, reached for her phone, and checked for text messages. Her heart skipped as she found what she was hoping for.

Fergus arrived at the ranch with Fire Dance and turned him out into the corral with hay and water. Your horse is ex-

hausted and still disoriented but otherwise looks sound. So rest easy for now, Cheyenne. I'll keep you posted.

Cheyenne read the text again, warmed by a deep sense of relief. She closed her eyes as the nightmare faded. Buck was comfort. He was safety. And the flicker of time she'd spent in his arms had felt more like home than anyplace she'd ever been. Her need to feel that way again had become a burning hunger.

His message had said nothing about seeing her again. Maybe he'd believed she was with Hayden. Unless she could summon the courage to take matters into her own hands, he could leave tomorrow without even saying goodbye.

Could she do it? What she had in mind wasn't just reckless, it was insane. What if he only saw her as a silly young girl? What if he wasn't alone? Or what if, even with Buck, she couldn't break through the logjam of fear that kept her paralyzed?

Make a fool of herself, and the booby prize would be a lifetime supply of shame.

But what did she have to lose? As things stood, Buck would never come to her. If she wanted him, she would have to risk the pain and offer him all she had to give.

Her mother lay in the opposite bed, snoring under the spell of the tea she'd drunk. Heart pounding, Cheyenne swung her feet to the floor and slipped her key card into the chest pocket of her shirt. After taking a moment to arrange her pillows in the semblance of a sleeping body, she tiptoed to the door, opened it, and slipped through.

As the door closed behind her, she glanced up and down the dimly lit hallway. Buck's door was only a few steps away. She could still go back. But not when everything she wanted was on the other side of that door.

Summoning her courage, she forced her feet to move, step by step until she was facing the door.

Taking a deep breath, she raised a shaking hand and knocked.

From the other side of the door she heard a faint stirring, a thud like something dropping to the floor, and an audible curse. “Hang on, damn it, I’m coming!”

Heavy footfalls approached the door. The safety chain rattled as the bolt slid back. The door opened a few inches. In the dim light, Cheyenne could see his expression change from annoyance to surprise.

“Cheyenne . . . what the devil?” His voice was thick and muzzy. “You can’t stand out there. Come on in.”

She stepped inside. The light that fell through the uncovered window revealed that he was bare-chested. One hand clutched the hem of a sheet that had been hastily wrapped around his waist.

“Are you all right, Cheyenne?” he asked. “Is your mother—?”

“She’s fine. She’s fast asleep.”

“Is there something you need?” He pulled the sheet tighter and tucked in the ends to make it stay put. His naked torso was all lean muscle, broad shouldered and flat-bellied, nicked here and there with scars.

“What I need is you,” she said. “I . . .” Her voice faltered. She forced herself to go on. “Do you understand what I’m trying to say?”

The slow release of his breath told her that he did. “What about Hayden?” he asked.

“There’s no Hayden. There never really was. It’s you I need, Buck. I’ve seen your gentleness. I trust you.”

“You’re expecting me to save you?”

Cheyenne had no reply. She felt small and foolish. “I should go,” she said.

"No, sit down." He motioned her to a seat on the edge of the bed. "We haven't had much chance to talk, have we?"

She sat gingerly. The covers were rumpled where he'd pulled out the sheet. He took his place beside her, close but not quite touching. She could sense his warmth. He smelled of hotel soap and good, clean man. Cheyenne checked the urge to reach out and touch him.

"You're so beautiful and full of life, Cheyenne," he said. "It would be all too easy for me to say yes. But you need to understand what you're asking. I'm a few years older than you are, and I've been around the block a time or two. I've had girlfriends. And if there's one thing I've learned about love—and lovemaking—it's that the good stuff can't be forced." His gaze met hers. "Does that make sense?"

She gave him a nod, her cheeks burning.

His arm slipped around her shoulders. "Someday, you'll find the right person, Cheyenne. When you do, everything will fall into place. You'll see."

"I'm in love with you, Buck." Saying the words was like stepping off a precipice.

A startled look flashed across his face. He lowered his arm and shifted on the bed to sit facing her. "Are you really saying that you love this worn-out, worthless excuse for a cowboy? You can't be serious."

"I'm very serious. I was already falling when you lectured me on the dangers of men in Las Vegas, and I told you that you sounded like my mother."

"Oh, yes. That's the line I always use to get the girls. It works every time."

"Stop joking, Buck. This isn't funny."

"Sorry," he said. "But if you mean what you said, we've got ourselves a problem."

"What kind of problem?" Cheyenne braced herself for heartbreak.

"I've loved you from the moment you dropped your key card at my feet. But with Hayden hanging all over you, I figured I didn't have a chance. I'm still not sure you know your own mind."

"But you kissed me."

"Just to see what would happen. It was a great kiss, but you backed off. I told myself that was all I needed to know." He stood, offering his hand to pull her to her feet. "Maybe you need to give this time," he said.

"You want me to leave?"

"No, but maybe you should. You're barely grown up. Me, I'm too old for games. When I play, it's for keeps. If you stay, that's what you'll have to understand."

Stunned by his words, Cheyenne hesitated. It was only for an instant, but long enough for him to notice. With a gentle hand on her shoulder, he turned her toward the door.

"Someday you'll thank me for this," he said. "Go, love. Go and live your life."

His hand dropped from her shoulder. Numb with disbelief, Cheyenne forced herself to take a step, then another. With each step, she felt more sure that this wasn't what she wanted. At the door, she paused and turned around.

The anguish in his face told her everything.

She stood perfectly still.

"Oh, you fool!" she whispered. "You big, proud, self-effacing idiot! As if anything you say could ever make me leave you!"

With an eager bound, she flung herself across the space between them. He caught her in his arms, but her momentum knocked him off-balance. They tumbled backward across the bed.

Deliciously tangled, they lay face-to-face, both of them breathing hard. Where her ear pressed his chest, she could hear the slamming of his heart.

Turning her head, she kissed one of his nipples, drawing it slightly into her mouth and giving it a little flick with her tongue. She'd never done anything like that before, but when a low growl rose from his throat, she did it again, feeling his flesh shrink and harden at her touch. She loved the taste of him, the way he smelled, and the glorious sensation of being cradled in his arms.

"If you keep doing that, I won't be responsible for my behavior," he muttered.

"That's the idea." It was strange how emboldened she felt. She had knocked on his door and literally begged him to heal the paralyzing fear that had haunted her since the rape. But the fear was gone, banished by a shared love with this strong, gentle man and the sense of safety that he gave her.

Moving upward, she offered him her mouth for a long, sensual kiss. Buck let her tongue play with his before responding with his own deep thrusts. He was encouraging her to take the lead, she realized, giving her control over her fear. For that, she loved him even more.

Now he took over, pulling up her tee to brush kisses down the curve of her throat, stroking her breasts, nibbling them, then moving lower. A warm, liquid weight stirred in the depths of her belly. As he slid her leggings down, she felt a shimmering pulse and a subtle ooze of moisture between her thighs to make her ready. So this was how it was supposed to be.

She moaned softly and tugged at the sheet that bound his hips. His caressing paused. "Are you—?" He didn't have to finish the sentence.

"Yes." Cheyenne had gotten an IUD after the rape, as soon as she knew she wasn't pregnant. A girl—especially a rodeo girl—couldn't be too careful. The thought flickered in her mind how lovely it would be to have this man's babies. But that would have to wait.

He nudged the sheet aside. Instinctively, Cheyenne closed her eyes. This was the moment she'd yearned for—and feared. Unbidden, the memory reared its ugly head—the terror of being trapped beneath that big, heaving body, the size of him, and the tearing pain, not just the pain, but the humiliation that had come with each thrust.

This was Buck. This was the man she loved. Still . . .

"Open your eyes, Cheyenne." His voice was gentle, coaxing. Lying on his side next to her, he kissed her. Then he rolled onto his back. "It's your night to ride, lady," he said. "I'm all yours."

"How did you know?" His understanding astounded her. "Oh, Buck."

He guided her hips, lowering her over his erect shaft. When he slid inside her it was as if they'd been fashioned for each other. No pain. Nothing but the silky friction of his flesh gliding against hers. A tear slid down her cheek.

She took a moment to settle into place. He was lying back on the pillow, gazing up at her. In the dim light, she could see that he was smiling. His mouth moved as if he were about to speak. She silenced him with a finger across his lips. "No words," she whispered. Then, instinctively, she began to move.

With every stroke, the exquisite sensations shimmered upward. Her eyes closed. Her head fell back. It was as if her whole body was singing.

She moaned, stroking harder as the intensity mounted. His strong hands clasped her hips, driving him deeper. Shudders rippled through her body, exploding as he gasped and spilled his seed inside her.

Spent, she lay in his arms. She might have chosen to stay like this forever, but this was their reality. "I need to go soon," she said. "Mother could be waking up before long."

"I've got to get going, too," he said. "I need to load Chief and get on the road. Then, when I get back to the ranch, I'll need to look after your stallion. If you're with your mother in the morning, I won't see you before I leave."

"So it's to be goodbye for now."

"We can keep in touch. I'll text you, or call if there's a good time."

"I can stay a little longer." She snuggled against him.

With a gentle kiss, he eased her away and sat up. "If you stay, I'll start wanting you again. That could be trouble for both of us. Go on; we'll work things out."

Reluctantly, she slipped out of bed, found her night-clothes, and pulled them on. "I love you," she murmured, bending to give him a light kiss.

"I love you, too. And this isn't over. Now let's get moving."

As he swung out of bed, She slipped out through the door. The hallway was empty. Back in the room, her mother was still snoring. Wide awake now, Cheyenne rearranged the bed and slipped between the sheets. Through the wall, she could hear the faint sounds of Buck moving in the next room, running water, getting ready to leave. The door closed. The elevator dinged, and he was gone.

As she lay in the darkness, her thoughts wandered to a fearful question. What if she were to go back to sleep, then wake to discover that the heaven she'd found in Buck's arms had been a dream?

Sam had spent a sleepless night going over every detail of the crime. Like pieces from the devil's own puzzle, the clues swam in his tired mind, joining, then separating, fitting, then crumbling where the edges came together. He was getting a migraine. But with time running out, there was nothing to do for it except take a painkiller and soldier on.

The urge to call Jasmine was like a siren's song in his

ears. He needed her cheerful voice, her commonsense advice. And he needed to know she was out there, waiting for him to clear up this god-awful mess so they could be together. But the call wasn't going to happen. He had promised to honor her wishes and keep his distance. The least he could do was keep that promise.

Now, as the eastern sky began to pale over Las Vegas, he sat facing the large window, his laptop, his phone, and a fresh cup of coffee on the table in front of him. It was Saturday morning, the day of the Run for a Million—a day when anything could happen.

As he sipped his coffee and reviewed the report he was preparing to send, Sam's phone rang. His first thought was that it might be Jasmine. But it was Nick's name that appeared on the call screen.

"I hope I didn't wake you." Had Nick's voice weakened over time, or was it just that Sam was so worried about him?

"That's a joke," Sam said. "I've been awake all night. I was about to send you my report, for what it's worth."

"You might want to hold off," Nick said. "We may have had a breakthrough on the murder weapon."

Sam's pulse lurched. The veterinary-sized hypodermic with its eighteen-gauge, one-inch needle, had been ruled to be the murder weapon when traces of fentanyl had been found in the vial. But there'd been no trace of prints or DNA to identify Frank's killer. What could have changed?

"Our techs had given up on finding anything," Nick said. "But then we got a new girl on the crew who'd worked for a horse vet. She noticed how the needle was attached to the syringe with what's known as a Luer Lock."

"That's a new one on me," Sam said.

"Me, too. I won't go into detail, but with a Luer Lock, the needle screws onto the syringe for a very secure fit. No one on my crew knew enough to unscrew the needle.

When they couldn't pull it off, they assumed the syringe and the needle were sold in one piece."

"So when your new tech unscrewed the needle—" Sam's heart was pounding.

"We found a trace of DNA. After the syringe was tossed in the creek, the lock kept the water out. And we got lucky. Whoever attached the lock, it appears they had trouble fitting the needle in place. As nearly as we can figure out, they wet the connection with saliva to make the threads slip and seal."

Nick paused to clear his throat. "What we found isn't perfectly preserved, but it should be good enough to test. We've sent the syringe to the central lab with samples of DNA from Roper, Darrin, Simone, and Lila. They're working on it now. If it's a match . . ." He let the conclusion hang.

CHAPTER THIRTEEN

Roper was up at dawn, showered, shaved, and dressed in the work clothes he would change before tonight's big event. Meanwhile, the day would belong to One in a Million—exercising, feeding, and grooming the big roan for the performance of a lifetime.

Until that performance was over, he would force his thoughts away from anything that might lay ahead. Sam had been making himself scarce, as if distancing himself for a final decision. If it came to the worst, Roper would still have the trial to try and prove his innocence. But his life would be a living hell for as long as it took.

Forcing the thought away, he left the room. There was no sign of life from across the hall, where Cheyenne was staying with their mother. Buck Tolson's room was empty, the door left ajar. Cheyenne had told him that Buck was sending Fire Dance to his ranch. Roper had planned to thank the man in person. But for now, that would have to wait.

Downstairs, he took time to sit back, savor the restaurant's good coffee and listen to the sounds of the world waking up—the clatter of pans from the kitchen, the hum of vacuum cleaners from the casino, the swish of a revolving door. Ordinary sounds that he could be hearing for the last time.

He imagined Lila waking up in her bed, her golden hair a silken web on her pillow, a sleepy little yawn on her face. He would have given anything to spend the night with her—something they'd never done. But her protective daughter was still on guard.

Roper finished his coffee and left cash on the table. Maybe later he would have a meal. But food would be the last thing on his mind today.

In the barn, One in a Million nickered and thrust his elegant head over the gate to greet the man he'd come to accept as his master. Even without his daily grooming, the stallion looked magnificent, bright and alert, his silvery roan coat gleaming in the morning light.

One in a Million was as strong mentally as he was physically, Roper reflected as he stepped into the stall. He'd witnessed the brutal murder of his owner and survived a traumatizing accident. But he remained as calm and wise as ever.

Roper had been reluctant to use him in competition because of his age. Only Lila had believed in the big roan and urged Roper to show him one last time. Roper had insisted on borrowing a younger horse—the flashy Fire Dance. But Lila had been right. This morning, One in a Million appeared ready to take on fifteen of the best horses in the world.

And for this day, nothing else could be allowed to matter.

After some light exercise, Roper gave the stallion a shower. Back in the stall, he was giving him a vigorous rubdown when he heard a voice behind him.

"My, doesn't he look fine?"

Lila had come into the stall. She stood at Roper's elbow, a radiant smile on her face. It was all Roper could do to keep from crushing her in his arms. He settled for a brief but tender kiss.

"This is a nice surprise," he said. "Where's your bodyguard?"

"Still asleep when I left her. She watched a couple of late movies last night. And Gemma is my daughter, not my babysitter, as I have to remind her. I told her I might pay you a visit this morning."

"Did Gemma have anything to say about that?"

"I didn't bother to ask her. And I'm not asking you either. One in a Million is *my* horse, in case you've forgotten."

"Getting sassy are you? You must be feeling better."

"I am. Much better. I thought I'd celebrate by helping you fancy up our boy here for his big night. When Frank used to show him, I would braid his mane and groom his tail. Didn't I, big guy?" She stroked the stallion's withers. He blew and nodded his head as if in agreement.

"I'll get started now, while his hair is still damp. See, I even packed my own kit." She took down the canvas pouch she'd slung over her shoulder and opened it. "First, we spray on some detangler. Then the fun begins."

"Can I help?" Roper asked.

"You can keep him still. But he should be accustomed to having me do this—at least he was."

One in a Million hadn't forgotten the routine. He stood patiently while Lila sprayed his damp mane and tail with a detangler. After combing the coarse dark hair to silky smoothness, she trimmed the tail and then started on the mane.

Roper stood back, steadying the stallion's head and admiring the skill of Lila's slender hands as they divided the strands into sections and braided them in intricate patterns. His eyes drank her in—the shape of her profile, the subtle pulse at her throat, the curve of her breasts beneath the thin cotton of her blouse. He memorized every detail, knowing that it might be all he'd ever have of her.

While she worked, they made small talk, as if today were no different than any other. "What do you think of your chances?" she asked. "Have you sized up the competition?"

"No need for that. The media's been all over them. Two previous winners are in the running, as well as a woman who's the European champion. One rider has his own TV show, and several others have racked up more than a million dollars in winnings. Then there are a few hopeful stragglers like me who are hoping for a miracle. Does that answer your question?"

"I suppose so." She tied off one braid and started another. "But you've got the best horse. He was born for this. You've got to believe in him—just like I believe in you."

He gave a slight shake of his head. "Damn it, I love you."

"But?"

He took a breath, dreading what had to be said. "But I need you to promise me something, Lila."

Her busy hands paused. She raised an eyebrow. "What?"

"Promise, and I'll tell you."

"That's not how this works. Tell me, and I'll think about it." She went back to braiding, her chin stubbornly set.

"Just this—and it isn't easy to say. If I'm to be arrested for Frank's murder, I don't want you involved in any way. If you're called as a witness, you can tell the truth. Otherwise, I don't want you implicated. You're not to visit me; you're not to talk to my lawyers. As far as you're concerned, I was just someone who worked for you. Do you understand?"

With a sharp intake of breath, she spun toward him.

Her eyes were blazing. "Who do you think you are, Roper McKenna, that you can tell me what to do? I'm the boss here. And if the worst happens, I intend to fight for you, to my last breath!"

"You're not listening. It's for your own good, Lila—for your reputation and for the risk that you could be charged as an accessory. Darrin and Simone always claimed that we were having an affair before Frank died."

"We both know that isn't true."

"Yes, but Mariah was spying for them. She saw us together after Frank's death. And we both know she isn't your friend or mine. She could do you some serious damage."

"I can deal with Mariah."

"Blast it, Lila, don't do this to me. I love you, and I need to know that, whatever happens, you'll be all right. I've got enough worries as it is."

"Then listen to my idea," she said. "This is Las Vegas. We could get married while we're here."

"What the—" Roper flinched as if she'd punched him. Sensing his reaction, the stallion snorted and jerked his head. "If this is a proposal, it's the craziest one I've ever heard of."

She took up her braiding again, fingers flying. "Just listen," she said. "If the worst happens and you're arrested, you'll need someone on the outside to fight for you. Who's that going to be? Your mother? From what I've heard of her, she might not be taken seriously. Your brothers and sister don't have the experience to deal with judges and lawyers. I handled Frank's business and legal affairs for years. And I have connections. As your wife, I'd have access to you and your defense—access I wouldn't have if we weren't married."

"And you couldn't be called to testify against me," Roper added. "Not that you'd have anything useful to say."

"That, too, yes. But—"

"Good Lord, Lila, don't you realize how that would look? If things were different, I'd marry you in a heartbeat. But this way? No. Absolutely not."

"Have you got a better idea? I want to help you, Roper. I can't just sit back and watch you suffer for something you didn't do."

She looked up at him from her braiding. The tears welling in her eyes tore at Roper's heart. She was so desperate to help him. And there was nothing she could do.

With a muttered curse, he opened his arms and drew her fiercely close. As she trembled against him, his terrors tumbled into the open—the false accusations, the wrong verdict, the grim, cold lifetime behind bars, away from this woman he loved more than his life.

"I meant what I told you," he said. "If I'm arrested, stay away. If I'm convicted, forget me and live your life. That's the best thing you can do for me."

She clung to him for a moment, then pushed away, wiping her eyes on her sleeve. "I'm a big girl," she said. "But that doesn't mean I have to do as you say. Whatever happens, when the time comes, there's just one thing you can count on, Roper McKenna. I will do whatever I damn well please."

With that, she went back to braiding the stallion's mane. Her back was ramrod straight, her chin thrust at a stubborn angle. But from where he stood, Roper could see the single silent tear that trickled down her cheek.

Sam treated himself to more coffee and a Danish in the restaurant. While he waited to sign for the meal, he checked his phone. He'd made several calls to the sheriff in Wichita Falls. Each time, he'd left a follow-up message related to the question of Hayden Barr's alibi and his background. So far, the messages had gone unanswered.

Most likely, the sheriff had more pressing matters on his

hands, like the investigation of Chet Barr's fatal plane crash. Or maybe there was nothing new to report. At least it might be helpful to know whether Hayden had flown home or stayed here in Las Vegas. Sam had kept his eyes open, but he hadn't seen Hayden since yesterday.

Several questions troubled Sam. Why hadn't Hayden flown directly home after Chet's death—or at least after winning the cutting competition? Was it Hayden who'd made the mysterious call to Darrin, or could it have been someone else? And where had Hayden been when Darrin was killed by the horse?

Hayden had shown a puzzling lack of grief over Chet's death, and he'd barely acknowledged the pregnant fiancée who'd perished with him. Sam was aware that Chet wasn't Hayden's natural father. Still . . .

But what was the use of letting his mind wander in circles when the results of the DNA test could solve his case? He was here to do one job. And distraction was only a waste of time and energy.

He signed for the breakfast and wandered back through the lobby. The casino was already coming to life, the slots dinging, the wheels spinning. Country music blasted from speakers in the background. He'd long since grown tired of hearing that music everywhere. There were times, like now, when he would give anything for some good New Orleans jazz.

Sam wandered outside for some quiet. The parking lot was already full. The Run for a Million would be starting at 6:30, preceded by a new competition. The Race to the Slide, with its $70,000 prize for the fastest and longest slide to a stop, was scheduled for 5:00. By the time the pre-show started at 6:00, the main arena would be filled with cheering fans.

Spotting Hayden in the crowd wouldn't be easy, but

Sam would keep his eyes open. Roper was the prime suspect in Frank's murder. But the lab would also have a sample of Frank's DNA. If the trace in the hypodermic was a Culhane family match, the suspects would be narrowed down to three—Darrin, Jasmine, and, by elimination, Hayden, which would mean more testing for a final result. Sam's money would be on Darrin—a relief to everyone concerned.

The blazing sun, reflecting off the cars, was making Sam's migraine worse. He turned around and went back into the hotel. The urge to call Jasmine was a constant burning. By now, he couldn't even be sure where she was. She could have caught an early plane back to California. She could have been caught up in Darrin's funeral arrangements. Or she could still be in her room at the Excalibur, passing the time while she waited for her Sunday flight.

Sam had booked his own flight back to Abilene for late the same day. He had promised to be there on Monday morning so Nick could start his cancer treatments. By then, if he hadn't arrested Frank's killer, the case would either be closed or given to another agent. When, or even whether, he would see Jasmine again remained to be seen.

He checked his phone again. No calls. With a curse of frustration, he pushed the elevator button and headed back to his room. For now, he was up against a wall. There was nothing to do but wait.

Sunlight glittered on the surface of the L-shaped swimming pool, one of several in the Excalibur's vast outdoor complex. The pool was surrounded by desert palm trees and separated from the outside world by a high wall. Tourist kids splashed in the shallows and dived into the deep end, while parents watched from the sidelines, their well-oiled bodies basking in the midday heat.

Jasmine reclined in a lounge chair, her face protected by sunglasses and shaded by a floppy-brimmed hat. Her long, golden legs lay exposed to the sun, displaying toenails that had been painted a jewel-like turquoise in the hotel beauty salon.

Checking the time on her phone, she sighed. Coming here to be with Sam had been a disastrous mistake. She could hardly wait to climb onto that plane tomorrow and fly back to California.

She'd had such hopes, but after a wonderful reunion the first night, everything had gone downhill. Sam couldn't be with her—not only because he was working but because he couldn't be seen with anyone who might be a suspect in her father's murder. Then Darrin and Simone had seen them and tried to blackmail her. And then—

Despite the blistering heat, a shudder passed through her body. She'd never gotten along with her brother. But she'd never wanted him dead. And now, with Sam out of touch, nobody was telling her anything. She didn't even know when and where the funeral service would be held or where Darrin would be buried. If Simone was in charge, she might not even be invited.

One person might know what was going on—Mariah usually had her ear to the ground. And Jasmine had always looked on her as an ally. Scolding herself for not having thought of it sooner, she took her phone from her purse and scrolled to the house number at the Culhane ranch.

"Hello, honey." The voice of the Culhanes' longtime cook and housekeeper reached out to her over the phone like a warm hug. "I was hoping to hear from you. You must be devastated about your brother—especially that awful way he died. Have you been able to reach your mother?"

"Mother's gone underground, if she's even in the country. She won't know about Darrin unless she sees the story in the news. I keep hoping to hear from her, but so far, there's been nothing."

"Well, don't you worry. Your mother's a smart woman. She can take care of herself. You'll hear from her when she feels safe to make contact."

"You were always a good friend to her, Mariah."

"Well, she and your dad always took good care of me. I miss them both. And you." Mariah sounded as if she might be wiping away tears. "Now, is there anything I can do for you?"

"I just need to know about Darrin's funeral," Jasmine said. "I suppose I should be there, out of courtesy to Simone."

"There isn't going to be a funeral," Mariah said. "Simone was too distraught for a funeral—she was right there when he was killed, you know. She had his remains cremated and sent to her in Dallas. Lord knows what she plans to do with them. Put them on the mantel maybe, the poor thing. At least the baby seems to be all right. Her mother—that's who I talked to—says it's a boy. Darrin never knew. He would have been so pleased."

"That's a shame. I suppose most of his estate will go to Simone and the baby. That's no problem for me. But some things will need to be sorted out. Does Simone still want to fight Lila for the house?"

Mariah sighed. "I don't think she's got the energy for it. Now that Darrin is gone, she might be happier someplace close to her family. Too bad. I would've enjoyed helping raise a little Culhane boy here. Lila will probably flood the place with those trashy McKennas. I made it clear that if she did, I wouldn't be staying on. I've got my standards."

"And how are you, Mariah? I haven't asked."

"Oh, my health is fine. And I'm enjoying the peace and

quiet of an empty house. You've no need to worry on my account."

"Good to know. I wish we could talk longer, but it's getting noisy here by the pool. Call me if you get any news."

Mariah hung up the landline phone in the kitchen. Jasmine was a dear—the closest thing to a daughter Mariah had ever known. She would be welcome in the house. But she was a free spirit who'd never be happy settling down on a Texas ranch. She'd most likely marry that FBI man and end up living in some big city.

Let her go, Mariah told herself as she cleared off the parlor coffee table and polished the glass surface. With Madeleine's disappearance, Jasmine's indifference, Frank's murder, and now Darrin's tragic death, there was nothing left of the family she'd served for half her life.

She'd come here as the bride of a ranch hand and found a place in the kitchen. When her husband had been killed and she'd lost the baby she was carrying, it was Madeleine and Frank who'd supported her, paid her expenses, and given her time off to recover. Their kindness had won her loyalty forever, even after their divorce.

But that wasn't all.

Frank's framed photo stood on the mantel. Even after his death, his smiling presence seemed to dominate the room. Mariah took the picture down and held it between her hands. Madeleine had shown her kindness after her husband's death. But it was Frank, and his late-night visits to her room, who'd made her feel like a woman again.

If Madeleine had known about those visits, she'd had the grace to keep silent. As for Lila—she hadn't known, of course, or Mariah would've been sent packing.

The trysts had grown less frequent with the years and finally ceased altogether. Mariah suspected that it was because her youth had faded. Even so, when Frank was killed, she had felt his loss as keenly as if she'd been widowed again.

Mariah replaced the photograph and surveyed the parlor with its comfortable leather furniture and stone fireplace. Through the archway lay the dining room with its great slab of a table and the kitchen, her true domain. This house had been her home for more than half her life. If things had gone differently, she might have been its mistress, with the designer clothes, the fancy cars, and the shared king-sized bed in the master suite upstairs. But that dream had never come true.

Now she faced the prospect of Lila, whom she barely tolerated, and the people she would invite in to share the place—not a Culhane in the lot of them.

The Culhanes had been family. Now her family was gone.

Jasmine tossed a towel over her bare legs. The afternoon sun was hot enough to burn—time to go back to her boring, air-conditioned room. But she was in no hurry. She could always enjoy a cold drink at the poolside bar.

The call to Mariah had left her unsettled. In a way, it would be a relief, not needing to attend Darrin's funeral. But where was the closure? Where was the chance to say goodbye to her only brother? She'd never liked him much, but they'd shared some happy memories. And they'd supported each other through the crises of their parents' divorce and the arrival of Lila. Now she felt strangely alone. She couldn't depend on her mother or even on Sam.

"Excuse me, miss." The male voice sounded relatively young. Maybe one of the pool boys. "I'm sorry to bother you, but do you happen to be Jasmine Culhane?"

Startled, she sat up and lifted the brim of her hat. He

was standing in silhouette with his back to the blinding sun, a tall, lean figure wearing a cowboy hat. His hand reached toward her, holding a mojito. "The bartender told me you liked these," he said. "I heard about your brother—so sorry for your loss. I'd spoken briefly with him on the phone and was looking forward to meeting him in person. Then I heard about that awful accident."

Jasmine sat up and took the icy drink from him, pressing it to her hot cheek before taking a sip.

"Thanks. That tastes good," she said, "Now, suppose you tell me who you are and why you just brought me a drink. If this is a pickup, you're wasting your time. I'm already taken, and he packs a pistol."

He moved a nearby deck chair to her side, sat down, and took off his hat. Out of the glare now, he appeared to be a little younger than she was and handsome like a very young John Wayne. His hair was dark, thick, and neatly trimmed, his jaw nicely squared.

As he shifted in the chair, giving her a glimpse of his profile, she felt an odd flash of recognition. She could've sworn that she'd never seen him before. But something about him was almost creepily familiar. But then, in her former profession, she'd met a lot of people. Maybe she'd signed an autograph for him back in the day.

She sipped the mojito, savoring the tangy chill as the liquid slid down her throat. He studied her with curious eyes. Jasmine was accustomed to being hit on by men, but she didn't get that vibration from this attractive young cowboy. It was time she found out what he wanted.

She met his gaze over the frosted rim of her glass. "I believe I asked you to introduce yourself," she said. "Speak up or leave."

"Sorry. You must think I'm an idiot. It's just that I'm overwhelmed, seeing my half sister for the first time."

Jasmine's first reaction was shock. Her second was suspicion. This cowboy had appeared out of nowhere with an unbelievable story. If he was lying, maybe trying to scam her out of some cash, he had a lesson to learn.

She set her emptied glass on a side table. "You really are an idiot if you think you can fool me. Who are you really?"

"My legal name is Hayden Barr," he said. "If you're following the events in the Run for a Million at South Point, I won the cutting challenge on Thursday. It was in the papers."

"Unlike some members of my family, I don't pay much attention to horse events. I had too much of that growing up. How did you know where to find me?"

"Your brother mentioned you were in town when we spoke on the phone. The rest was easy. Again, I'm so sorry for your loss."

"Thank you for your sympathy," Jasmine said. "But what I really want to know is what proof you have that we're related. If you don't have that proof, we're finished here."

"Understood." He fished a folded sheet of paper out of his hip pocket. "My mother died of cancer when I was fourteen. On her deathbed, she told me that nine months before I was born, she'd had an affair with Frank Culhane—an affair they'd ended because they were both married to other people. I'm Frank's son—your half brother."

Jasmine forced herself to take his revelation calmly. If Hayden Barr was telling the truth, she wasn't alone. She had a brother, a possible friend and confidante. The news could be wonderful. But what if he was lying? Or what if he only wanted to take advantage of her? Red lights flashed in her head.

"My father got around. That part doesn't surprise me," she said. "But your word isn't proof. Is Frank's name on your birth certificate?"

"No. My mother's husband, Chet Barr, is listed as my

father. But this DNA test I had done confirms the truth." He unfolded the paper and thrust it into her hands. Jasmine studied it a moment. Something, she realized, was missing.

"Wait," she said. "This test confirms that you're not related to Chet Barr. But that's all. You didn't test your DNA against my father's. You've got nothing here."

"I didn't have his sample for the test," Hayden said. "But look at me, Jasmine, if I may call you that. I've seen his photos—there's one on the wall in the equestrian complex. I look a lot like him—the thick hair, the eyebrows; it's almost like looking into a mirror."

Jasmine studied his earnest face. "Well, maybe not quite a mirror. I do see a resemblance, but that doesn't constitute legal proof." She gave him a laser-focused glare. "Exactly what is it you want from me, Hayden?"

"I want a sample of your DNA," he said. "If the test shows that you're my sister, that would be enough to prove that Frank Culhane was my father."

His request put Jasmine on instant alert. Maybe the young cowboy was on the level. But DNA could be used in ID theft, blackmail, and other crimes. Her DNA would have been on the mojito glass. Maybe he'd planned to take it, she thought. But glancing down, she saw that the glass had been whisked away by the efficient hotel staff. He would have to get it directly from her.

"And then what?" she asked. "Assuming you could get proof, what would you do with it?"

"Change the name on my birth certificate. And get to know my new family, if they'll have me."

"Your new family would be me. The rest of the Culhane bloodline is either dead or unborn. We're finished here, Hayden. I'm not reckless enough to give my DNA to a perfect stranger, especially if he claims to be my brother."

As she looked back at the cowboy, his image began to blur. Even through her sunglasses, the light behind him was blinding. Spasms of nausea churned in her stomach.

She struggled to stand, but her legs felt as if they'd liquified beneath her. Maybe she'd gotten too much sun. Or—God forbid—maybe she shouldn't have trusted that mojito.

"You need to lie down, Jasmine." Hayden was helping her up, supporting her by the arms and shoulders in a solicitous manner that wouldn't draw attention. "Let me get you up to your room. Here, I've found the key card in your purse. The elevator is just inside. Come on. Don't worry, Sis. I've got you."

CHAPTER FOURTEEN

Cheyenne had begun to feel like a caged animal, cooped up in the hotel room with her mother. As the hours crawled past, she'd forced herself to remember how her mother had spent nights tending sick children without a word of complaint, and how she'd sacrificed nice things for herself to meet her family's needs—a pretty dress for Cheyenne, quality boots and hats for her younger sons, a new wheelchair for her husband.

Rachel had been an exemplary mother, giving her all with meager thanks and scarcely a word of complaint. The least she deserved was a little patience and understanding from her daughter in this unfamiliar place.

And Cheyenne wouldn't be a captive much longer. The afternoon sun was low in the sky. The Race to the Slide event was scheduled to start at 5:00 in the main arena. It should be fun to watch. No judges and no scores—just the fastest run to the longest sliding stop. If she could talk her mother into going, they could stay in their seats for the Run for a Million. Afterward, they had a pass to go back behind the stands and meet Roper.

Rachel was napping, stretched out on her bed with her

shoes off and a blanket over her legs. If she was still asleep by the time their room service meals arrived, Cheyenne would wake her. Then, if all went well, they would eat and get ready to go down to the arena.

Cheyenne's hopes would be with Roper tonight—not only in the competition, but afterward, when Sam Rafferty's decision would determine the course of his life. Either he would be a free man, or he would be a prisoner.

Maybe she would get to meet Lila, Roper's boss and the woman he loved. For her brother's sake, Cheyenne was prepared to like her. But Rachel would have her claws out, ready to draw blood. It might be best to keep the two women apart.

Cheyenne had been checking her phone all day. This time, her heart skipped as she saw the new text and began to read.

Just wanted to let you know that Chief and I made it home this afternoon. I checked on Fire Dance first thing. Physically, he looks good—no visible injuries, and he's eating and drinking a little. But he's still terrified. I can't get near him. If I try, he runs away when he can. Or if he's cornered, he rears and threatens. It is a good sign that he doesn't attack. I'll keep working with him and let you know how he's doing.

Now comes the hard part. Last night was wonderful. What you gave me was beyond precious. But I won't hold you to anything you said. You're young, gifted, and beautiful. And you could do so much better than a run-down cowboy with nothing to offer you but his heart.

There's something I need to tell you, Cheyenne—something I should have told you sooner. When you know, you'll understand why I'm cutting you loose.

When I was eighteen, I went to prison for rape and served three years. The girl was seventeen—my high school sweetheart. We were just a couple of dumb kids fooling around.

What happened between us was entirely consensual. But when I decided to break up with her and go to college, she went to her parents and accused me of forcing her. Her father was a judge. She was believed without question. I didn't have a prayer.

I don't have to tell you what three years behind bars was like. After I'd served my time, college was out of the question. My parents had died while I was locked up, and my younger sister had been taken in by relatives. I brought her home and got the family ranch running again.

I would have told you this up front. But I sensed that you needed me. I needed you, too. What if I'd told you the truth? Would you have let me touch you? Or would you have run away in horror?

I hope, as time passes, that you will come to understand and forgive me. Meanwhile, I'll continue to work with Fire Dance. If I can get him to the point where he's safe for you to handle, I'll have him delivered to you. If not—we agreed on what we would do. Let's hope it doesn't come to that.

Your friend always,

Buck

Hands shaking, Cheyenne reread the message. Her first impulse was to fling the phone against the wall. Her second impulse was to cry like a brokenhearted child.

Their lovemaking had been so tender and so real. What had possessed Buck to think his troubled past would make any difference? He'd made a youthful mistake, and things had gone bad for him. She could understand that.

But why hadn't he trusted her enough to share his secret? Why would he use it to justify ending their relationship?

She could call him—maybe send him an impassioned text. Or she could rent a car, drive to Ten Sleep, Wyoming, and fling herself into his arms.

But what if she was making too much of this? What if she was just another pretty toy who'd shared his bed, and now he was making excuses to step away?

"Cheyenne?" Her mother was stirring on the bed. "Is our food here yet? Is it time to get up?"

"Hang on. I'll be right with you, Mother." Cheyenne closed the message, wiped her eyes, and put her phone in her purse. She needed to pull herself together, think about where she stood, and come up with a decision. But there'd be no time for that now.

Back in the room, Sam plugged his phone into the charger and opened his laptop to update his report. He'd expected this day to be a busy one, reviewing evidence, conducting interviews, following last-minute leads, and possibly making an arrest. Instead, it had been a day of watching and waiting.

Everything could hinge on the contents of the DNA report. But the day was winding down, and he was still waiting to hear from Nick. The sheriff in Wichita Falls hadn't returned his calls either. Hayden's possible link to Frank Culhane's murder raised questions he couldn't afford to leave unanswered. He remembered the hours back in Chicago that he'd spent on stakeout, waiting for something that could happen any minute—or not. This was the same feeling.

Too restless to work, he put the laptop away and prowled to the window. Beyond the glass, spreading to the horizon, Las Vegas baked and shimmered in the summer heat. At least the Race to the Slide would be starting soon. He planned to watch it and stay for the Run for a Million. Maybe he'd see Hayden there. Or maybe he'd get the phone call that would move his case to conclusion. Whatever happened, he would have to be alert and ready to act.

Even if it meant hurting somebody he respected.

His nerves tightened as he turned away from the window, holstered his Glock, and clipped a set of handcuffs to his belt. Ignoring a shadow of apprehension, he slipped on a light denim jacket and left the room.

Jasmine opened her eyes. The light was bright enough to make her squint. The only sound she could hear was the blare of a television from somewhere out of sight. She was lying on her side, something soft and scratchy against her face. A blanket, maybe. So she must be on a bed. But how did she get here?

She shifted, trying to sit up. Only then did she discover that her wrists were tied behind her back and her ankles were bound with something hard and thin—zip ties, she surmised. Her pulse slammed as she realized she was a prisoner.

Her head was throbbing, and her mouth was as dry as parchment. What had happened? She struggled to clear her head. Why couldn't she remember?

Rohypnol . . . The word rose from a dark place in her mind. *Roofies*, the white tablets were called. The date-rape drug. Any woman who'd worked in Hollywood would know enough to be aware of them. Maybe she'd been given some in a drink. But she couldn't remember drinking anything. Her shorts and tank top were intact, and her body didn't feel as if she'd been raped. Surely she would know.

Twisting, she tried to see around the room. Her gaze found the open suitcase on the luggage rack, overflowing with clothes. Her clothes. She was in her own hotel room at the Excalibur. But was she alone?

That question was answered by the sound of a flushing toilet from the other side of the bathroom door. After a pause, the door swung open. A lanky figure emerged and walked toward her.

"Hello, Big Sister," said Hayden Barr.

As he grinned down at her, the partial memory returned—the poolside meeting, the mojito she'd been foolish enough to accept. She couldn't remember getting up to her room or being tied, but the picture was clear enough.

A darker picture was also clear. He wouldn't have drugged her, brought her back to the room, and tied her hands and feet if he'd meant to let her go.

She had no doubt that Hayden planned to kill her.

What she didn't understand was why.

"Let me go," she said, masking the cold fear that had congealed like tallow in her stomach. "Whatever you want, you don't have to punish me to get it."

"Don't I?" He pulled up a chair and settled next to the bed. "You don't even know what I want."

"Then suppose you tell me. Cut me loose, and I'll listen."

"No need for that. I've got you right where I want you."

Jasmine fought to contain an explosion of rage. That, she sensed, would be giving him what he wanted.

"At least you could tell me what's going on," she said. "Why am I here? What have I ever done to hurt you?"

"Nothing," he said. "You're probably a good person. Your only crime is being in my way." He crossed his legs, leaning back in the chair. "I'll tell you what. We've got plenty of time. For entertainment's sake, ask me anything you want. I'll answer truthfully. I've got nothing to hide. All right?"

"I need the bathroom first. Can you help me up for that?"

He shook his head, the grin never leaving his face. "Sorry, no. Just cross your legs. First question?"

Fine. She would play his wretched game while she tried

to figure out an escape. "Here goes," she said. "Are you really Frank Culhane's son?"

"Yes. My mother didn't lie, Neither does my mirror. I just need the DNA for legal proof."

"You can have my DNA if you'll let me go."

"It's too late for that," he said. "You already know too much. Besides, I've already got your DNA. I took a sample while you were out. Next question."

"Did my father know about you?"

"My mother claimed to have told him. But that's all I know. We never heard from him."

"So you never met him?"

"I wanted to. I even called him once and asked to get together. He said that if every bastard who claimed to be his showed up on his doorstep he'd have himself an army. He hung up, and I never called back."

Jasmine could sense the pain of rejection in his words. "So, did you kill him?" she asked.

"No. I swear to God I didn't. It might've crossed my mind. But I had nothing to gain by it. I guess somebody else had a different idea."

"How did you feel when you heard he was dead?"

"Sad. Sorry for what I'd missed." Pausing, he looked as if he had more to say. But he simply shrugged. "Haven't you about run out of questions?"

"Just one more. Chet Barr, the father who raised you, is a respected man with, as far as I understand, a fortune in land, cattle, and fine horses. You're his heir. Isn't that enough? Why would you even care about connecting with your birth father's family?"

Hayden was silent. Jasmine sensed that she'd struck a nerve—the reason he was here, now, preparing to commit an unspeakable crime.

"There's a lot you don't know," he said. "My legal

father—Chet—was just killed in a private plane crash. When I leave here, I'll be going home to his funeral. I'll inherit the ranch, and the debt that goes with it. But I never was a son to him. He knew I wasn't his, and he never treated me like his own blood. I was more like a hired hand, especially after my mother died. Finally, I confronted him about the way he treated me. He admitted he'd never felt any love for me. I was only a reminder of his wife's affair. That was when I decided to connect with my blood family.

"I did my homework first. I learned he had two children by his first wife, neither of whom had given him much satisfaction. The daughter was a playgirl and failed actress—well, what would you call yourself? The son was a sissy-pants lawyer who hated horses. I hoped your father would welcome me to the family—a son by blood who shared his love for horses and ranching. But no—first, he wouldn't even talk to me. Then, before I could change his mind, it was too late."

"But you kept trying. You contacted Darrin before he was killed. And then me, wanting my DNA. Our father was already gone. What were you thinking?"

Hayden stood. "Figure it out for yourself. I'm through talking."

He was gazing out through the glass, as if measuring the angle of the sun, when the answer struck her. Hayden didn't just want to be a part of the Culhane family. He wanted to qualify for a share of Frank's estate. And the fewer Culhanes there were, the larger his share would be. Clearly, he hadn't killed Darrin. But maybe he'd planned to. Maybe he'd set up the situation, and fate had carried out his wish. He may have even killed Frank. He was certainly capable of lying about it.

If he succeeded in killing her, Jasmine reasoned, that would leave Darrin's unborn baby as the only legal blood heir, with Lila and Simone as widows. All three of them could be in danger.

The question was, why was Hayden doing this? Maybe his inheritance from Chet Barr had been drained by debt. Or maybe he just wanted to have something tangible from his birth father. The bottom line was, there was no sane reason behind what he was doing.

But then, maybe Hayden wasn't sane.

How was he planning to kill her? Jasmine didn't see a weapon anywhere. But on the far side of the room, a sliding-glass door opened onto a balcony fronted by a chest-high wrought-iron rail. If she was immobilized, it would be easy enough to boost her over the rail and let her fall sixteen stories to her death, then arrange the scene to look like suicide.

But he couldn't get away with it in broad daylight. He would have to wait until after dark, when most people would be watching the Run for a Million, either in the arena or on closed-circuit TV.

He would have to cut her bonds to make a convincing show of suicide. She would fight for her life if he set her free. But he could inject her with a drug, render her unconscious with a blow, or twist her head and break her neck while she was still bound. Then he could cut the zip ties and toss her helpless body off the balcony.

The last time Jasmine had faced death, her mother had stepped in and saved her life. But her mother was beyond reach now. And so was Sam. Tonight would be his last chance to arrest her father's murderer and close the case. Mingling with the crowd that poured into the arena, he would be focused on his job, alert to everything around him.

Her safety would be the last thing on his mind.

The arena's outside doors opened at 4:30. Like water through the floodgates of a dam, the crowd poured in. Fans wandered among the vendor booths, lined up at the concessions counter, or hit the concourse to find their seats. This was the big night, with the Race to the Slide starting at 5:00, the Run for a Million opening ceremony at 6:00, and the main event at 6:30.

The festive air crackled with excitement. Country music blared over the shouting, laughing buzz of the crowd. The aromas of popcorn and hot dogs wafted from the concessions stand.

Dressed to blend in, Sam stood near the concourse entrance, watching for people he knew. It was early yet, but he wanted to keep track of who was here and where they could be found.

Stepping out of the way, he checked his phone again. In this noisy place, it would be easy to miss a call. But there was nothing new on the screen—nothing from Nick and nothing from the sheriff in Wichita Falls. Sam muttered a curse. In his line of work, there was nothing harder than waiting.

Admonishing himself to be patient, he set the ringtone to vibrate and slipped it into the chest pocket of his western-style shirt. Glancing up again, he saw Lila making her way toward him through the crowd, trailed by her pale shadow of a daughter.

"Hello, Agent." She wasn't smiling. A smile would have been insincere. For all Sam knew, she probably hated him.

"Mrs. Culhane." He matched her formal tone. "I'm glad to see that you and Gemma were able to be here."

"Of course we're here," she said. "One in a Million is my stallion. Some people tend to forget that."

"Well, I wish him the best of luck," Sam said. "He's a magnificent animal."

Lila ignored his comment. "The last time we met, I asked you to keep me informed. But I've heard nothing."

Sam exhaled. He should have been better prepared for

this. "I know what you're asking," he said. "But I'm afraid I can't discuss an ongoing case with you. Even if I could, I wouldn't have much to tell you. All I can say is that I'm waiting for more information."

"I understand." Her mouth spoke the words, but her lovely violet eyes pleaded with him. *Please, please don't arrest him. You know he's innocent.*

"I have a couple of questions, if you don't mind," Sam said. "Do you happen to know Chet Barr's son, Hayden?"

"Barely. I met him when we had Fire Dance at the ranch. I heard about his father's crash on the news. Awful."

"I need to talk to Hayden, but I can't locate him anywhere. I was just wondering if you'd seen him."

"Wouldn't he have gone home to arrange his father's funeral?"

"I thought so, too, but when I spoke with the sheriff there, he hadn't arrived."

"That's strange. Really strange."

Sam could almost read the hope in her eyes—that maybe Hayden, not Roper, was the new suspect in Frank's murder. For now, he would let her keep that hope. But tracking down Hayden was mostly a matter of covering his bases. Only if the DNA on the murder weapon turned out to be Culhane, but no match for Darrin or Jasmine, would Hayden become a person of serious interest.

Hayden did have motive and means. Opportunity would be a stretch, but Sam couldn't rule it out. Damn, what he wouldn't give for that call from Nick. Until it came, his hands would be tied.

He watched Lila and her daughter cross the lobby and head toward the concourse, pausing to look at a selection of T-shirts in a vendor's booth. Gemma, as always, was very protective of her mother. If she thought that Frank was mistreating Lila in any way . . . But no. The idea of soft-spoken Gemma leaving school in the middle of the night, luring Frank to the stable, and jabbing the powerful man with a syringe was too far-fetched to even consider.

But things were about to get interesting.

Three people had just come in through the main entrance—Cheyenne, her mother Rachel, and a lanky cowboy that Sam recognized as Stetson McKenna, the oldest of the young rodeo stars.

Stetson walked ahead with an air of indifference. He'd seen his share of big events, and this was just one more. Cheyenne looked preoccupied and exhausted. Rachel, a full head taller than her daughter, clasped Cheyenne's arm. Dressed in a denim skirt and a faded, western-style blouse with a leather bolo, she was looking around the lobby, taking in the crowd. When a trio of giggling girls in crop tops, skimpy cutoff denim shorts, and cowgirl boots passed in front of her, she pursed her lips and shook her head as if to say, *What's this world coming to?*

In the next moment, her gaze fell on Lila and Gemma standing by the T-shirt stall. Her spine stiffened. She raised her head like a mare sniffing trouble on the wind.

"Go on ahead and find our seats, Stetson," she said. "We'll be along shortly."

Sam checked his phone again. After seeing that there were no new messages, he moved in closer to where Lila stood with Gemma, holding up a blue tee with a horse logo on it for her daughter's approval. Experience had taught him that sometimes he could learn more from an overheard conversation than from an interview.

Pulling Cheyenne along, Rachel marched straight up to Lila. "Mrs. Culhane," she said, not bothering with an introduction, "I think it's time we met."

"My pleasure, Mrs. McKenna. I'm glad you could be

here." Lila laid the shirt on the counter and extended a hand.

Rachel ignored the gesture. "I have every right to be here," she said. "My son will be riding tonight. He invited me to come and watch him."

"I know," Lila said. "He'll be riding my stallion. So we'll both be pulling for them to win, won't we?"

Rachel's only reply was the raising of an eyebrow. A heavy silence descended between the two women. The two daughters exchanged sympathetic glances. This wasn't their fight.

"I'll get right to the point, Mrs. McKenna," Rachel said. "I don't like you. And I don't approve of the way you're influencing my son."

"Roper's a grown man," Lila said. "I couldn't influence him if I wanted to. If we have a relationship, it's as much by his choice as by mine."

Rachel's eyes narrowed. "I know you think you're too good for our kind. But the McKennas are a God-fearing family. You're a woman of the world. Even if you wanted to, you could never be one of us."

"That was never my intention, Mrs. McKenna. I respect your ways. But I have my own ways, my own morals and values. They're as good as yours. But they aren't the same."

"See?" Rachel hissed. "By your own admission, you're a sinner, a Jezebel. And you're dragging my son down with you. There's a lovely young woman who goes to my church—sweet, modest, and pure as an angel. She'd be a perfect wife for Roper. But he won't even agree to meet her. You've corrupted his soul—led him down the path of sin and sensuality."

"I think you've said enough." Lila's voice was cold. "We both know where we stand. Go now. Enjoy the competition. We're done here."

With a nod to her daughter, Lila turned to walk away.

But Rachel wasn't finished. She flung the words at her enemy's retreating back.

"No thanks to you, Roper's about to be arrested for murder. I'm his mother. I know he's innocent, I can prove it, and I'll do anything to save him. Can you say the same?"

Gripping Cheyenne's arm, she stalked away, headed for the concourse, where Stetson had gone. Lila caught Sam's eye. He made his way to her side. She was trembling. The ever-vigilant Gemma appeared at her side with a small, opened bottle of water. Lila drained it in a few gulps.

"You heard that?" Lila asked Sam.

"I did."

"I knew Roper's mother didn't like me," she said, "but I've never felt such hatred."

"My guess is that she's scared," Sam said. "One way or another, she's losing her son."

"I'm scared, too," Lila said. "And having her attack me like that doesn't help."

"This is an emotional time for everyone connected with Roper," Sam said. "Save yourself some grief and cut the poor woman some slack."

"That's easy for you to say. You're the one playing God with people's lives. How does it feel?" Lila demanded.

The words stung more deeply than Sam had expected. "It's like being an ordinary man with human feelings, trying to do the right thing," he said. "I respect Roper. I don't want to find him guilty. But the final decision has to depend solely on the evidence. That's what I'm waiting for."

As he spoke, his phone began to vibrate. Lila stared at him as he lifted it out of his pocket.

"Go on inside," he ordered her, turning away. "I've got to take this in private."

Chapter Fifteen

The call was from the sheriff in Wichita Falls. Sam stepped into a nearby meeting room to take it. "Sorry for not getting back to you sooner, Agent Rafferty," the sheriff said. "Things have been crazier than fire ants on a mule around here."

"What about Hayden? Has he come home?"

"His horse did. One of his buddies brought it back. He said Hayden wanted to stay in Vegas for the Run for a Million—maybe do some business for the ranch. We could do the funeral when he got home. Mighty strange behavior for a son, I'd say. Has he showed up on your end?"

"Not that I know of," Sam said. "I'm at the arena now. I'll be watching for him. Do you want me to call you if I see him?"

"Yes, if you don't mind. We need to talk to him."

"Is there anything else I need to know?"

There was a pause. "I guess its okay to tell you, your being FBI and all. The part-time girl who cleans the ranch house claims that a couple of days before Hayden left for Vegas, she heard an awful hullabaloo of a fight between him and Chet."

"Did she say what it was about?"

"Yup. According to the girl—Addie—Chet told Hayden that his girlfriend was pregnant with a boy. Chet meant to marry her and make their baby—his blood son, he said—an equal heir to his estate. Hayden blew up, said he hadn't worked like a field hand all his life to share his legacy with a snot-nosed brat. From there, things got worse. Hayden called the girlfriend a whore and Chet a stupid old man who couldn't keep it in his pants. Chet ended up throwing him out."

"What about the girl—Addie?"

"She says they didn't notice her. She finished cleaning and cleared out. According to the work crew, Hayden and Chet patched things up the next day. But Hayden still didn't look too happy."

"What about the plane crash?" Sam's mind jumped ahead.

"The FAA folks are still going over the wreckage. I'll be waiting to hear what they find. But either way, we need to get Hayden home and question him. If you see him, give me a call. Don't tell him what you know. We'll take it from there."

"Do you happen to have his cell phone number?"

"Yes. We've tried to call, but he doesn't pick up."

"Could you give me the number?"

"Sure. I'll text it."

"Thanks. I don't suppose you've established an alibi for the night Frank was killed, have you?"

"Sorry, we've tried, but nobody remembers that far back."

Ending the call, Sam left the room and stepped out into the noisy, crowded lobby. It made sense that Chet's news would drive Hayden to seek out his natural family. That would be when he'd presumably called Darrin. But Frank was long dead by then. It didn't make sense that Hayden would have killed him.

Hayden was a weak suspect at best. So why, as Sam made his way toward the concourse, did a sudden thought stop him in his tracks?

If Hayden was indeed Darrin's mysterious caller, why would he propose that they meet in the middle of the night, in the horse barn? And why would Darrin have agreed to it?

But that wasn't Sam's problem right now.

He checked his phone again. Nothing from Nick. Maybe there was a problem with the DNA from the syringe. Maybe it was contaminated, or there wasn't enough for a decent test. Or maybe it didn't match up with any of the murder suspects. The suspense was giving him an ulcer. And his migraine, which he'd banished earlier with extra-strength painkillers, was coming back.

He owed answers to Nick, to the Culhane family, and to the cause of justice. But at times like this, all he wanted was to be done with this accursed case, reconnect with Jasmine, and spend every night for the rest of his life making love to her.

Hayden had turned on a live TV broadcast of the events in the Run for a Million. He sprawled on the sofa, eating chips and drinking the second can of a six-pack of Bud Light that room service had left outside the door.

From where she lay on the bed, still bound with zip ties, Jasmine couldn't see the TV. But she could hear it, blasting in the room, turned high to muffle any noise she might make.

The curtains had been drawn over the sliding-glass doors to block the glare of the late-afternoon sun. It was barely 5:30, with plenty of summer daylight left. But what if her idea about his waiting until dark was wrong? He could kill her anytime. There were plenty of ways to make a murder look like a suicide. He could slice her wrists and leave her in the bathtub or pump her full of barbiturates and alcohol. Or maybe tie a plastic bag over her head.

In her less-than-brilliant career as an actress, she'd had minor parts in a number of big-name TV crime dramas: *CSI*, *Law and Order SVU*, *Criminal Minds*, and *NCIS*. Never the star, she'd played secretaries, mistresses, strippers, teachers, and prostitutes. But mostly she'd played the victim. Usually her character had died. But once in a while, she'd managed to escape. Now, as she lay on her side with her ankles bound, her wrists lashed behind her back, and her captor a stone's toss away, Jasmine thought about those times and tried to remember how she'd gotten free. In one show, she'd pretended to have a seizure. In another, she'd used a shard of broken glass to cut through the ties. In yet another, locked in a car trunk, she'd kicked out a taillight and flagged a passing car.

But these situations were staged. This was real, and unless Hayden—her ever-loving brother or, more correctly, her half brother—cut her loose so she could fight or run, she was toast.

How could he do this to his own flesh and blood?

The thought kindled a hot blaze of fury in her. Damn it, she wasn't ready to end her life like the women she'd played for the TV cameras. She wanted to live—to save animals and contribute to the good of the world. She wanted to marry Sam and fill their home with the blue-eyed babies her mother had always hoped for.

She tried to picture her mother now—Madeleine Carlisle Culhane, a force of nature, powerful as a lioness and just as fearless. Frank had been a weakling beside her. Maybe that was why their marriage had been troubled from the start.

Where are you now, Mother? Where is your strength, your courage? Is it inside me? Can I find it?

The light through the curtains was not as bright as before. The day was fading. Hayden got up from the couch, massaged the small of his back, and started toward the bathroom. Pausing, he glanced back at Jasmine.

"Stay put now," he said, giving her a grin before stepping inside and closing the door.

This could be her only chance. Jasmine strained at the zip ties that bound her wrists and legs. But the plastic strips held fast. She couldn't walk. She couldn't use her hands. She was helpless. But there had to be something she could do to change the dynamics of the situation.

She could hear him using the toilet in the bathroom. She had seconds to act. Twisting toward the far side of the bed, she rolled onto her belly. From there, hunching and crawling like an inchworm, she managed to reach the edge of the mattress and drop into the narrow space between the bed and the wall. She had no plan—only what was possible.

The bed was low, with less than a foot of space between the metal frame that supported the box spring and the carpeted floor. Jasmine could hear the toilet flushing as she squirmed her way under the bed. She was slender, but the fit was so tight that she was literally wedged. There wasn't even room to raise her head.

The carpet that pressed into her face was musty and smelled of stale beer. Fear soured her stomach, making her nauseous. She couldn't hide forever. But she had no place to go. All she could do was lie still and wait.

The arena stands were full. Fans cheered wildly as horses and riders competed in spectacular slides from a full gallop to an explosive skid that sprayed the sawdust mix into waves.

Sam's aisle seat gave him a view of the crowd below. He could see Lila's blond head where she sat with her daughter in the front row. The dark-haired McKennas were farther back, Rachel sitting between her son and daughter. Stetson was cheering and hooting with the crowd. Cheyenne slumped in dejected silence. Love gone wrong, maybe?

He had yet to see Hayden, and he was still waiting for the call from Nick. The sense of time running out was like blood dripping from a fatal wound. His thoughts wandered briefly to Jasmine. Was she still at the Excalibur waiting for her flight, or had she found another way out of town? Would she even let him know? Maybe he should give her a quick call, just to make sure she was all right. He scrolled to her number.

Jasmine's phone was still in her purse. She could hear the muffled ringtone and then the faint voice she recognized as Sam's, leaving a short message before the call ended. For a few seconds, there was nothing except the sound of the TV. Then the bathroom door opened. With her ear pressed to the floor, Hayden's steps reverberated like the footfalls of a giant.

He stepped into the room and stopped, probably noticing the empty bed. "Where are you, Big Sister?" He was moving around the room, looking behind the furniture. She heard him open the door, check up and down the hallway, then slam it shut.

Now he stood next to the bed, scarcely an arm's length away. She could see the toes of his boots below the hem of the bedspread. Barely able to move, she held her breath as he lifted the spread, dropped to his knees in the small space, and bent low enough to see her. Jasmine's pulse went wild as he chuckled, then spoke.

"So there you are. Clever girl. But you might as well give up and come out. You're not going anywhere."

Jasmine stayed silent. He might have found her hiding place, but he still had to get her out. A childhood story surfaced in her mind—the chuckwalla, a desert lizard that could escape enemies by hiding in a rock crack and inflating its body to fit so tightly that a predator couldn't pull it out. What a time to remember such a thing. But maybe that lizard had something to teach her.

The phone in her purse rang again. Sam's voice. Clearer this time. "I know what we agreed on, but please call me, Jasmine. I just need to know you're okay."

As the call ended, Jasmine's lips formed his name.

It was dark under the bed. The light that fell on Hayden's face cast his features into a grotesque mask of light and shadow. She'd surmised earlier that he might be mentally ill. But maybe he was more than that. Maybe he was a monster. Whatever he was, she wouldn't submit to her fate. If she was going to die, she would die fighting.

Worried, Sam stared down at his phone. Jasmine was known to be stubborn. He wouldn't put it past her to ignore his calls. But what if she was in some kind of trouble?

The phone vibrated in his hand. His pulse quickened. But the caller wasn't Jasmine or Nick. It was the sheriff.

"I've been hoping you'd find Hayden for us," he said. "Any luck?"

"I haven't seen him," Sam said. "Why? Has something else happened?"

"We just got the report from the FAA. They finished their investigation of the plane wreckage. They found a leak in the fuel line. The damage was done with sulfuric acid. The stuff eats through aluminum like a rat through cheese. Have you heard of that?"

"I have." Sam remembered Lila's car wreck a few weeks ago at the ranch. The fuel line leakage had been timed to happen on the freeway. Only a swerve to avoid a goat on a back road had caused a rollover and saved her from a much worse accident. The crime had been traced to Darrin, but his mother's intercession had saved him from arrest.

"The leak wouldn't have started till the plane was in the air," the sheriff said. "We're looking at a murder case now. And Hayden's our chief suspect—hell, our only suspect. We've got a manhunt on our hands. If you see him, take him into custody and call me."

Sam ended the call, his thoughts churning. Hayden, it appeared, had wanted his full inheritance badly enough to kill for it. He must have wanted the Culhane inheritance, too. Killing Frank didn't fit the timing, but he could have done it. Next was Darrin. Hayden could have set his half brother up for murder in the barn. But Darrin's tragic death had done the deed for him. That left only one living blood Culhane relative . . .

Jasmine.

Jasmine kept silent as Hayden cursed her from the side of the bed. His shoulders were too bulky to fit under the frame. But if he flattened himself face down on the floor, he might be able to reach her with an arm. Sooner or later he would think of that. And Hayden was strong. If he could get a grip and pull her out, he would probably be angry enough to beat the life out of her.

"Come on out, you little bitch," he snarled. "If I have to drag you out, you'll pay for it! When I'm through with you, that pretty face will look like roadkill!"

Jasmine's silence defied him to try. She lay taut and waiting like a trapped animal. Whatever she did next would depend on him.

From somewhere in the room, Hayden's phone rang. He glanced up but didn't try to answer it. "Maybe that's your boyfriend," he said to Jasmine. "I'll let it ring for now. He'll find you soon enough. By then, I'll be gone without a trace. He'll never know you didn't kill yourself. I was planning to wait, but if he's onto us, it'll have to happen soon."

Jasmine didn't reply. Silence was her only weapon.

"Say something, damn it!" he exploded. "Beg for your life!" He paused, the TV the only sound in the room. "If I have to come after you, you'll be sorry!"

As he flattened himself on the floor, Jasmine prepared to fight for her life. She waited as his arm slid under the bed, close enough to reach her. His fingers groped for something to hold onto—her shoulder, her face.

Raising her head a fraction of an inch, she sank her teeth into the fleshy part of his hand between the thumb and forefinger.

He yowled as she bit down with the strength of desperation, locking her jaws so hard that he couldn't pull away. She tasted the wet saltiness of blood, tasted flesh. He screamed and struggled, but only when Jasmine's strength began to fail did she let him go. He staggered to his feet. A trail of blood drizzled from his hand to soak into the carpet.

He reeled for a moment. Then, with a bellow of fury, he gripped the side of the metal bed frame, lifted it, and flipped the entire bed onto its side, leaving her exposed on the floor.

He loomed over her, his face contorted in rage and his right hand dripping blood. He stanched it with the hem of his shirt. "You asked for it, you she-devil," he muttered. "Get ready to die."

Hiding her fear, she met his gaze. "You might want to make new plans, Little Brother. You thought you were going to get away with murder. But you've lost. Your blood is in the carpet and on the bed, and even on me. Whether you kill me or not, as soon as your DNA is identified, you'll be as good as behind bars."

His features froze as the truth struck home. "As I see it, you've got a choice," she continued. "You can kill me and be sentenced for murder, or you can leave me alive and do time for kidnapping and assault."

His expression changed, grew more confident. "You think you know me," he said. "You won't feel so damn smart when I tell you that I've got nothing to lose."

"Nothing to lose?" She was momentarily stunned. "Are you telling me you've killed others?"

His grin widened. "I could kill you for the pleasure of it and be no worse off."

"Did you kill my father?"

"He was my father, too. But no, I didn't kill him, though maybe I should have. As I told you, when I called him and said I was his son, he wouldn't even talk to me. Our father wasn't a nice man, big sister. But I don't have to tell you that, do I?"

"You say you've nothing to lose. But you've nothing to gain, either. What's the point of killing me now? You can't live a normal life anymore. You'll either be on the run or in prison."

"I could kill you for this." He held up his hand, still oozing blood from the shirt hem that wrapped it. "But since you're my sister, I'll give you an even chance before I go."

Bending, he scooped her off the floor in his arms, carried her into the bathroom, and laid her down, still bound hand and foot, in the luxury-sized bathtub. After closing the drain, which was at her feet, he turned the cold water spigot on full force. Jasmine gasped as the icy stream touched her skin. She struggled to sit, but the tub's enameled surface was slick, and she couldn't use her hands to push herself up.

Hayden looked down at her and grinned. "Good luck, Big Sis. Try not to drown."

Then he turned and left, with the water running and the TV blaring full volume in the other room. She heard the door to the hallway open, close, and lock. She was alone.

Sam had made repeated calls to Jasmine's phone and to the number the sheriff had given him for Hayden. When no one answered, he tried to tell himself there was nothing to worry about. Jasmine could be in the hotel pool or at dinner. Maybe she'd caught an early flight, or maybe she was still angry with him.

He needed to be here, watching the arena and waiting for Nick's phone call. But the silence had begun to eat at him. Something was wrong.

Overcome by worry, he pocketed his phone and left the arena. He would still be able to get Nick's call, and the main event hadn't started yet. With luck, he shouldn't be gone more than fifteen or twenty minutes.

The Excalibur wasn't far, but a cab would be faster than walking. He caught one outside and, minutes later, was let off at the Excalibur's main entrance.

At the desk, he showed his FBI credentials and learned from the clerk that Jasmine was still registered at the hotel.

"Has anyone seen her or talked with her today?" he demanded.

"I couldn't say. We've got our hands full with the overflow from South Point."

"Try calling her room on the house phone."

"Certainly." The clerk punched in the number. Sam heard

several rings, but there was no answer. "We could send someone up to check."

"I'll go. Just give me a key card."

Card in hand, Sam raced to the elevator.

The water was freezing cold. It was still streaming out of the faucet, getting deeper in the tub by the minute. Soon it would be over Jasmine's head. She'd tried pushing herself up to a sitting position, but her hands were trapped behind her, and her bound feet could find no purchase on the tub's slippery bottom. The spigot was just above the tub, but the levered flow control and another lever for the drain plug were located on the tile wall above the tub, too high for her to reach.

How long had she been here? Time had lost its meaning. She only knew that her body was too numb to feel cold or pain, and she could no longer control her chattering teeth.

The TV was still blasting in the other room with live coverage of the Race to the Slide. Sam would be there, in the arena, doing his job. Challenging him to choose between her and his work had been one of the hardest things she'd ever done. She'd already known what his choice would be. But how could she settle for playing second fiddle to his career? Much as she loved Sam, she deserved to be first.

At least he'd tried to call her. She remembered his worried messages on her voicemail. Maybe those messages were the last she would ever hear from him.

Her mind was clouding over. A whisper in her head urged her to give up, to end the fear and sink into nothing. She closed her eyes, then forced them to open again. No—she wasn't going to die like this. She had to keep fighting.

Now she began rocking from side to side, using her whole body to splash water over the side of the tub. At first she thought it might be making a difference. But then she realized that most of the water was falling back into the tub. And the motion was exhausting. As her strength ebbed, the water rose higher. She struggled to hold her head up, but she was losing the battle. And the water was cold, so cold . . .

Mama . . . where are you, Mama . . . ?

From the other room came the shrill ringing of the house phone. That was the last thing she would remember.

As Sam yanked the key card out of the lock and shoved open the door, he could hear the TV and the sound of running water. The room was in shambles, the bed tipped onto its side and fresh bloodstains trailing across the carpet. Jasmine's open suitcase, its contents spilling over, sat on the luggage rack. But there was no sign of her.

The bathroom door was closed. From the other side, he could hear the water running. Heart in his throat, Sam turned the knob and opened the door.

The tub was overflowing onto the floor. Clad in shorts and a tank top, Jasmine lay in the tub. Her eyes were closed, her face covered by a sheen of water.

With an anguished moan, Sam snatched her into his arms and lifted her out of the tub. Her skin was clammy, her hands and feet bound with zip ties. Feeling her throat, he detected a thready pulse. She was alive, thank heaven, but he didn't know how long she'd been in the water. He could still lose her.

He turned off the water and carried her into the next room. Before he could perform CPR, he needed to cut her hands loose. Moving to the couch, he laid her on her side. He had just slashed through the zip tie with his pocket knife when she stirred, coughed, and opened her eyes.

"Sam . . ." Her voice was a feeble whisper. Overcome,

he clasped her close. Her teeth were chattering. "S-Sam, you came."

"Don't try to talk." He found a blanket from the wreckage of the bed and bundled it around her, then took a moment to slash the zip tie around her ankles. Her bare feet were like blocks of ice. He cradled them in his hands.

"We've got to get you warm, and we can't do it here. I'm calling for an ambulance." He punched in the police code. There were no new calls on his phone.

"I don't n-need an . . . ambulance." Her teeth were still chattering. "I'll be fine."

"Don't argue with me. You almost drowned. You could have water in your lungs."

"All right . . . but please, until they come, just hold me."

Sam adjusted the blanket around her and settled her onto his lap. He still had a job to do, but he would have to work around that. Right now, nothing was more important than this precious woman.

She snuggled against him, her hair wet and stringy against his chin. "It was Hayden," she said, still speaking with effort. "He drugged me and brought me up here. He was going to kill me. He planned to make it look like suicide so he could claim my share of the estate. But I took care of that idea. That's his blood on the carpet. At least you'll have plenty of evidence."

"I'm not surprised that you fought him and drew blood. That would be like your mother's daughter." Sam bent and kissed her. Her lips were cold. His arms tightened around her.

"He put me in the tub and left me like that," she said. "He's mentally ill, Sam. No sane person would do what he did. He meant to kill Darrin, too, before the accident with the horse. And he said he'd killed other people, too."

"Did he say that he'd killed your father?"

"I asked him. He swore that he hadn't. I believe him. Why would he lie if he meant to kill me?"

Too bad, Sam thought. Finding Hayden guilty of Frank's murder would have simplified everything. Now he was left with just one suspect.

"Once I'm in that ambulance, I want you to go back to work, Sam. The hospital will take care of me. I've taken up enough of your time."

"Don't even think about it," Sam said. "I've got my phone if I need it. And the Run for a Million is just starting. There's plenty of time for me to get back to the arena. I'll ride in the ambulance with you, and I won't be leaving the hospital until I know you're all right."

"Oh, Sam." Her teeth were still chattering. "You don't have to prove anything to me. I know you love me. And I know you have responsibilities. I should never have asked you to choose."

"That's enough talk." He found another blanket and wrapped her in it, tucking it around her feet. "Let's make you some coffee and get you into some dry clothes."

He turned away to hide a surge of emotion. A few more minutes, or even seconds, in that tub, and he would have lost her. Hayden would pay for his crimes, and Sam still had a killer to arrest. But right now nothing mattered except taking care of the woman he loved.

Chapter Sixteen

"This is it, old boy. It's our time to shine."

Roper stood beside the great bay roan stallion, speaking softly, as if talking to himself. Still in his stall, One in a Million was groomed to perfection—his coat brushed to a metallic glow, his mane braided, his hooves polished, and his legs freshly wrapped with bright turquoise tape. Under his familiar saddle, which had been oiled and buffed, he was wearing a colorful new saddle pad, handwoven of fine Mexican wool.

Roper was all in black—western-style shirt, black jeans, and a black Resistol hat. The color was meant to focus attention on the horse and away from the rider.

As he waited for the opening ceremony, Roper could feel the adrenalin surging in his blood. The stallion seemed to feel it, too. He was tense and alert, restless with energy.

Both horse and man were ready to go. But there would be some time to wait. Roper had drawn the number fifteen spot out of sixteen riders. He would walk into the arena with the others for the opening ceremony. After that, he would remain behind the scenes, watching the Jumbotron or closed-circuit TV, and tracking each score until his turn came.

The Race to the Slide was finished, the winner celebrated with a buckle and an oversize duplicate check. Now it was time for the big show, a spectacle of live music, lights, and patriotic displays, designed to whip the crowd into a state of excitement for the competition ahead.

Roper stood in line with the other riders, waiting while a pretty girl on a galloping horse carried the flag around the arena, followed by a big-name country star singing the national anthem.

By now, Roper knew most of the riders. The leading contender was the biggest money winner in the sport. He'd already won the Shootout and was on target to win the one prize that had always eluded him—the Run for a Million. His son, a gifted young horseman barely out of his teens, was also competing, as was the son of another powerful breeding and reining dynasty, as well as the rider who'd won the prize twice in the past two years. There were two women in the mix and a couple of international champions. And then there were a few newcomers like Roper, unknowns who'd made it here on hope, dreams, and luck.

In Roper's case, that luck had included a tragic death. It was Frank Culhane who'd first won a place in the contest. That thought almost made Roper feel like an imposter. But Frank's horse was here. One in a Million had won Frank's place at the Cactus Classic last March. And he'd won the same place for Roper at the elimination derby last month. The big roan had earned every right to be here.

Roper had believed he needed a younger horse to compete. That was the reason he'd borrowed Fire Dance from Chet Barr and kept Onc in a Million as backup. But now he realized how wrong he'd been. Fire Dance's loss was a tragic twist of fate. But One in a Million had proven himself. He was ready. This was his night.

The arena was dark now, heightening the drama of music, lights, and fire as a prelude to the introduction of the riders. Fifteenth in line, Roper walked out of the gate and into the spotlight.

He was conscious of the eyes that were fixed on him and the hopes that rode with him. Lila, as an owner, sat in the VIP row with her daughter. His own family sat a few rows back. Cheyenne, the baby sister who'd been with him all the way, would be cheering him on. Rachel, his mother, would be sitting with her spine rigid, her eyes looking straight ahead, the way she sat in church. She was out of her element but determined to share her son's triumph and take credit for raising him by the Good Book. Stetson was just having a good time, probably thinking ahead to his next big rodeo. The two younger boys hadn't even bothered to come. It was as if the family was already breaking up and drifting apart.

And somewhere, out of sight, Agent Sam Rafferty would be watching and planning his next move.

But Roper couldn't think of that now. If he was about to be handcuffed and hauled away for murder, all he could do was make the most of the time he had left. The Run for a Million had been his dream. He would live that dream—until it ended.

Cheyenne watched her beloved brother stride out into the spotlight, so tall and proud that it brought tears to her eyes. Whether he won or not—and she knew the odds—she would never forget this moment. Right now, the dread that might come after was a closed door, to be opened later.

She glanced at her mother, who was sitting beside her. Rachel's work-roughened hands were tightly clasped in her lap. Her lips were pressed into a hard line, holding back her emotion. Cheyenne's mother had never been one to show her feelings, except for anger. The tenderness and love inside her were kept locked away like the precious contents of a treasure box.

Moments later, after a round of applause, the riders vanished, and the lights came on. The grooming machine made a final pass over the deep layer of specialized rodeo dirt that covered the arena floor. With everything in readiness, the competition began with the first rider.

Cheyenne checked her phone, hoping that Buck might've regretted his last message. But she should have known better. Buck had made a serious decision. The next move would have to be hers. Knowing Buck, a text wouldn't be enough to persuade him he was wrong. As soon as this event was over and she got her mother home to the ranch, she planned to head straight for Ten Sleep, Wyoming, wherever that was and whatever way would get her there. She needed to tell him face-to-face that she didn't care about his past. And if telling him wasn't enough, she would show him.

Tension rose in the arena as the scores piled up. Lila leaned forward in her seat, watching each horse and rider, measuring their skill against her hopes for Roper and her stallion.

She'd seen enough reining competitions to understand how the complicated scoring system worked. Reining horses were judged on their execution of a series of maneuvers within a set pattern—circles, stopping slides, rollbacks, direction changes, and others. Each move was scored separately. At the end of the run, the scores were combined and any penalties subtracted. In a championship meet like this one, a score of less than 220 points was lackluster. A score in the high 220s was excellent. Anything over 230 would be in the winning range.

With half the contestants to go, the leading score was 228. But some of the best riders, including Roper, had yet to compete. That score was sure to be beaten.

Beside her, Gemma was lost in her phone. The girl had little interest in the sport. But Lila watched every move of the magnificent horses, struggling to keep her mind off the question tearing at her heart.

What would she do if Roper was found guilty of murdering her husband?

She'd heard the vicious rumors, but it wouldn't have been because of her. She and Roper had barely known each other before Frank's death. But Frank's refusal to let Roper compete had chafed him more than she'd realized. She saw it now in Roper's discipline and determination. Tonight was the culmination of a dream. It was what he'd wanted all along. Had he wanted it badly enough to kill for it? Sam Rafferty seemed to think he had.

But why was she questioning her own heart? She loved Roper, and she believed in his innocence. He was going to need her in the days ahead. She would be there for him.

In the hospital, Jasmine had been put to bed and treated for mild hypothermia. Due to the danger of water in her lungs, the doctor had decided to keep her overnight for observation. Sam had kissed her and left her dozing beneath warm flannel blankets. It was time to get back to work.

A police officer had taken her statement at the hospital and put out an APB for Hayden. Sam had also called the sheriff in Wichita Falls, who already had a warrant to arrest him. The law was closing in on Jasmine's half brother. But right now, Sam had even more pressing responsibilities.

The officer gave him a ride back to South Point. As he took his seat in the main arena, Sam made the mental shift back to his case. He'd checked his phone repeatedly for text messages and missed calls. But he'd heard nothing from Nick. By now, he was getting worried. Cancer could be unpredictable. What if his old friend and boss had been taken to the hospital?

He would wait for Roper's performance, Sam decided. If he still hadn't heard, he would call the Bureau in Abilene. Without the results of the DNA test, his hands were tied.

At least he'd made it back here before Roper's turn to compete. There were six riders to go. Roper would be second to last. On the scoreboard, the leading rider had 231 points, whatever that meant. Sam had watched Roper practice, but he'd never seen a reining competition or taken the time to learn about the sport. To him, it was about as suspenseful as watching paint dry, with every horse and rider doing the same exact routine. Some were obviously better than others, hence the points awarded. But to Sam they all looked the same. He'd take a good basketball game any day.

But he hadn't come here to watch a horse show. His instincts told him that Frank Culhane's killer was here in the arena. He had one last chance to find proof—and, given the delay in hearing from Nick, he might not be able to depend on the DNA.

Shutting out the distraction of the contest, he tried to concentrate on what he knew—the interviews he'd conducted, the clues he'd found.

The answer had to be right in front of him. Damn it, what was he missing?

Roper stood clear of the gate, a hand resting on his horse's saddle as the groomer made one last pass around the arena. There were three riders left to compete—Vance Harlow, an older, seasoned veteran of the competition, Roper himself, and Berta Jansen, the Dutch national champion.

The leading score stood at 231—a daunting number. Morgan Dollarhide, from a Montana family of champion riders, was probably already counting his prize money. But anything could happen in the arena, and Roper still had hope.

Vance Harlow was out of the gate now. Roper mounted up and watched, his mind following each maneuver—slide, rollback, spin, small circle widening to full circle with a direction change, another slide, then another circle, and a full gallop to a sliding stop.

Roper could see the dejection on Harlow's face as he rode back through the gate. His palomino horse had stumbled slightly on the direction change—enough of a penalty to lower his score to 223, but he gave Roper a good luck sign as he passed.

At last, after what had seemed like an eternity of waiting, it was Roper's turn. No time to think of winning or losing or who might be watching, no time to think of what might happen after he was finished. One in a Million carried him into the arena.

The big roan was calm and solid beneath him, responding to the slightest touch of Roper's knees. His gait was sure and steady, taking his rider through each maneuver, almost as if he could have performed them with an empty saddle—a blinding spin, a flawless rollback, a final slide that sent up a fountain of dirt.

They ended to a roar of applause. Roper patted the stallion's neck. Whatever else happened tonight, One in a Million had not let him down.

When the score—233—was announced and posted, Roper felt a wave of light-headedness. He was in the lead.

But anything could happen; and when Berta Jansen

rode her husky grulla gelding into the arena, Roper could tell she wasn't ready to give up.

Tall and plain, with her straw-colored braids flying behind her, Berta rode as if the hounds of hell were after her. With the flashing spins, the pounding runs and explosive slides, the performance might have been a disaster. But her horse never missed a beat and never put so much as a hoof out of place.

Even before her score—233.5—was announced, Roper knew that he had dropped to second place—which was not without honor. The $350,000 prize would be welcomed and well used. But it wasn't the hoped-for million. While Berta took her victory lap, he dismounted and braced himself for whatever was to come next.

Sam left his seat and made his way down the steps, toward the area inside the gate, where Roper would be waiting with his horse. Surprisingly, Roper's run on One in a Million had stirred Sam's emotions. Knowing the history of the pair and the effort it had taken to create that beautiful performance had made it meaningful for him. But what was he to do now?

He had yet to hear about the DNA results. He'd tried calling, but there was no answer at the Bureau, and he was hesitant to disturb Nick on his cell phone. But he couldn't delay much longer. The time had come for a decision.

He wouldn't feel confident about making an arrest until he knew about the DNA. But meanwhile, what was he supposed to tell Roper? Should he go ahead and arrest the man when he could still be innocent? Or should he throw up his hands, abandon the case now, and risk wrecking his career?

There were no good choices.

He had reached the lower part of the arena, with most of the seats and the concourse above him. From here, he could see that Roper's family, as well as Lila and her daughter, had gone back into the waiting area behind the gate to congratulate him. There would be others back there as well—Berta Jansen and her supporters, other riders, and most certainly the press, including TV cameras, hardly the setting for a discreet arrest.

He would wait, Sam resolved. He would give Roper his moment of glory and give his family the chance to share his triumph. Then, after the crowd had cleared out and Roper was putting the stallion away, that would be the time to approach him.

If he decided to make the arrest, he would need to call for backup from the local police or U.S. Marshals Service. He didn't expect trouble, but Roper would need to be taken into custody and transported.

Heaven help him, this still didn't feel right. It was times like this that almost made him hate his job.

Sam checked his phone again and sat down to wait. The minutes crawled past. By now, the seats were empty. The fans had left, the judges and dignitaries had cleared out, and the Jumbotron had gone dark. He was getting restless when the phone rang.

The name on the screen was Nick's.

Sam's pulse rocketed as he took the call.

"Sorry to be so slow getting back to you," Nick said. "What's happening on your end?"

"Nothing. Roper came in second, and now I'm sitting in an empty arena, just waiting. Did you hear from the lab?"

"Yes. Just now. Since the results weren't quite what we expected, the lab folks ran the test twice, to make sure. That's what took so long. Sorry for that. I know you've been waiting."

Sam's mouth had gone dry. "So, is the DNA a match to Roper's?" he asked.

"Yes . . . and no."

"Blast it, Nick—" Sam muttered a curse.

"I'm no expert, but I'll try to explain. It was a partial match. Some of the markers in our sample were a perfect match to Roper's. But not all of them."

Sam exhaled the breath he'd been holding. "So the DNA you found isn't Roper's. So whose DNA is it?"

"It didn't match any of our other samples. I'd say it belongs to a relative of Roper's. A close relative, likely a family member."

"But that doesn't make—" Sam's jaw dropped as the truth struck him like a thunderbolt. "Oh, my God!" he muttered. "I've got to go, Nick. I'll fill you in later."

He made a quick call for backup. Then, taking time to think, he walked around the side of the arena toward the gate.

With each step, a missing piece from his mental puzzle crashed into place. The two matching stories. The barking dog. The skunk. Roper chasing the animal away, putting the dog in the barn, returning through the dark kitchen and finding his mother there, clad in her full-length chenille robe—the robe she'd flung on over the clothes she'd been wearing when she returned home by way of the front door.

The skunk had been a wild card. Roper wasn't supposed to have been awake. But in the end, his presence had furnished Rachel with an alibi. All she'd needed to do was tell the truth.

Only one question remained. Why would a religious woman like Rachel risk her immortal soul by murdering her neighbor?

Hopefully, Sam was about to find out.

Glancing up toward the concourse, he saw the two uniformed officers who had just come into the arena. They'd been patrolling the crowds outside, so they'd been close by. Sam gave them a nod and continued toward the space inside the gate, where most of the crowd was still gathered.

Berta Jansen had already gone, and the TV crew was packing up, but Roper, still in the saddle, was doing a last-minute interview with a blond female reporter. She stood next to the horse, smiling up at him as if she were hoping he'd ask her out.

Sam could tell that Roper had seen him. His expression froze before he glanced away. Sam avoided making eye contact. Roper would welcome the news that he was no longer a murder suspect. But how would he take the discovery that his mother was about to be arrested?

At first, Sam couldn't see Rachel. Then he spotted her and her two children at the rear of the crowd. Separated from Roper by a jam of people, they were waiting for a chance to get through. Sam stayed back, biding his time, sizing up the emotionally charged situation. Making an arrest was one of the most dangerous parts of his job. The wrong move at the wrong time could touch off a tragedy.

With the interview finished, the TV crew retreated, and the crowd began to thin out. Sam could see Lila now, waiting with her daughter, back toward the entrance to the barn.

Roper had noticed the two uniformed officers coming down the steps. His mouth hardened. His shoulders tensed. For a moment, Sam feared that he might panic and try to make a break on the horse. But Roper held firm, sitting tall astride One in a Million, with the stallion's hooves planted solidly on the sawdust-covered floor.

Rachel broke away from Stetson and Cheyenne and pushed through the crowd toward him, her arms outflung as if to embrace her firstborn son. Roper shifted in the saddle, preparing to dismount. Sam moved in closer.

At that moment, something happened to the stallion.

One in a Million snorted. His nostrils flared. His ears went back. A scream of rage erupted from his throat as he made a lunge for the woman in front of him.

Caught off guard, Roper was nearly thrown from the saddle. As he flung himself against the reins to pull back the horse, Sam caught Rachel by the waist, yanking her off her feet and dragging her to safety.

It was over almost before it began. Roper had the quivering, snorting stallion under control, and Sam was helping Rachel to her feet. Her face was pale. She was unhurt except for a shallow gash where a hoof had grazed her cheek. Sam handed her the clean handkerchief from his pocket.

As she dabbed at the blood, her gaze flickered toward the horse. "He remembered, didn't he?" she said in a quiet voice. "I was wondering if he might."

Sam unhooked the handcuffs from his belt. "Rachel McKenna, I'm arresting you for the murder of Frank Culhane. You have the right to remain silent—"

"Never mind those fancy words, Agent." Her demeanor was one of icy calm. "And you can put those cuffs away. I'll go peaceably. And I waive my right to silence because I have something to say, and I want these good people to hear it."

Sam could see the two officers closing in. He nodded.

The crowd fell into a hush as she began to speak. "Yes, I killed Frank Culhane. But I didn't just kill a man. I killed a monster—a creature who preyed on young girls and women—a creature who took advantage of my pure, innocent daughter and stole her virtue.

"The Good Book says, 'Thou shalt not kill.' But he had to be stopped—and I'm not sorry I stopped him. My family's honor demanded it. Now I hope to live my life in a way that will atone for my sin and earn God's grace."

She turned to Sam. "This isn't how I wanted things to end, Agent Rafferty. I was hoping you would just go away and leave us in peace. That was not to be. But I would never have let you arrest my son. I would have come forward and confessed first."

"I understand." Sam nodded to the two officers. They took their places on either side of her. One took out a pair of cuffs and linked her wrists behind her back. "Ready?" he asked Sam.

"Ready. I'll go with you, make some calls, and take care of the paperwork. She'll need to be extradited to Texas. Let's go."

They'd started for the exit when Cheyenne caught up with them. Flinging her arms around her mother's neck, she sobbed like a child, murmuring words that Sam couldn't make out.

"Enough, girl." There was steel in Rachel's voice. "It's time to be strong. Dry your tears. Go home and take care of your dad and brothers. They're going to need you."

Chapter Seventeen

Still in shock, Roper stood outside the visitors' room at the Clark County Jail, waiting for his mother to be processed. He'd been given permission to see her tonight, but he couldn't get her out without a bail hearing. Lila had generously pledged her half of their prize money to the cause. But for a murder charge, even $350,000 might not be enough. And since Rachel would be extradited to Texas, where the crime had taken place, bail probably wouldn't be an option here.

At last, he was called in and shown to a booth with a metal chair and a phone. Rachel sat facing him behind a thick glass pane with a matching phone. Her hair was disheveled, and she was clad in a baggy orange jumpsuit. *His mother.* The sight of her made him want to rail and curse. But her expression was surprisingly calm.

What could he say to her?

She spoke first. "Hello, son. Are you all right?"

"I will be. But it's you I'm worried about."

"Don't be worried. I'm where the good Lord wants me to be. Did Stetson and Cheyenne come with you?"

"They wanted to. But the folks here would only allow

one visitor. I sent them back to Texas with the stallion. Cheyenne begged to stay. But never mind that. I'm here to help, and we don't have much time. Do you have a lawyer yet?"

"I don't need a lawyer. I killed that monster of my own free will. I'm going to plead guilty and accept God's punishment." Her serenity was almost Buddha-like. In spite of what she'd just said, it was hard to believe this woman had killed in cold blood.

"You're going to need a lawyer, Mother. It's a complicated system, and you don't know the law. You'll probably be sent back to Texas soon. But if a lawyer is offered to you, let them help."

"We'll see. In the meantime, I'll be perfectly safe. Go home, take care of your dad and your sister. They're going to need you."

"I understand." Roper despised his own helplessness. "But isn't there anything I can do for you?"

"One thing. It would be a comfort to have my Bible."

"I thought of that," Roper said. "Your Bible is at the front desk. I had to leave it. But the lady said you could have it once it's been cleared by security."

"Then that's good enough for me. Go home now. And trust that things will work out according to God's plan."

Their time was up. A guard had come to take Rachel back to her cell. Another guard showed Roper out. As he passed the front desk, he caught the woman's eye. "You'll see that she gets that Bible?"

The woman nodded. "I'll see to it."

Roper left the jail and crossed the parking lot. It was night, but the bright lights of Las Vegas obscured everything in the sky except the moon. Stetson and Cheyenne had taken the stallion in the new trailer rig, leaving Roper the family car. Before visiting the jail, he'd checked out of the hotel and packed the trunk for the drive back to Texas.

He was dog-tired, but there was no way he'd be able to sleep.

Lila would be flying back to Texas tomorrow. After that, the two of them would piece together the changed fabric of their lives and try to create something real and lasting.

Guzzling the energy drink he'd bought earlier, Roper climbed into the car and headed for home.

Cheyenne sat buckled into the passenger seat of the truck. Too wired to doze, she gazed blankly at the headlights sliding past the window. After more than two years on the rodeo circuit, riding shotgun with Stetson was nothing new. He didn't talk much, just blasted his music on his favorite radio station, hour by hour. Cheyenne could usually tune it out. But tonight she'd lost her earbuds, and the bedlam of wailing guitars and screaming voices was like earned punishment to her overloaded brain.

It was her fault, all of it—Frank's murder and her mother's arrest. She'd kept quiet about Frank's rape for two years. She could have kept the secret safe forever. But no, she'd finally flung it at her mother in an outburst of anger. She'd meant to hurt Rachel, and she had. But she'd had no idea of the biblical fury she'd awakened in that stoic, God-fearing woman.

Roper had sent her a brief text, saying that he'd seen their mother in jail and that she was safe, calm, and resigned to her punishment. Roper would be on the road now, a few hours behind them. Too bad Stetson couldn't let her out at the next off-ramp and have Roper stop and pick her up. At least she'd be with someone she could talk to.

She found her phone and scrolled to Buck's text. Every time she read it, the pain deepened. She hadn't known how to respond to him, but now, as she composed a reply, the words began to come.

When I read your message, all I wanted was to drop everything, rush to Ten Sleep, and convince you that your past didn't matter to me. That's still what I want. But something has happened, something heartbreaking, that's going to delay me for a while.

Fingers flying, she told him her story—the quarrel with her mother and the confession of the rape, Frank's murder, and the shocking discovery that her mother had been the killer.

I don't know what's going to happen. I suppose my mother will spend years, if not the rest of her life, in prison. My father is an invalid, and she took care of him. She asked me to take her place in the family. I'll do my best, but I'm not her, and I don't know how well I can manage. I'm not ready to give up my life—or you. If that sounds selfish, I can't help it. Roper will be around, although he'll be working and probably married soon. But I'm guessing my other brothers will go their own way. I don't know if I'll ever have a chance to get a cutting horse and train with it. I only know that the one thing I can't give up is the hope of being with you—sharing life on your ranch and giving you all my love.

By the time Cheyenne finished the message and sent it, tears were spilling out of her eyes. She had poured out her heart to Buck. Would he respond, or had he already made up his mind to let her go?

A few minutes later, his reply appeared on the screen. Cheyenne hesitated, bracing herself for what she was about to read. Maybe she'd been too bold. Maybe he had really wanted to end their relationship. She opened the message.

Cheyenne. If I could, I would take you in my arms and hold you. What a tragedy for you and your family. As for your response to my message, it's what I desperately wanted. But I'm still concerned that you don't understand what you're asking.

Let me explain some of the realities you'd be facing if you were to come here.

Ten Sleep is a beautiful little town at the foot of the Bighorn Mountains. My ranch is surrounded by forest and grasslands, and there are many wild animals—deer, elk, moose, wild horses, and even bears. That's the good part. But Ten Sleep is in the middle of nowhere. There are tourists around in the summer season, but in the winter, the population dwindles to about 250 brave souls, so you couldn't expect much social life, especially if you're not into hunting and fishing. Winters are long and harsh. I get around on a snowmobile and spend most of my time trying to keep the animals alive. If you were here, you'd be doing that, too.

The ranch has been in my family for generations. That's one reason I'll never live anywhere else. But there's another reason. That arrest I told you about, when I was eighteen, is still with me, like a life sentence. My name is on state and national registries for anyone to find. People here are my friends. They know me and know my story. But if I were to move away, wherever I might go, I would have to check in with the police. Then, whenever a crime was committed, they'd be knocking on my door. I wouldn't wish that on myself, and I certainly wouldn't wish it on you. I'm sorry if that shocks you, but that's the reality you'd have to face if you were with me. Think it over. If it's too much for you to process, I'll understand.

If you're still on board, this is what I'd like you to do. Take some time to make your decision—say, until next spring, after the winter's over. We can stay in touch, get to know

more about each other. I can work with Fire Dance and keep you posted. You can deal with your family situation, weigh your options, and make up your mind either way. If, by spring, you still want to come, I'll welcome you with open arms. But make sure you're ready to commit to this life. It would break my heart to have you come and then leave again. As I told you, I'm a man who plays for keeps.

Love, Buck

Jasmine's flight to LA was scheduled to leave Harry Reid International Airport at 10:15 on Sunday morning. When Sam arrived at the hospital to pick her up for their short, shared cab ride, she had already checked herself out. Dressed in the designer track suit she'd worn the night before and carrying her purse, she was waiting in the main lobby when he walked in.

She stood and walked to meet him. Sam took her in his arms and kissed her, long and deep, not caring who saw them. No more hiding from the world.

"You look like you just came from the spa," he said.

"Did you get my suitcase out of the room?"

"It's in the cab, packed and ready to go. Are you sure you'll be all right?"

She looked radiant, even without makeup. But given what she'd been through the day before, Sam knew she'd need time to heal. Unfortunately, he couldn't be there to help her. His own flight for Abilene would be leaving an hour after hers from a different terminal. With Nick starting chemo on Monday, he couldn't delay his return.

"I'll be fine," she said. "Chantal, my roommate, will be meeting my plane. She'll take good care of me."

"But not for long, I hope."

As soon as things settled down with his job, Sam planned to find a bigger apartment or even a house for the two of them. But what if he was taking too much for granted? Their love affair had been smoking hot, but they'd spent almost no time as an ordinary couple doing ordinary things. And they'd made no formal plans for the future.

They'd survived danger and forbidden love. But could they survive real life together?

Their cab was waiting at the curb. Sam stowed her bag and helped her into the back seat. The ride to the airport would be a short one.

As the cab pulled away, she rested her head against his shoulder. "We need more time, Sam," she said. "What are we going to do about that? Like, you know, dating?"

"Can you come to Abilene?"

"Will you have time for me? I'm not good at the part-time girlfriend thing."

"Part-time isn't what I have in mind. But you're right, we need to get to know each other. And not just in bed."

"But not just out of bed either." She giggled.

The cab was pulling into the airport. Sam was crushed by a sense of impending loss. This woman was his soul mate. He'd be crazy to risk losing her. The words welled up in him and spilled over.

"Blast it, Jasmine. After what we've been through, I can't just let you fly off into the blue without some kind of understanding. So help me, I don't have a ring or a decent place to live. I don't know how demanding my job will be. But I love you, and as soon as I can get my feet on the ground, I want the whole package—wedding, house, kids, everything. And I promise I'll be there for you every step of the way. This might be the crummiest proposal you ever heard, but what do you say?"

She lowered her gaze. Sam's heart sank. Was she about to turn him down? He waited for her to speak.

"Before I answer I have a confession—a secret I've been keeping from you," she said. "If I tell you now, it's only because I don't want anything hidden between us. If you can't live with what you're about to hear, feel free to take back your proposal."

"Just tell me."

"It's about my mother. When I was with her in Austin, she was seeing Louis Divino—not just as a lover but as a business partner. One day, he intercepted a phone call from you to me. He was about to kill me for it when she shot him—right in the back of the head. She got me out of there and got somebody to clean up the mess. As you know, my mother has . . . connections.

"With Divino dead, she tried to take over his organization. But he had friends. When they came after her, she had to flee the country. That's the last I heard from her. I don't even know if she's alive. So tell me, Sam, as an FBI agent with rules, how would you deal with this situation?"

Sam answered without hesitation. "Rules aside, Madeleine is one of my favorite people—and now I have her to thank for saving your life. As to what I would do, I would take her innocent daughter, shelter and protect her, love her, and give her those blue-eyed grandbabies the lady always wanted. Does that answer your question?"

"I suppose it does."

"Is that a yes?" The cab was pulling up to the curb in front of the terminal.

"It's a yes. And I plan to hold you to it." She flung her arms around him for a long, passionate kiss. "Call me tonight, okay?"

With that, she climbed out of the cab, retrieved her suitcase, and, with a wave and a smile, vanished into the terminal. Sam settled back for the ride to the next terminal, a smile on his freshly kissed lips. Jasmine was passionate, generous, impulsive, and a trifle spoiled. Life with her was bound to have its ups and downs. But it would never be dull.

Lila hugged her daughter goodbye and watched her board the Southwest flight from Las Vegas to Fort Worth. Gemma had been a devoted nurse, but she was eager to get back to school. Except for a slight pang of motherly regret, Lila was not sorry to see her go.

Lila's own flight to Abilene, where she'd left her car, wouldn't be boarding for another couple of hours. She took her time walking down the concourse to the numbered gate. As she settled into a seat, a wave of exhaustion swept over her. The past week had been an emotional roller coaster—first the incident with the trailer and Millie's tragic loss, then the attack on Gemma, Darrin's death, and the shocking resolution to Frank's murder. Would there ever be an end to it all?

She'd hoped to be with Roper, celebrating One in a Million's flawless second-place performance. But Roper was so devastated by his mother's arrest that nothing else seemed to matter—not even the proof of his own innocence. Celebrations would come, but no time soon.

If Roper was crushed, his family—brothers, sister, and invalid father—would be equally stricken. For her, she realized, being there for Roper would mean being there for all of them. She would open her home and her heart to the McKennas. When she married Roper, they would become her family, too.

Mariah wouldn't be happy about that. Lila remembered their conversation and the cook's threat to quit the first time a McKenna set foot in the house. Now the time was at hand. Soon Lila would know whether Mariah's threat had been a serious one.

Calling ahead might be wise. That would give Mariah time to prepare for the changes. If she chose to leave, that would be her decision. But hopefully she just needed a reminder that she wasn't the one in charge.

Lila scrolled her phone to the house number and placed the call. The phone rang several times and went to voicemail. That was fine, Lila told herself. Leaving a message would be less confrontational than speaking with Mariah directly.

At the tone, she began to speak.

"Mariah, I'm at the airport now. I'll be home tonight. There'll be no need to fix anything for me. But tomorrow I want to take some food to the McKennas and maybe have them over later for a meal. They've lost their mother, and they're going to need our support and friendship.

"You've expressed your feelings about this issue, and I understand. But if you'll do your job without complaint and give the McKennas the respect they deserve, I'm prepared to offer you a twenty percent raise in salary. We can discuss this tomorrow after breakfast. There'll be some changes ahead, but I hope you can accommodate them with good grace. We'll talk later."

Mariah replayed Lila's voice message, her expression hardening into a determined scowl. So that's how it was to be. The line had been drawn. She could accept the new conditions or leave.

None of this came as a surprise. She'd expected it—even the offer of money. She'd hoped to have more time to prepare, but it was what it was.

She'd spent the past few days cleaning the house from top to bottom, polishing every surface to a gleam. It was a final act of love for the home that had been hers, yet never hers, much like its owner. For years, this place had been her pride and joy—the Culhane house, the finest in the county. But those days were over. The Culhanes as a family were no more. When Lila remarried, which was bound to happen, even the name would be gone.

It was time.

She finished packing her suitcase and carried it out to her car. It surprised her, the small number of possessions that were worth taking. She had money in the bank. She could buy whatever she needed and go anywhere she chose.

Only one thing remained to be done.

Starting with the master suite upstairs, she visited each room. In either hand, she carried a can of gasoline. Walking swiftly but carefully, she spilled enough of the flammable liquid on carpets and furniture to leave a trail behind her, all through the house.

The trail ended on the front porch.

After moving her car to a safe distance, Mariah struck a match and touched it to the gasoline. She stepped back to watch as the flame caught, flared, and raced through the open front door into the house.

Within minutes, the Culhane mansion had become a roaring inferno. By then, Mariah was in her car, driving up the road.

She didn't look back.

Epilogue

Late April, eight months later

The northern Wyoming prairie swept like a vast sea of grass on both sides of Cheyenne's new Ford F-250 truck. Swards of fresh native green, dotted with early-spring wildflowers, rippled in the cool morning breeze. Northbound flocks of migrating ducks and geese etched their V-shaped formations across the azure sky. In the distance, forested hills rose above the prairie, topped by the rugged Bighorn Mountains.

Cheyenne touched the brake as a family of pronghorn antelope bounded across the road and flashed out of sight. She had seen deer, elk, coyotes, and bison since starting out from Casper after breakfast. But she still had a long drive ahead of her—north on Highway 25 all the way to Buffalo, then a sharp right and a sixty-mile drive through the mountains to Ten Sleep and her new home.

In the eight months since she'd decided to join Buck in Wyoming, she'd done a lot of growing up. During that time, the two of them had exchanged countless texts and phone calls, and Buck had even managed a few visits when he was competing at horse events in Texas. By now, they were comfortable together, and their passion was as strong as ever. She felt secure in her decision to start a new life in a new setting with the man she loved.

Other situations had resolved themselves as well. Rachel had been given a life sentence. But she would be serving her time in the French Robertson women's unit ten miles north of Abilene, which would make it easy for family members to visit. The last time Cheyenne had seen her, she'd talked enthusiastically about the Bible study group she'd organized. She'd also become involved in some of the counseling and mentoring programs. "This is where God wants me to be," she'd said. "These women need me. I'm content to be here, paying for my sin and doing His work."

Kirby had been another problem. Lonely and missing his wife, he was becoming more irascible by the day. Roper and Cheyenne had shared his care, but the arrangement wasn't working well for any of them.

Finally, a new retirement home had opened in Willow Bend. Kirby seemed happy enough there. The food was good, and he'd made a few friends. More important, he was getting some therapy for the back pain that had kept him drinking. Visits to Rachel in prison had only distressed him. At her suggestion, Roper had stopped taking him. The couple communicated now by letters and rare, awkward phone calls. Not all endings could be happy.

The Culhane house had burned to the ground. Lila and Roper, who'd married in a quiet ceremony, had moved into the larger of the two guest bungalows and made it their home. Instead of rebuilding the house, they'd invested the insurance money in a medical and physical therapy clinic for horses. The facility, which was still under construction, already had a waiting list of clients.

Another wedding had taken place in Abilene. Cheyenne hadn't been invited, but Lila, who'd attended with Roper, had told her about it. Jasmine was a glowing, pregnant bride. Sam's boss, Nick, still recovering from chemo, stood as his best man. The couple had received some nice gifts, but one gift, as Sam had told Roper, was puzzling. A package had arrived by messenger with no card, no postmark, and no return address. Inside was an exquisite cashmere christening blanket and an envelope with a very generous cashier's check inside.

"I think someone's keeping an eye on them," Lila had said to Cheyenne. "Madeleine was always a stealthy one. This has her touch all over it. Let's see how long she can stay underground after that baby comes."

Everyone had their story, some sad. Hayden had crashed his plane into a mountain while fleeing arrest. He'd left behind a debt-mired ranch and proof that he'd engineered the deaths of Chet Barr, his fiancée, and her unborn child.

Cheyenne had placed a bid on Hayden's cutting horse, Steely Dan. But the beautiful champion paint had brought out an army of high bidders, and she'd lost. Maybe that was for the best. The future she'd planned didn't include a life on the competition circuit. She'd sold Jezebel, her barrel-racing mare, to a wealthy breeder who would give her a good retirement. The sale had helped pay for Cheyenne's new truck.

After a stop in Buffalo to fill the gas tank and grab a quick bite, she'd taken the sixty-mile cutoff through the Bighorn Mountains to Ten Sleep. The country's spectacular beauty left her breathless. It was everything Buck had described and more.

Coming out of the hills, where the road leveled off, she'd seen them, the wild horses he'd told her about—a band of them, thundering over the prairie, manes and tails flying, bays, roans, paints, palominos, grullas, and blacks; mares, stallions, and tiny, long-legged foals. Mesmerized, she followed them with her gaze until they vanished from sight.

Seeing the horses reminded her that she had a decision to make—a final decision about Fire Dance.

"Your stallion survived the winter in good shape," Buck had written. "I can pet him, and he seems to get along with other horses. But after months of trying, I can't get a saddle on him. He bolts at the sight of it. I think it's safe to say that this horse will never be fit for riding. We talked about this, but since you're coming, what we do with him will be your decision."

Twenty minutes later, she was driving through the ranch gate. Ahead now, she could see the house—heavy timbers, glass, and natural stone, with a wide front porch. Buck was standing on the porch with his two cattle dogs. As she pulled into the yard and climbed out of the truck, he strode out to meet her.

For a long moment, he held her in his arms, kissed her, then stepped back, looking her up and down. "I can't believe you're here," he said. "Do you still want to take care of Fire Dance first? That's what you told me."

"Yes, let's do it now," she said. "Take me to him."

The red stallion was alone in the outer paddock. He was shifting restlessly, moving back and forth along the fence line, nickering and calling. "He's been like this for days," Buck said. "Listen."

At first, Cheyenne heard nothing. Then the sound came her on the breeze, faint, sweet, and so chilling that it raised the hair on the back of her neck. It was the sound of wild horses.

"Where are they?" she asked. "I don't see them."

"They're out there, beyond the trees," Buck said. "Fire Dance knows where they are."

"It's time, isn't it?" she said.

"Go ahead. He's your horse." He pointed her toward the gate.

Heart pounding, Cheyenne slid back the bar and swung the gate open. With a joyful snort, Fire Dance reared, passed through the gate, and thundered off across the prairie, drawn by the sound that sang in his blood.

Cheyenne and Buck stood watching him go. As he pulled her into his warmth, Cheyenne felt a sense of everything as it should be. Fire Dance was home at last. And so was she.